新聞英文搭配詞

學會 collocation，擺脫中式英文

臺灣師範大學翻譯研究所　**廖柏森** 博士 著

眾文圖書股份有限公司

推薦序

從搭配詞開始，培養自然道地的英文語感

本書作者廖柏森教授和我一樣在大學任教，在幫助學生學習英文的過程中，我們都遇到相似的困境：大學階段英文學習的重點究竟是什麼？從國小到高中，文法與單字都已經學了超過十年了，進入大學之後該如何學好英文呢？廖柏森教授的新書《新聞英文搭配詞：學會 collocation，擺脫中式英文》提供了一個可以實作的解答。

正如廖柏森教授在自序中所述，搭配詞 (collocation) 是「字與字之間的組合或共現關係」，亦是約定俗成的習慣用法，可以讓英文表達更加道地、自然，更符合英文的「語感」。因此，「學會自然且道地的英文」正是本書最重要的目標。學習搭配詞語的困難點在於，無法以固定的語法規則明確界定某些字詞如何搭配，僅能依賴多聽、多閱讀來培養字詞搭配的語感。因此，不少讀者以為僅能靠個人的「直覺語感」去判斷搭配字詞的語用真實度，似乎不需要刻意學習。其實不然，本書正好適合想學好英文的讀者以搭配詞語作為「意群」(meaningful chunks)，強化情境或語意的關連程度後，讀者便能以「舉一反十」倍增強化英文單字力，增強寫作或口語表達的語用力或溝通力，並提升英文「真實感」。

此書以新聞主題來區分文境 (context) 的搭配詞使用，讀者系統性深化學習意群後，閱讀時即能以文境關連方式來使用英文搭配詞語，進而理解更真實的語感。以本書「環境災害」主題中地震 (earthquake) 的搭配詞語為例，若想深入了解地震的意群，可以從地震相關名詞（如「震央」epicenter、「震源」hypocenter、「斷層」fault 及「餘震」aftershock）學

起，進而學習描述地震大小的形容詞（如「毀滅性的」devastating、「強烈的」massive/severe、「輕微的」mild/moderate），以及與地震有關的動詞（如「摧毀」devastate/ravage、「襲擊」hit/strike、「搖動」jolt/rattle 等）。學習此一環境災害主題時，若能比對海嘯 (tsunami) 的搭配詞，可以明確知道 tsunami 的用法與 earthquake 極為相似，兩個字都可以和 strike, ravage 搭配，表示「侵襲」之意，不同的是 tsunami 還會跟其他動詞搭配，例如被海嘯吞沒 (engulf)、被海嘯沖走 (sweep/wash away)。這些其實都不是艱深的英文字詞，然而在不同主題下（地震或海嘯），可提供「文境」的意義連結，在大腦記憶中形成較深的刻痕，學習自然事半功倍。

為何這樣一本書對於培養英文的語感特別重要呢？第一，僅學習單字及文法會造成學習的片斷性，且脫離文境的學習方式，不僅「忘記的比記得的多」，也無法真正了解語用的適當性及語意的關連程度。第二，儘管大量閱讀可以在文境中理解或推論語意及語用，然而僅靠閱讀需花費較久的時間才能累積系統化的詞語搭配力。本書透過有系統的方式介紹各種新聞主題來學習搭配詞語，既可強化英文的語法、語用與語意，並可同時深化英文新聞的閱讀力及英文表達力。

非常感謝廖柏森教授編寫了這本教學、自修皆適用的新聞英文搭配詞專書。此書的英文搭配詞涵蓋十分豐富的主題，包括政治法律、財經商務、軍事戰爭、科技電腦、環境災害、大眾傳播，收錄的都是與現代生活息息相關的英文用語。廖教授在每一個主題單字的搭配詞後附上大量的例句，還提供「相關詞彙之搭配使用」，透過片語、句子和新聞段落，方便讀者延伸相關單字的搭配詞語學習。同時，考慮到讀者自學需求，每個單元後面都附上了「搭配詞練習」，方便讀者檢視學習效果。廖柏森教授以其翻譯與語料庫研究的學術根底，以及深厚的英文素養，將這些重要新聞

主題的英文搭配詞語統整，成為英文學習者學習搭配詞語的利器。讀者熟悉本書的搭配詞語後可以獨立閱讀英文新聞內容，開闊視野，這也是本書最高的學習目標。

國立中正大學語言中心副教授

林麗菊

推薦序

內容新穎、例證豐富，
是學習新聞英文的進階版好書

　　許多人在學習英語的過程中，常因字彙量不足而難以暢所欲言，加上英語使用過度類化、受中文母語表達習慣的干擾，多以不適切的搭配詞來敘述，與實際英語用法相去甚遠，深陷詞不達意的窘境。所謂的搭配詞即為 "the right combination of words"，學習者若能掌握約定俗成的英語用法、了解詞語間的連結關係，看到某名詞即聯想到與其搭配的動詞、形容詞與介系詞，必能以符合語法的英語通暢表達。換言之，搭配詞使用得當，可使學習者的口說與寫作能力更接近以英語為母語者的道地表達習慣，有效提升學習英語的精確度。

　　熟識廖柏森教授多年，深感他不僅是位學識淵博、有著儒雅風範的學者，更是位令人敬重的「多產」、高效能作者。他的著作一向是各大專院校教師的指定用書，我在世新大學新聞系的「全方位新聞英語」課程中，不僅以廖教授編寫的《新聞英文閱讀與翻譯技巧》作為指導學生新聞中翻英技巧的教學用書，亦選擇這本書的前身《決勝英語搭配力》作為引領學生踏入「詞彙搭配」世界的一把鑰匙，藉此向學生強調正確搭配各類英語詞彙的重要性。課程中，我依災難、社會、政治、經濟與生活等五類新聞時事題材，挑選適合作為中譯英素材的文本，經小幅編修後作為中譯英新聞的作業，讓學生由簡入繁、循序漸進地學習將中文新聞譯為英文新聞。

　　在課程中，我亦要求學生每週研讀《決勝英語搭配力》，透過學習詞彙搭配了解道地的英文，引導學生不再只按字面意義，以中文思考模式譯出表面上看似正確，卻不一定恰當的「中式英文」(Chinglish)。此外，我

也於期中與期末給予學生兩次測驗，檢視其是否研讀書籍中的搭配詞語。學生在期末分享參與課程的感受時，皆表示歷經一學期的訓練已不再害怕英文新聞寫作及翻譯；更強調因研讀該書後，體會英語詞彙搭配的重要性，不再只是照字面翻譯，而能學著揣摩正確用法，使得譯文更加通順。

我之前在課堂使用《決勝英語搭配力》已見良好教學成效，近日更欣聞廖教授在該書出版多年後作一全面翻修，更名為《新聞英文搭配詞：學會 collocation，擺脫中式英文》，特別針對新聞英文的常見議題和詞語搭配作更深入詳盡的解說，例句、段落和練習內容也都更新為最近的時事，更符合讀者的學習需求。在教授新聞英文過程中，我會將各類新聞中出現頻率高、功能性較強的單字分類、歸納，幫助學生更有效率地聯想、記憶單字。而閱讀廖教授新編的《新聞英文搭配詞》，發現此書更是學習新聞英文的進階版好書。書中內容乃廖教授將過去於《經濟日報》擔任編譯的豐富經驗及學術研究加以整合，並充分利用語料庫擷取真實語料，再根據新聞領域分為：政治法律、財經商務、軍事戰爭、科技電腦、環境災害、大眾傳播等六大類。書中詳盡介紹各類新聞主題的搭配詞語，並以詞性分類幫助讀者熟稔各詞彙與其搭配的形容詞、動詞、副詞及介系詞的正確串連方式。

舉例而言，環境災害類新聞中，「地震」(earthquake) 是極為常見的主題。書中以詞性分別列出「地震」的搭配用法，例如可搭配 earthquake 的動詞有 cause/generate / set off（引發）、predict（預測）、survive（存活）、withstand（抵擋）；可搭配 earthquake 的形容詞有 devastating（毀滅性的）、great/huge/major/massive/powerful/severe（強烈的）、mild/minor/moderate/small（輕微的）。加上眾多例句說明，方便讀者在短時間內就學會如何以英文描述各種情況或災情的地震。

書中的詞彙與例句多取材自國際知名的英文新聞媒體，各詞彙與搭配用法有一千六百組、例句亦超過五百句，內容新穎、例證豐富，中英對照的編排更有助於讀者參閱。而書中所設計的「新聞英文搭配詞自我評量」及參考書目中附上的「新聞英文搭配詞學習資源」都有利於讀者快速有效地習得新聞英文常用搭配詞。無論是想學習新聞英文寫作或翻譯者，都可透過本書早日脫離「中式英文」的夢魘，培養詞彙搭配的意識來閱讀英文新聞，奠定最紮實的搭配詞基礎，進而寫出合乎語法的英文新聞報導。

　　目前市面上與搭配詞相關的書籍、辭典及網站日益增多，但專屬於新聞英文搭配詞的書籍則相對較少。廖教授重新編纂的《新聞英文搭配詞》是新聞學理與實務經驗的結晶，不僅為教師打造實用度極高的教學參考書，更提供讀者最有效的自修寶典，為有意鑽研新聞英文的讀者開啟學習的新頁，是一本可讀性與實用性兼具的教戰手冊。

世新大學新聞系副教授

推薦序

不僅是學習新聞英文的利器，
也是提升英語能力不可或缺的書籍

　　能為廖柏森教授的新作寫序，深感榮幸。廖教授的著作向來是各大專院校教師的指定用書，不僅內容深入淺出，更以有系統的方式編寫，讓英文學習變得有趣而淺顯易懂，造福了無數莘莘學子。廖教授的專業知識博大精深不在話下，他的為人更是謙遜，並樂於提攜後進，是一位令人尊敬的學者。

　　現在英語學習資源豐富，不論聽說讀寫都有各種學習管道，相當方便。但這是否意味著現今大學生的英文能力也跟著達到一定水準，足以應付國內外不同的英語需求呢？答案卻不見得是肯定的。各大學之所以制定英文畢業門檻，就是擔心學生一畢業，或還沒畢業，英文能力就走下坡而失去競爭力。此外，根據美國教育測驗機構 ETS 於 2017 年公布的多益英語測驗（聽力及閱讀）分數排名，台灣在 47 個國家中排名 37（平均分數 544），落後第 17 名的韓國（平均分數 676）以及第 30 名的中國大陸（平均分數 600）。雖然分析排名結果仍需將其他因素（如考生年齡）列入考量，但由此略可窺見，現今豐富的英語學習資源似乎和學生的英文程度不成正比。由此也可看出，學習英文需要對的工具，才能達到事半功倍的效果。

　　廖教授的新作《新聞英文搭配詞：學會 collocation，擺脫中式英文》就是一本難能可貴的英語學習書。全書聚焦英文的搭配詞 (collocation)，除歸納整理大量的搭配詞語外，還收錄了使用該搭配詞語的範例，包括片

語、句子和段落，且範例皆出自國際知名英文新聞媒體。英文學習最大問題之一，就是字彙量夠多，但仍說寫出讓英語母語人士一頭霧水的英文。追根究底，問題往往出在未能使用正確的搭配詞。英文搭配詞一方面常有固定伴隨使用的字詞（包含動詞、形容詞等），另一方面也經常不是字面上的意思。我在教學時常常遇到學生在考試後問我，他的答案雖然與標準答案不同，但意思相通，是否也可以算是正確的呢？學生以中文的意思來理解英文句子，按照中文意思來選擇英文單字，自創詞組，結果變成了中式英文，這就是缺乏搭配詞的意識，或沒有學好搭配詞的結果。

廖教授的新作補足了此一學習漏洞。此書既可作教學用書，也可自修使用，適合所有想要培養搭配詞意識、藉此提升英文能力的讀者。搭配廖教授傳神且簡潔有力的中文翻譯，讀者更能感受到英文搭配詞的趣味。

本書有以下特色：

1. 依新聞分門別類，涵蓋 6 大新聞主題；
2. 將新聞英文常用關鍵字搭配不同詞性，方便學習；
3. 附有大量例句，讓讀者迅速了解搭配詞的使用方式；
4. 附有大量練習題，方便檢測學習效果；
5. 提供豐富的線上語料庫和辭典資訊，供讀者進一步學習。

一般英文字典雖然有些也附有搭配詞語，但廖教授的新作依主題分類，是相當方便的學習及參考工具書。書中收錄的搭配詞語雖然以新聞英文為主，但也相當適合用於一般寫作及口語表達，換言之，此書不僅是學習新聞英文的利器，也是想要提升英語能力不可或缺的參考書籍。

相信此書不僅能幫助初、中級學習者培養搭配詞意識，打好學習基礎，也能讓有一定程度，卻總是覺得英文不夠道地、不夠自然的讀者突破

現況，更上一層樓。在此祝福所有讀者學習愉快，對廖教授的中英文寫作及翻譯功力再次深感佩服。

輔仁大學英文系助理教授

作者序

　　臺灣的英文學習者在用字遣詞時往往只按照字面意義，表面上看似正確，但不一定恰當。尤其從英美人士的觀點來看，常覺得我們的英文表達怪怪的，不太自然。換句話說，就算我們自認為使用的英文字義是對的，但英語母語人士並不是這樣用，這就表示我們很有可能創造出所謂的中式英文 (Chinglish)。

　　很多人理解英文字義的方式是查閱字典，但英文字典中許多字彙的中文意義看起來非常接近，而實際用法卻有差異。例如用來表示「目標」的英文字有 goal 和 aim，但英美人士要說「達成目標」時常說 reach a goal，而不說或很少說 reach an aim；表示「規則」的英文有 rule 和 regulation，但「違反規則」通常說成 break the rules。又如「大雨」的英文是 heavy rain，可是要表達「大風」就不能用 heavy wind，只能用 strong wind；相對的，要表達「大雨」就不能說 strong rain，因為 heavy 不能搭配 wind，而 strong 無法搭配 rain。一般字典偏重個別字義的解釋，較少提供詞語間的連結關係，學習者唯有透過大量密集接觸詞語搭配，才能彌補傳統字典的不足。

　　所謂的搭配詞 (collocation)，簡單來說就是字與字之間的組合或共現關係 (co-occurrence)，某些字彙與其他字彙共同出現在一起的機會比較高，甚至已經約定俗成而為大眾習慣使用。例如中文成語就是一種高度慣例化的搭配，我們會說「絞盡腦汁」，但如果學習中文的外國人說成「絞完腦汁」、「絞光腦汁」、「絞碎腦汁」，儘管構詞方式正確，意義也很接近，但我們就是覺得不對勁。使用英文也是如此，我們絞盡腦汁想出很多英文表達方式，但對於英美人士而言總是覺得不夠自然道地，也很難解釋到底是哪裡錯了，其實通常就是詞彙搭配不當的問題。

中英詞彙搭配模式不同，無法以字面意義一一對應翻譯。筆者從過去的教學經驗中，發現臺灣同學的英文表達方式常受母語中文的干擾，而產出不適當的英文搭配，例如以下常犯的錯誤：

中文搭配	不當英文搭配	適當英文搭配
學習知識	learn knowledge	acquire/gain knowledge
查字典	check a dictionary	consult a dictionary / look up the word in a dictionary
感到頭痛	feel a headache	get/have a headache
今天早上	today morning	this morning
酸雨	sour rain	acid rain
古代歷史	old history	ancient history
毒蛇	toxic snake	poisonous snake
提升英文能力	raise English ability	improve English skills
改善問題	improve a problem	deal with / solve a problem
改進壞習慣	improve a bad habit	break a bad habit
提出辭呈	raise one's resignation	tender one's resignation
提出警告	raise a warning	give a warning
開支票	open a check	write a check
度過難關	cross one's difficulties	overcome one's difficulties
作研究	make research	conduct/do research
作夢	make a dream	have a dream
參加宴會	join a party	go to a party
成本降低	cost down	cut costs keep the cost down

一般字典雖然能對個別英文字彙提供定義翻譯和解釋，但是對字與字之間的搭配關係卻力有未逮。而且背誦、記憶個別單字的學習方式，收效往往不大。很多人背過就忘，或者就算背起來也不知如何使用，只能靠中文的語感或直覺來使用英文字彙，結果就成為不恰當的中式英文。因此學習英文不能只記憶孤立的單字 (isolated words)，用脫離文境 (context) 的方式記誦單字只是見樹不見林，使人自以為學了很多單字，一旦要使用時卻無所適從，徒增挫折感。另外，有些學者提倡大量閱讀，以篇章中的具體文境來推論字彙意義和用法。這種學習方式雖然有效，但通常需要長期的學習時間，並不一定能讓學習者注意到詞彙之間的搭配關係。因此我們有必要培養詞彙搭配意識來輔助閱讀文章，才能快速提升英文字彙能力。

本書編寫即是基於上述觀點，從一個單字引申出去學習更多相關搭配的字彙，可以讓我們在認知理解時產生意義的連結 (association of meaning)，加深印象並提升記憶的效能。再加上以詞性為分類的基礎，以詞組作為有意義的語塊 (meaningful chunks) 為單位來學習，如此一來，不僅可習得詞組中單字的意義，更能學到這些單字與其他不同單字之間的關係和用法，還可進一步掌握詞組、片語、句型和段落的意義，於短時間內增進學習英文的效能。

舉例來說，筆者過去曾於《經濟日報》擔任新聞編譯工作，在撰寫股匯市行情時常有詞窮之感，描述行情大好時總不能老是用「上漲」來形容，以免過於平板單調。於是我就收集相關意義的詞彙搭配，諸如「上揚」、「揚升」、「勁升」、「勁揚」、「飆漲」、「狂漲」、「銳增」、「漲幅驚人」、「牛市大漲」、「價量齊揚」、「開出紅盤」、「一片紅通通」、「帶動強勁漲勢」、「漲幅創下歷史新高」等等，都分類整理在筆記本中。日後使用起來果然得心應手，大幅增進個人的編譯效率，而文字效果也較為生動多元。學習英文也可如法炮製，把意義接近的相關字彙搭配集結在一起，例

如描述「上漲」相關的英文詞彙有 increase, gain, rise, grow, climb, go up, move up, jump up, surge, soar, escalate, peak, close in bull market 等眾多搭配形式，說明速度和幅度不等的「上漲」，這些字一起學習可達事半功倍之效。而持續學習大量不同專業領域的搭配詞，也可使我們的英文口說寫作和口筆譯更加自然精確，更接近以英語為母語者的表達方式。

本書的詞彙搭配和例句大都取材自國際知名的英文新聞媒體，包括報紙如 *The New York Times*《紐約時報》、*The Wall Street Journal*《華爾街日報》、*The Washington Post*《華盛頓郵報》；雜誌如 *Time*《時代雜誌》、*The Economist*《經濟學人》；電子媒體如 *ABC News*《美國廣播公司新聞》、*BBC News*《英國廣播公司新聞》、*CNN*《美國有線電視新聞網》；新聞通訊社如 *Associated Press*《美聯社》、*Reuters*《路透社》，以及國內英文媒體如 *The China Post*《英文中國郵報》、*Taipei Times*《臺北時報》、*Taiwan Panorama*《台灣光華雜誌》等眾多來源。新聞文體題材廣泛，用字豐富多元，不論是政治軍事、財經社會，乃至於廣告娛樂等，都是學習各種生活情境和專業領域英文字彙的最好教材。而為凸顯詞語之間的搭配關係，筆者也特地將英文新聞原文長句加以改寫，刪除贅字和不必要的細節資訊，以方便讀者閱讀學習。

本書以新聞中的常見字彙為核心概念，衍生大量相關的詞語組合和用法。例如 stock（股票）這一章就把全球主要股票指數的英文列出，同時說明股票行情漲跌的句型用字和相關術語。再如 military（軍事，軍隊）一章就提供軍隊編制、特種部隊和各種武器的英文名稱。而在 rain（雨）一章中，除了學習各種型態的大小雨、陣雨、梅雨、暴雨的英文外，也會提到和雨相關的習語和俚俗語。從這些核心字彙和新聞主題可延伸出大量相關詞彙，而且同一類別的搭配詞如財經或環保相關主題一起學習，更能使效果相乘加倍。讀者不論是面對平面或電子媒體的英文新聞報導，一定

會經常閱聽書上這些搭配詞彙，而熟悉本書內容不僅有助於理解英文新聞精要之處，更可快速提升整體英文實力。

　　此外，本書一開始先提供新聞英文搭配詞的自我評量測驗，書後還附上新聞英文搭配詞的學習資源，包括線上中英對照新聞、搭配詞辭典、語料庫網址和參考書目等，希望協助讀者進一步精通新聞英文搭配詞的用法。不過英文的詞彙眾多，加上字與字的搭配形式豐富，而本書能收納的字彙畢竟有限，只能當作一個學習的起點。因此筆者也建議讀者，除了使用本書學習之外，平日在閱讀各種英文文本時，不妨也將字彙的搭配模式記錄下來，整理在自己的筆記本或電腦檔案中，有空就拿出來瀏覽複習，增強自己的英文搭配實力。

　　最後要說明的是，本書的前身是 2012 年由所以文化出版的《決勝英語搭配力》。在 2017 年著作版權合約到期後，筆者將全書作一通盤整理，增添新聞英文搭配詞彙，加深加廣說明文字，翻新段落譯例和暖身練習，希望能去蕪存菁加以補強，使篇幅更加充實，內容更為多樣，譯例更貼近讀者的生活經驗，讓本書轉型升級為學習新聞英文的利器，也有助提升一般英文和口筆譯能力。經過一年的修訂工程，現交由眾文圖書公司重新排版付梓，以嶄新面貌問世，期待舊雨新知繼續支持，筆者無任感荷。

國立臺灣師範大學翻譯研究所教授

Contents

Part 1

新聞英文
搭配詞
自我評量

學習新聞英文搭配詞前，請讀者先檢測一下自己的英文搭配詞語能力，寫完後再對照題目後的參考答案，有助於你更了解英文詞性的搭配方式和重要性。但同時也請讀者注意，以下中文譯文只是作為練習時的提示，並不代表中英文的詞語搭配皆可一一對應。

動詞 + 名詞

請依照「動詞 + 名詞」的搭配方式，於下列空格中填入你認為最適當的搭配詞彙，畫線和粗體的中文字可提供你翻譯的提示。

1. 台塑集團決定**擴大**對越南合資鋼鐵廠的**投資**。

   Formosa Plastics Group has decided to _____ its **investment** in a joint steel venture in Vietnam.

2. 巴黎今夏房地產價格將**達**新**高**。

   Prices for real estate in Paris are set to _____ new **records** this summer.

3. 將來必須興建更多的托兒所，以**符合**高品質兒童照護的**需求**。

   More nurseries will have to be built to _____ the **need** for high-quality child care.

4. 國防部表示，將**發布聲明**回應總統的調查命令。

   The Defense Ministry said it would _____ a **statement** in response to the President's investigation order.

5. 這次的颱風對農作物**造成**嚴重的**損害**。

   This typhoon _____ serious **damage** to the crops.

6. 有些購物狂用催眠的方式來幫助自己**戒除**這個壞**習慣**。

   Some shopaholics use hypnosis to help them _____ the bad **habit**.

7. 這位教授的理論**招致**許多**批評**。

   This professor's theories _____ a lot of **criticism**.

8. 政府採取措施**限制販賣**菸草產品給青少年。

   The government took measures to _____ the **sale** of tobacco products to teenagers.

9. 我們的政府是認眞想**處理**汙染**問題**。

   Our government is serious about _____ the pollution **problem**.

10. 目前的趨勢開始**產生**一些**影響力**後，進一步的問題就會浮現。

    When current trends have begun to _____ some **impact**, further questions will arise.

11. 暴動過後士兵被派來**恢復秩序**。

    Soldiers were sent in to _____ **order** after the uprising.

12. 這位部長**駁斥**政府被外國媒體「陷害」的**指控**。

    The minister _____ **accusations** that the government was "set up" by foreign media.

13. 這位導演的新片**引起**許多人的**興趣**，每個人都在談論這部電影。

    This director's new film has _____ a lot of **interest**. Everybody is talking about it.

14. 鴻海將**取得訂單**，成爲 iPhone 的唯一組裝廠。

    Hon Hai will _____ **orders** to become the sole assembler of iPhones.

15. 在無法兼顧長工時和家庭需求的情況下，她在一年內**增加**了 10 公斤。

Unable to juggle long work hours and the needs of her family, she
_____ 10 **kg** in a year.

形容詞 + 名詞

請依照「形容詞 + 名詞」的搭配方式，於下列空格中填入你認為最適當的搭配詞彙，畫線和粗體的中文字可提供你翻譯的提示。

1. 川普總統首次海外出訪受到**熱忱歡迎**。

   President Trump received a _____ **welcome** on the first overseas trip of his presidency.

2. 這種藥一般被視為是避孕最**可靠的方法**。

   This pill is generally regarded as the most _____ **method** of contraception.

3. 政府機構中男性和女性的**人數不成比例**。

   There is a _____ **number** of men compared to women in the government agencies.

4. 青少年抽菸似乎是個**愈來愈大的問題**。

   Smoking seems to be a _____ **problem** among teenagers.

5. 那不是一個很**有說服力的解釋**。

   That's not a very _____ **explanation**.

6. 過去兩週以來，部隊**一再嘗試**突破敵人陣線。

   For the last two weeks the army made _____ **attempts** to break through enemy lines.

7. 我和我的朋友對於政治有著完全**相反的觀點**。

   My friend and I have sharply _____ **views** on politics.

8. 很不幸地，某些家庭常出現**家暴**。

   Unfortunately, _____ **violence** is a regular occurrence in some families.

9. 如果當初有更多**特定資訊**會更有用。

More _____ **information** would have been useful.

10. 暴徒於獨立紀念日的慶祝活動中攻擊俄羅斯駐華沙大使館，波蘭政府對此表達「**深切遺憾**」。

Poland has expressed " _____ **regret**" after rioters attacked Russia's embassy in Warsaw during Independence Day celebrations.

11. 教授講課結束後，展開了**熱烈的辯論**。

After the professor's lecture, there was a _____ **debate**.

12. 七大富裕民主國家週六於義大利結束高峰會，對氣候變遷並無**一致的共識**。

Seven wealthy democracies ended their summit Saturday in Italy without _____ **agreement** on climate change.

13. 對**持久和平**的希望不幸地正快速消退中。

Hopes for a _____ **peace** are unfortunately fading fast.

14. 發展**共同的興趣**和嗜好可減少婚姻中的衝突。

Developing _____ **interests** and hobbies can decrease conflict in marriage.

15. 法國總統舉辦晚宴，歡迎來參加夏季青年奧運**開幕儀式**的國際**貴賓**。

The President of France held a banquet dinner to welcome international _____ **guests** who had come to attend the _____ **ceremony** of the Summer Youth Olympic Games.

參考答案

上述問題的正確答案可能不只一個，以下答案僅供參考：

1. cordial	2. reliable	3. disproportionate	4. growing
5. convincing	6. repeated	7. opposing	8. domestic
9. specific	10. deep	11. heated	12. unanimous
13. lasting	14. common/shared	15. distinguished, opening	

副詞 + 動詞 / 副詞 + 形容詞

請依照「副詞 + 動詞」或「副詞 + 形容詞」的搭配方式，於下列空格中填入你認為最適當的搭配詞彙，畫線和粗體的中文字可提供你翻譯的提示。

1. 川普首次**公開譴責**近來在美國境內反猶太人的威脅。

   Donald Trump has _____ **condemned** for the first time recent anti-Semitic threats in the US.

2. 儘管憂鬱會**嚴重影響**生活品質，但常被忽略或置之不理。

   Although it can _____ **affect** quality of life, depression is frequently overlooked or dismissed.

3. 學生需要機會**批判分析**其溝通時的內容、組織和用字。

   Students need the opportunity to _____ **analyze** the content, organization, and lexis of communication.

4. 大多數學生**極力強調**字彙教學的需求。

   The majority of the students _____ **emphasized** their need for vocabulary instruction.

5. 這種疾病在西方世界**突然快速增加**。

   This disease is **increasing** _____ in the western world.

6. 此類研究對於教學**可能有深刻的**衝擊。

   This line of research **has potentially** _____ impacts on educational practices.

7. 德國總理梅克爾**堅信**德國和美國的關係堅定不移。

   German Chancellor Angela Merkel **believes** _____ in strong German-US relations.

8. 俄羅斯官員**嚴厲批評**北大西洋公約組織和其他西方機構。

Russian officials have _____ **criticized** NATO and other Western institutions.

9. 該研究**強力主張**使用合作團體可促進認知發展。

The research **argues** _____ that the use of collaborative group contributes to cognitive development.

10. 川普對於俄羅斯介入 2016 年大選的指控已經**愈來愈**感**挫折**。

Trump has grown _____ **frustrated** by allegations of Russian meddling in the 2016 election.

11. 該研究結果的描述是不**具實證基礎的**。

Descriptions of the research results are not **empirically** _____.

12. 我相信這個方法在**科學上是健全的**。

This is the approach which I believe is **scientifically** _____.

其他詞性

請依照每題題後的詞性指示,於下列空格中填入你認為最適當的搭配詞彙,畫線和粗體的中文字可提供你翻譯的提示。

1. 他**解決問題的方法**在於學習過程的初期。(名詞)

   His _____ **to the problem** would lie in the initial learning process.

2. 京都議定書**旨在**削減空氣汙染對世界的破壞效應。(介系詞)

   The Kyoto Protocol **aimed** _____ reducing the devastating effect of air pollution on the world.

3. 他的評論顯示他對此問題完全**缺乏了解**。(名詞)

   His comments showed a complete _____ **of understanding** of the problem.

4. **一連串的爆炸**後,飛機就解體掉落到地面。(名詞)

   There was **a** _____ **of explosions**, and then the plane broke up and fell to the ground.

5. 在某些文化中,**丟臉**是非常嚴重的事。(名詞)

   In certain cultures, _____ **of face** is a very serious matter.

6. 父母**對**子女的**影響力**最大。(介系詞)

   Parents have the most important **influence** _____ their children.

7. 這件事有個層面似乎**值得一提**。(形容詞)

   One aspect of this matter seems _____ **mentioning**.

8. 年長人士接受訪談，**目的在於**了解他們對於自身行動不便的感受。
（介系詞）

Older people were interviewed _____ **the aim of** finding out how they felt about their physical disabilities.

9. 意見調查顯示，女性的政治觀點明顯**不同於**男性。（介系詞）

An opinion survey showed women had significantly **different** political views _____ men.

Part 2
新聞英文常用詞彙及其搭配詞

I. 政治法律類

government

(n.) 政府

► 答案請見 p. 20

⚙ 請就以下中英譯文選出適當的搭配詞。

Opposition leaders say they will not ① **recognize** ② **admit** the new **government**.

反對黨領袖表示，他們不會**承認**新**政府**。

臺灣的中央政府體制為「一府五院」，「一府」指總統府，英文名稱就官方組織而言稱為 Office of the President，就建築物而言則稱為 Presidential Office Building。而「五院」為「行政院、立法院、司法院、監察院、考試院」，「院」音譯為 Yuan，乃臺灣獨有的英文機構名稱，其他國家的政府機關並不會使用。臺灣政府組織 (government organization) 中重要府院部會機構的官方英文名稱如下：

1. Office of the President 總統府
2. Executive Yuan 行政院
   - Ministry of the Interior 內政部
   - Ministry of Foreign Affairs 外交部
   - Ministry of National Defense 國防部
   - Ministry of Finance 財政部
   - Ministry of Education 教育部
   - Ministry of Justice 法務部
   - Ministry of Economic Affairs 經濟部

- Ministry of Transportation & Communications 交通部
- Ministry of Health and Welfare 衛生福利部
- Ministry of Culture 文化部
- Ministry of Labor 勞動部
- Ministry of Science and Technology 科技部

3. Legislative Yuan 立法院

- Committees 委員會

4. Judicial Yuan 司法院

- Supreme Court, High Courts & District Courts
  最高法院、高等法院、地方法院
- Supreme Administrative Court & High Administrative Courts
  最高行政法院、高等行政法院
- Commission on the Disciplinary Sanctions of Functionaries /
  Public Functionary Disciplinary Sanction Commission
  公務員懲戒委員會

5. Control Yuan 監察院

- Committees 委員會
- National Audit Office 審計部

6. Examination Yuan 考試院

- Ministry of Examination 考選部
- Civil Service Protection & Training Commission
  公務人員保障暨培訓委員會
- Ministry of Civil Service 銓敘部

☑ v. + government

v.	government	中譯
bring down / overthrow		推翻政府
denounce		譴責政府
discredit		抹黑政府
embarrass		使政府難堪
lobby		遊說政府
petition	government	向政府請願
pressure		向政府施壓
recognize		承認政府
reform		改革政府
urge		敦促政府

搭配詞例句

- Fujitsu workers from around the UK will lobby the government to act on their complaints about changes to pay and pensions.
  英國各地的富士通員工將遊說政府，希望政府就公司改變他們的薪資和退休金一事採取行動。

- Our Constitution guarantees your right to petition our government.
  我們的憲法保障你向政府請願的權利。

- They are pressuring the government to allow them to perform religious rites.
  他們正在向政府施壓，要求政府允許他們舉行宗教儀式。

• Traders have urged the government to completely withdraw duties on imports of tea.
貿易商已敦促政府全面廢除進口茶葉的稅。

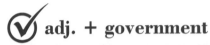 **adj. + government**

adj.	government	中譯
authoritarian/totalitarian		獨裁／極權政府
caretaker/interim/provisional/temporary/transitional		看守／臨時／過渡政府
civilian		平民政府
communist		共產政府
conservative	government	保守政府
federal		聯邦政府
incumbent		現任政府
legitimate		合法政府
municipal		市政府
socialist		社會主義政府

搭配詞例句

• There have been a series of protests against the authoritarian government's latest measures.
近來有一連串反獨裁政府最新措施的抗議。

● The faction leaders are set to formulate a joint position on an interim government.
各派系領袖將在過渡政府中組成共治的體制。

相關詞彙之搭配使用

·coalition government 联合政府

片語	
... has badly damaged the reputation of the government	…已大損政府威信
a demonstration against the government's new laws	反對政府新法的示威活動
anti-government demonstrations	反政府示威活動
bloodless coup	不流血政變
civil/public servant government employee	公務員
government in exile	流亡政府
government restructuring	政府組織再造
long-awaited restructuring of government	期待已久的政府組織再造
term of office	任期
to decline to recognize the new government	拒絕承認新政府
to form a coalition government	成立聯合政府
to negotiate a treaty of mutual recognition with the new government	與新政府協商，討論出一相互承認的條約
to share power in a coalition government	在聯合政府中共享權力

·legislation 立法

句子

● It's no surprise that the country's <u>legislature</u> is largely for <u>rubber-stamping</u>.
這個國家的<u>立法機關</u>多淪為<u>橡皮圖章</u>，並不令人意外。

··

● Following weeks of media speculation, President Tsai Ing-wen's <u>administration announced a cabinet reshuffle</u> late Friday.
歷經數週媒體的揣測後，蔡英文<u>政府</u>週五晚間<u>宣布內閣改組</u>。

說明 動詞 shuffle 有「打亂順序」的意思，例如 shuffle the cards 為「洗牌」，而「一副洗好的牌」是 a shuffled deck of cards，其中 shuffle 字尾加 -d 就轉成形容詞。此句中 shuffle 加上字首 re- 成為 reshuffle，是指「改組」，可當動詞或名詞用。reshuffle 前面搭配 cabinet 就成為「內閣改組」，搭配 government，則為「政府改組」。要注意的是，government reshuffle 是指更換政府部會首長，不同於前一頁提及的 government restructuring（政府組織再造），意思是調整政府機關的組織編制。

··

段落

Panama <u>has severed diplomatic ties with</u>[①] the Republic of China, the latest setback for Taiwan on the international stage as Beijing continues its efforts <u>to cow and constrain</u>[②] Taipei. In an announcement Tuesday, Panamanian President Juan Carlos Varela announced his government <u>was establishing diplomatic relations with</u>[③] mainland China, calling it a "true country." Varela thanked Taiwan for its years of support, but said his country saw new possibilities in establishing ties with Beijing.
(*China Post*)

巴拿馬<u>與</u>中華民國<u>斷絕外交關係</u>，由於北京政府持續對臺北<u>恐嚇打壓</u>，導致臺灣在國際舞台上遭受此最新挫敗。巴拿馬總統瓦雷拉在週二宣布，該國政府<u>與</u>中國大陸<u>建立外交關係</u>，並稱其為「真正的國家」。瓦雷拉感謝臺灣長年來的支持，但表示巴拿馬與北京建交會帶來新的發展可能。(《英文中國郵報》)

說明

① 「外交關係」可用 diplomatic ties/relations 表示，前面搭配動詞 sever（切斷）或 break（打破）即為「斷絕外交關係」。一旦斷交就容易陷入 diplomatic isolation（外交孤立）或 diplomatic predicament（外交困境）。

② cow 當名詞時是「母牛」或「乳牛」的意思，但此處當動詞用，意思是「恐嚇」、「威脅」，而 to cow and constrain 是共用的搭配，可指「恐嚇打壓」。

③ 「建立外交關係」的「建立」常用 establish，也可用動詞片語 set up，例如「建立全面外交關係」為 to set up full diplomatic relations。另一相關的搭配詞組「正式恢復外交關係」則可用 to formally restore diplomatic relations 或 the resumption of formal diplomatic ties 來表示。

搭配詞練習

⚙ 請從方格中挑選正確的搭配詞來完成以下的句子。

prevents	urged	embarrassed	overthrow

1. The scandal has gripped the country and deeply *embarrassed* the **government**.

   這件醜聞引起全國關注，並**讓政府**深感**難堪**。

2. This measure *prevents* **governments** from making new budget cuts quickly.

   這項措施可**防止政府**快速削減新的預算。

3. He is accused of leading a regional militant group seeking to *overthrow* the **government**.

   他被控領導一個地區性的武裝組織，意圖**推翻政府**。

4. Protesters from all over the country *urged* the **government** to abandon the cuts.

   來自全國各地的抗議民眾**力促政府**放棄撙節政策。

解答：1. embarrassed 2. prevents 3. overthrow 4. urged

暖身練習解答：①

politics/political

(n.) 政治 / (adj.) 政治的

▶ 答案請見 p. 27

暖身練習

⚙ 請就以下中英譯文選出適當的搭配詞。

Those who have mastered the art of **office** ① **politic** ② **politics**
seem to have more doors open to them at work.
深諳**辦公室政治**之道的人，在工作上似乎有更多的機會。

<u>politics</u> 主要指「政治事業」、「政治手段」、「政治觀點」和「政治學」
等意思。其中當「政治觀點」使用時為複數可數名詞，當「政治學」使用
時則為單數不可數名詞，因此後面所接的動詞型態不同，例如以下例句：

- Your politics are your beliefs about how a country ought to be
  governed.
  你的政治觀點就是你認為國家應如何治理的信念。

  · govern >治理

- Politics is a subject that is open to interpretation and debate.
  政治學是一門可供詮釋與辯論的學科。

  解釋　　　　辯論

  說明　學科名稱如 physics（物理學）、mathematics（數學）、statistics
  （統計學）、economics（經濟學）、<u>ethics（倫理學）</u>、<u>aesthetics（美學）</u>、
  poetics（詩學）等，都與 politics 一樣字尾為 -ics，且皆為不可數名詞，後
  面接單數動詞。另外，「政治學」也可稱為 political science。

politics 可以衍生出許多相關詞彙，例如動詞 politicize 是「政治
化」，其形容詞 politicized 是「政治化的」，而「政治化的議題」即為
politicized issue。名詞 politician 或名詞片語 political figure 是「政治人

物」，而「狡猾的政客」可稱為 crooked/cunning politician，「傑出的政治家」則是 distinguished/prominent politician，其中 politician 一字也可以用 statesman 取代。此外，形容詞 politic 和 political 的意義容易混淆，發音和重音也不同。首先，politic 是「精明的」，與政治無關，重音在第一音節；political 是「政治的」，重音在第二音節，例句如下：

- It would not be politic for you to leave the meeting early.
  你若提早離開會議，是很不明智的。

- Environmental science has become highly political.
  環境科學已經變得相當政治化。

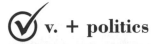 v. + politics

v.	politics	中譯
enter / go into / participate in		參與政治
influence/shape	politics	影響政治
interfere/intervene/meddle in		干預政治
play		玩弄政治手段

搭配詞例句

- The Government is not encouraging people to enter politics.
  政府並不鼓勵人民參政。

....

- There's a myth that the church shouldn't meddle in politics.
  宗教不應干預政治是種迷思。

....

- "Playing politics" at work is just about gaining the support of people with the ability to put your ideas into practice.
在職場上「玩弄政治手段」，其實就是使有能力的人幫你把想法付諸實現。

 **political + n.**

political	n.	中譯
political	activist	從事政治運動者
	animal	政治動物，熱衷政治的人
	asylum	政治庇護
	campaign/movement	政治運動
	chaos/jolt/turmoil	政治混亂
	clampdown/coercion/persecution/repression/suppression	政治箝制／迫害／壓迫
	correctness	政治正確
	dissident	政治異議人士
	impasse/standoff	政治僵局
	interference/intervention	政治干預
	issue	政治議題
	leadership	政治領導階層
	minefield	政治地雷區
	moderate	政治立場溫和人士
	neutrality	政治中立
	populism	政治民粹

political	prisoner	政治犯
	refugee	政治難民
	responsibility	政治責任
	stability	政治穩定
	stand	政治立場
	suicide	政治自殺

搭配詞例句

- He moved to a country in the European Union and was granted political asylum there.
  他遷往歐盟某個國家,並獲得政治庇護。

  說明 此句搭配 political asylum 的動詞為 grant,意指「准予」、「給予」。其他常和 asylum 搭配的動詞還有 apply for(申請)、ask for(請求)、seek(尋求)等,如 seek political asylum 為「尋求政治庇護」,而「尋求庇護的人」就稱為 asylum seeker。

- The police have become a tool for political suppression.
  警方已成為政治迫害的工具。

- A political dissident has to learn how to face suppression and spend his life in a prison.
  政治異議人士必須學習如何面對壓迫和牢獄生活。

- The Presidential Office denounced China's political intervention in Taiwanese businesses seeking investment in mainland China.
  總統府譴責中國對臺商在大陸投資的政治干預。

相關詞彙之搭配使用

片語

... maintain political neutrality ... remain politically neutral	…保持政治中立
apolitical organization	非政治性組織
political and financial support from the government	來自政府的政治與財務支持
political appointments to posts in public administration	公職的政治任命
politically correct language and behavior	政治正確的語言和行為
to discuss politically sensitive issue	討論政治敏感議題
to ensure women's rights to education, employment, access to justice and political participation	確保婦女受教育、工作、訴諸司法和政治參與的權利
to release all political prisoners immediately and unconditionally	立刻無條件釋放所有的政治犯

句子

- Trade protectionism is a <u>politically motivated</u> defensive measure.
  貿易保護主義是一種<u>出於政治動機</u>的防衛措施。

- <u>Politics at work</u> does not occur in a vacuum, but rather through interactions with others.
  <u>職場上的政治</u>不是憑空發生，而是與他人互動所產生的。

段落

The usual political arguments at Thanksgiving dinner <u>may be silenced</u>[①] this year thanks to America's <u>polarizing political climate</u>[②]. A new survey by the Cato Institute shows that most Americans <u>no longer feel comfortable talking about</u>[③] their political beliefs. According to the survey, 71 percent of Americans "believe that <u>political correctness has silenced important discussions our society needs to have</u>[④]." Meanwhile, 58 percent of Americans believe the "political climate prevents them from sharing their political beliefs." The survey found that Democrats are more open with their political views than Republicans. (*Daily Mail*)

在美國<u>極端的政治氛圍</u>籠罩下，今年的感恩節晚餐<u>可能聽不到往常的政治爭論</u>了。卡托研究機構一項新的調查指出，多數美國人<u>難以再暢談</u>自己的政治理念。調查指出，71% 的美國人「相信<u>政治正確已經使得民眾不再討論社會所需的重要議題</u>」，而 58% 的美國人相信「現在的政治氛圍使得他們不再與人分享自己的政治理念」。這份調查還發現，民主黨人士的政治觀點較共和黨人士為開放。(《每日郵報》)

說明

① The usual political arguments ... may be silenced 的 be silenced 是被動語態，指「被噤聲」，也就是不再如以往可以任意討論政治。

② polarize 原是動詞「極端化」，此處 polarizing 是現在分詞當形容詞用，意思是「極端的」，修飾名詞片語 political climate。political climate 若直譯成「政治氣候」，聽起來生硬不自然，可轉化譯為「政治氛圍」。

③ feel comfortable talking about... 是常見的搭配，意思是「愉快談論…」，前面加上 no longer（不再）即成否定用法。

④ political correctness 一般直譯為「政治正確」，是指在語言和行為上避免冒犯或歧視弱勢族群如身心障礙者、少數族裔等。近年來美國社會因出現矯枉過正的現象，某些人士認為政治正確可能箝制言論自由，導致本文所言的 political correctness has silenced important discussions our society needs to have。另外，此句中的 silenced 是主動語態。

搭配詞練習

⚙ 請從方格中挑選正確的搭配詞來完成以下的句子。

stability	responsibility	interfere	Politicians

1. Indonesia supported the ongoing efforts to achieve **political _Stability_** as a prerequisite for achieving sustainable economic development.
   印尼持續力求**政治穩定**，作為經濟永續發展的先決條件。

2. The Government could not take any **political _responsibility_**
   政府無法承擔任何**政治責任**。

3. _Politicians_ interfere in mass media reporting, and influential journalists _Interfer_ **in politics**.
   政治人物干預大眾媒體報導，有影響力的記者則**干預政治**。

party
(n.) 政黨

暖身練習

⚙ 請就以下中英譯文選出適當的搭配詞。　　　　　▶ 答案請見 p. 34

The basic purpose of ① **forming** ② **building up** a political **party** is to get in power.
成立政黨的基本目的就是要取得政權。

　　party 當名詞時常指「派對」、「集會」等，例如「舉辦派對」可搭配一個有趣的動詞 throw（丟，擲；舉辦），成為 throw a party，而「參加派對」則為 go to a party 或 attend a party。「參加派對的人」可以稱為 partygoer，而「熱衷參加派對的人」可稱為 party animal；相反地，如果是「把派對氣氛弄糟的人」就稱為 party pooper。

　　在政治上，party 是指「政黨」。臺灣幾個主要政黨的英文名稱如下：

- Chinese Nationalist Party (Kuomintang/KMT)：中國國民黨
- Democratic Progressive Party (DPP)：民主進步黨
- New Power Party (NPP)：時代力量
- People First Party (PFP)：親民黨
- Taiwan Solidarity Union (TSU)：臺灣團結聯盟

具「政黨」意涵的 party 搭配詞如下：

✅ v. + party

v.	party	中譯
disband/dissolve		解散政黨
establish/form/found / set up		成立政黨
join	party	加入政黨
support		支持某政黨
vote for		投票給某政黨

搭配詞例句

- They can do more to attract different minority groups to join the party.
  他們可以多做一點事，吸引不同的少數族群人士加入該政黨。

....

- About 65 percent of the voters in Florida's Republican primary said they supported the Tea Party.
  佛羅里達州共和黨初選約有 65% 的選民表示支持茶黨。

....

✅ adj. + party

adj.	party	中譯
conservative		保守政黨
fascist		法西斯政黨
governing/ruling		執政黨
left-wing	party	左翼政黨
political		政黨
right-wing		右翼政黨

搭配詞例句

- The ruling party has lost more than 40 percent of its legislative seats to rivals, but will remain the largest bloc in parliament.
  執政黨在國會失去逾 40% 的席次，但仍會是國會的最大黨。

- A major political party in Mexico has chosen a female presidential candidate for the first time.
  墨西哥一主要政黨首次選出女性的總統候選人。

 party **+ n.**

party	n.	中譯
party	chairman/chairperson/chairwoman/chief	黨主席
	congress/convention	黨代表大會
	discipline	黨紀
	headquarters	黨部（headquarters 字尾要加 -s）
	heavyweight	黨內大老，黨內重要人物
	manifesto	政黨宣言
	member	黨員
	membership	黨籍
	nominee	政黨提名人
	platform	黨綱
	spokesman/spokesperson/spokeswoman	政黨發言人
	whip	黨鞭

搭配詞例句

- Su has received several calls from residents in New Taipei City asking him to run for the position of party chairperson.

  蘇貞昌接到不少新北市民的電話，要他出來競選黨主席一職。

- He was soliciting support from local party headquarters chairpersons.

  他尋求地方黨部主任的支持。

  說明 headquarters 在英文新聞中也常用縮寫 HQ。

相關詞彙之搭配使用

片語

be expelled from the party expulsion from the party	被開除黨籍
Chinese Communist Party (CCP)	中國共產黨
inter-party cooperation	黨際合作
intra-party competition	黨內競爭
to cross party lines	跨越黨派
to deregister the opposition party	解散該反對黨
to revise the party's platform and charters	修改黨綱、黨章
to take the helm of the party	領導該政黨
violation of party rules	違反黨紀
vote-buying at a party election	黨內選舉時買票

句子

- The Ministry of Foreign Affairs has responded positively to a Democratic Progressive Party (DPP) <u>lawmaker's</u> proposal to invite former US president Barack Obama to visit Taiwan.

民進黨<u>立法委員</u>提議邀請美國前總統歐巴馬訪問臺灣，外交部對此表示樂觀其成。

說明 lawmaker 也可代換成 legislator，都是指國會的「立法者」，在臺灣則是立法院的「立法委員」。

段落

Taiwan's parliament descended into chaos for <u>a second consecutive day</u>[1] with lawmakers wielding chairs above their heads and throwing water balloons as they <u>brawled over</u>[2] a controversial infrastructure project. The plan is one of President Tsai Ing-wen's <u>signature proposals</u>[3] and includes building light rail lines, food control measures and green energy facilities. But the opposition Kuomintang party is against the project, saying it favours cities and counties faithful to Tsai's ruling Democratic Progressive Party (DPP) and has been devised to secure support for the party ahead of next year's regional elections.
(*Channel NewsAsia*)

臺灣的<u>立法院連續第二天</u>陷入混亂，<u>因</u>審查高度爭議的前瞻基礎建設計畫爆發衝突，立法委員高舉椅子揮舞並相互丟擲水球。這是蔡英文總統提出的<u>重要計畫案</u>，其中包括輕軌建設、食安管控和綠能設施等。但在野的國民黨反對此計畫，他們表示前瞻計畫只對親蔡英文執政的民進黨縣市有利，而且是民進黨用來為明年地方選舉固樁爭取支持的手段。(《亞洲新聞台》)

說明

① a second consecutive day 也可以說成 two days in a row，表示「連續兩天」。

② 動詞 brawl 是「爭吵」、「打架」，搭配介系詞 over，brawl over... 是指「為了⋯爭吵打架」，等於 fight over...，例如 My dogs are fighting over food.（我的狗在爭搶食物。）另外 brawl 和 fight 也可當名詞用，常搭配動詞 erupt（爆發），例如 A fight erupted between ruling and opposition lawmakers in the Taiwanese parliament.（臺灣立法院執政黨與反對黨立法委員之間爆發衝突。）

③ signature 原意是「簽名」，可引申為「識別個人或事物的重要特點」，如 signature dishes 是「招牌菜」、signature tune 是「主題曲」、signature style 是「個人獨特風格」等。此處的 signature proposals 就是體現蔡英文總統施政理念的「重要計畫」。

搭配詞練習

⚙ **請從方格中挑選正確的搭配詞來完成以下的句子。**

establish	ruling	political
deregistered	conservative	opposition

1. He intended to _____ a _____ **party**.
   他曾打算**成立**一個**政黨**。

2. South Korea's _____ _____ **party** changed its name to try to
   shore up sagging support in a key election year.
   南韓**保守的執政黨**更改黨名，希望藉此在選舉關鍵年挽回下滑的人氣。

3. The Zambian government is said to have _____ an _____
   party led by ex-Foreign Affairs minister Harry Kalaba.
   據傳尚比亞政府已**解散**由前外交部長哈利‧卡拉巴領導的**反對黨**。

解答：1. establish, political　2. conservative, ruling　3. deregistered, opposition
暖身練習解答：①

law

(n.) 法令，法律

暖身練習

⚙ 請就以下中英譯文選出適當的搭配詞。　　　　　▶ 答案請見 p. 41

I am definitely optimistic that I can start ① **doing** ② **practicing law** again.
我對於重新**從事律師工作**一事非常樂觀。

　　law 與其他字組成的字相當多，如 lawmaker 為「立法委員」或「國會議員」，lawyer 是「律師」（視國家或業務不同也可能稱為 counselor、attorney、solicitor 或 barrister），lawsuit 是「訴訟案件」，lawbreaker 是「違法者」。另外，從名詞 lawbreaker 也可聯想到其形容詞 law-breaking（違法的），相反詞是 law-abiding（守法的），而「守法的公民」就是 law-abiding citizen，例如以下例句：

- Immigrants are more law-abiding than native-born citizens.
  移民比本國出生的公民更守法。

　　另一個與 law 有關的衍生字是在 law 前面加 out-，成為 outlaw，當名詞用時指「歹徒」，也可當動詞使用，意思是「使…成為非法」，也就是「立法禁止」，如下例：

- Many states have outlawed cell phone use while driving.
  許多州都立法禁止開車時使用手機。

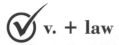 **v. + law**

v.	law	中譯
act within / obey/observe/uphold		遵守法令
advocate for		擁護法令
amend/revise		修訂法令
annul/repeal/rescind		廢除法令
approve/pass		核准法令，通過法令
break/violate		違反法令
draft		草擬法令
enact/introduce	law	頒布法令
enforce		執行法令
flout		藐視法令
go to		上法院，打官司
make		制定法令
practice		從事律師工作
reject		拒絕接受法令
sign		簽署法令

搭配詞例句

- Seven states have passed laws requiring that employers accommodate pregnant women.
  有七個州通過法令，要求雇主必須照顧到懷孕員工的需求。

- When the state will begin enforcing the law was not immediately clear.
  州政府何時將開始執行這項法令還不清楚。

- He was forced to go to law with his brothers to get back his property.
  他被迫與自己的兄弟打官司，討回家產。

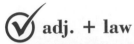 adj. + law

adj.	law	中譯
administrative		行政法
civil		民法，大陸法系
common		普通法，英美法系
constitutional		憲法
criminal		刑法
international	law	國際法
martial		戒嚴法，戒嚴令
natural		自然法
out-of-date		過時的法令
proposed		提議的法令
strict/stringent		嚴格的法令

搭配詞例句

- The company is stoutly protected by international law.
  該公司受到國際法妥善的保護。

- During the 38-year Martial Law period from 1949 to 1987, Taiwanese were deprived of basic rights such as the freedoms of expression and assembly.
  從 1949 至 1987 年共 38 年的戒嚴法實施期間，臺灣人民被剝奪了言論和集會自由等基本人權。

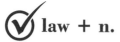 **law + n.**

law	n.	中譯
law	degree	法學學位
	enforcement	執行法令
	firm	法律事務所
	school	法學院
	violation	違反法令

搭配詞例句

- Prosecution officials said 8 opposition lawmakers were being investigated for alleged election law violations.
  檢方表示，有八位反對黨的國會議員疑似違反選舉法而遭到調查。

相關詞彙之搭配使用

片語

anti-money laundering laws	反洗錢法
Assembly and Parade Act/Law	集會遊行法
be protected under copyright law	受著作權法保護

equality before the law	法律之前的平等
lack of law and order / lack of rule of law	缺乏法治
law and order / rule of law	法治
law enforcement agency/authorities	執法機關
law enforcement officer/official	執法官員
multiple federal felony charges	指控數項聯邦重罪
to file a defamation/libel/slander lawsuit against...	對…提出誹謗告訴
to provide legal advice/counseling to...	對…提供法律諮詢
to take the law into your own hands	自行執法治罪

句子

- We are equal under the law.
  法律之前，人人平等。

- No one is above the law—not even the President.
  無人能凌駕於法律之上，即使總統也不例外。

- There should be a law against it.
  應該立法禁止這件事。

- It is against the law to take something that does not belong to you.
  拿走不屬於你的物品是違法的。

- Following the national affairs conference on pension reform, the government has begun work on amending the law to push reform.
  在國事會議討論年金改革後，政府已開始著手修訂法令以推動改革。

- Germany <u>has strict/tough laws on</u> hate speech and symbols linked to the Nazis.

德國<u>對於</u>與納粹有關的仇恨言論和象徵符號<u>有嚴格的法律禁制</u>。

....

段落

Taiwan has <u>passed landmark animal protection laws</u>[①] imposing fines for the consumption of dog and cat meat as well as jail time for those who kill and <u>torture animals</u>[②]. <u>The Animal Protection Act amendments</u>[③] approved by the Legislative Yuan on Tuesday punish the sale, purchase or consumption of dog or cat meat with fines ranging from NT$50,000 to NT$2 million. (*China Post*)

臺灣通過指標性的動物保護法案,將對食用狗肉和貓肉者處以罰鍰,而殺害或虐待動物者則判處徒刑。週二立法院通過《動物保護法》修正案,將針對販售、購買或食用狗肉或貓肉者開罰新臺幣五萬至兩百萬元。(《英文中國郵報》)

說明

① law 指「法規」或「法條」時是可數名詞,如 pass a law(通過一項法規)。此處的 landmark(地標,指標)搭配 laws,意思是「具有指標意義的法案」。

②「虐待動物」還可說成 animal abuse,如 They are found guilty of animal abuse.(他們虐待動物被判有罪。)

③ 一般字典把 act 和 bill 皆譯為「法案」,兩者容易混淆。bill 是送交立法機關審議的議案或草案,通過後成為正式的法律才稱為 act。此處 The Animal Protection Act 是「動物保護法」,其後接 amendments 是指對現行法律的「修正案」,如著名的美國憲法第一條修正案,保障言論和新聞出版自由,就稱為 First Amendment。

搭配詞練習

⚙ **請從方格中挑選正確的搭配詞來完成以下的句子。**

repealing	violating	making
amending	lawmakers	firm

1. Protesters were charged with _____ the **law**.
   抗議者被控**違法**。

2. Several _____ have proposed writing food banks into law to better help the disadvantaged while reducing waste of food and daily necessities.
   好幾位**立法委員**提案制定食物銀行法案，以更有效幫助弱勢族群，並減少食物和日常必需品的浪費。

3. The legislature has the function of _____ **new law** or _____ or _____ **existing law**.
   立法機關具有**制定新法**、**修訂**或**廢除現有法令**的功能。

4. He originally went to work for a prestigious **law** _____.
   他一開始是到一間知名的**法律事務所**工作。

解答：1. violating　2. lawmakers　3. making, amending, repealing　4. firm

暖身練習解答：②

41

judicial

(adj.) 法院的，司法的

暖身練習

⚙ 請就以下中英譯文選出適當的搭配詞。　　　　　　▶ 答案請見 p. 47

One side is likely to be disappointed by the **judicial** ① **judgement**
② **decision**.

一方可能會對此**法院判決**感到失望。

　　judicial 是形容詞，意指「法院的」或「司法的」，不要與另一個形容詞 judicious 混淆。judicious 的意思是「明智的」、「謹慎的」，例如 judicious use of natural resources（謹慎使用自然資源）。而與 judicial 相關的司法用字有 judge（法官）、jury（陪審團）、jury duty（陪審義務）、juror（陪審員）、jurisdiction（司法管轄權）等，例如 hung jury 或 deadlocked jury 是指「陪審員無法達成一致裁決的陪審團」；beyond this country's jurisdiction 則是「超出這個國家的司法管轄權」。而 judicial 後面搭配名詞也會產生許多與法律相關的詞組。

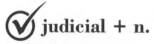 **judicial + n.**

judicial	n.	中譯
judicial	branch/system	司法體系
	court	法庭
	decision	法院判決

	ethics	司法倫理
	independence	司法獨立
	interpretation	司法解釋
judicial	investigation	司法調查
	proceeding	司法程序
	reform	司法改革
	remedy	司法救濟

搭配詞例句

- Corrupt judicial systems in Albania and neighboring countries deter needed foreign investment.
  阿爾巴尼亞以及鄰近國家的司法體系腐敗，使得他們所需的外資不願進入。

- Arab states neither have such judicial independence nor are their leaderships subject to the law.
  阿拉伯國家缺乏司法獨立，他們的領導階層也不受法律約束。

- At present, we still have a long way to go in our judicial reforms.
  目前我們的司法改革還有一大段路要走。

相關詞彙之搭配使用

片語

a landmark ruling	重要判決
be served with a subpoena to give evidence	收到傳票，被要求提供證據

be subpoenaed as a defense witness in the trial	在審判中被傳喚作爲被告證人
capital punishment death penalty/sentence	死刑
civil case/litigation	民事案件
claim for damage	要求損害賠償
court-martial	軍事法庭
court of appeals	上訴法院
criminal case/litigation	刑事案件
deferred indictment	緩起訴處分
diplomatic immunity	外交豁免權
facing charges of murder and misconduct	被控謀殺與行爲不檢
force majeure clause	不可抗力條款
infringement upon rights	侵權
life imprisonment/sentence	終生監禁，無期徒刑
obstruction of justice	妨礙司法
out-of-court settlement settlement of dispute outside the court	庭外和解
serving a sentence of imprisonment	監禁服刑
suspended sentence	緩刑
to bail ... out	將…保釋出獄
to begin a court session	開庭
to jump bail	棄保潛逃
to place/put on probation	處以緩刑

to plead guilty	認罪
to plead innocence / to plead not guilty	辯稱無罪
to release on bail	交保獲釋
to release on parole	假釋
to release without charge	無罪釋放
to remand in custody	還押候審
to stand trial	受審
without the possibility of parole	沒有假釋機會

句子

- A witness was called to give a testimony in court.
  一名目擊者被傳喚至法庭上作證。

- A Mississippi jury fails to reach a unanimous verdict in the trial of a man accused of burning a woman to death.
  密西西比州的陪審團針對一名男子被控縱火燒死女性案，無法作出一致的裁決。

- The Taipei District Prosecutors' Office filed charges citing Offenses Against Children's Development against the kindergarten owner.
  臺北地檢署依妨害幼童發育罪嫌起訴幼稚園的負責人。
  說明 此處 charge 當名詞用，意思是「控告」、「控訴」，前面搭配動詞 file（提出，提起），file charges against... 為「控告⋯」、「起訴⋯」的意思，file 也可代換為 press, bring 等，例如 They have decided to press charges against me.（他們決定要控告我。）如果要表示「撤銷告訴」可搭配動詞 drop，即 drop the charges。

段落

Former President Park Geun-hye stared straight ahead and denied that she engaged in bribery and leaking government secrets[①] at Tuesday's start of the criminal trial[②] that could send South Korea's first female leader to prison for life[③] if she is convicted[④]. (*AP*)

在週二的刑事審判庭開始時，南韓前總統朴槿惠直視前方，否認她行賄和洩露政府機密。如果被判有罪，這位南韓第一位女性領導人可能遭終身監禁。（《美聯社》）

說明

① 在 bribery（賄賂）和 leaking government secrets（洩露政府機密）兩項罪名前可搭配動詞片語 engage in...（從事…）。

② criminal trial 為「刑事審判」，與此相對的「民事審判」則為 civil trial。

③ send someone to prison 等同於 put someone in jail（把某人關進監獄），後面加 for life 是指 life sentence（終身監禁）。

④ 此處 convicted 接在 be 動詞後面，是被動語態，意思是「被判有罪」。convict 當動詞用時指「判決有罪」，後面接介系詞 of 再接罪名，例如 He was convicted of murder.（他被判犯下謀殺罪。）convict 當名詞用時則是指「判決有罪的犯人」。

搭配詞練習

⚙ 請從方格中挑選正確的搭配詞來完成以下的句子。

judges	interpretation	Court	investigation	reforms

1. Such a dispute may require **judicial** _____ of the definition of a hazardous waste.

   這種爭議可能需要**司法解釋**，說明危險廢棄物的定義為何。

2. Seven of Europe's top anticorruption _____ called for sweeping **judicial** _____ in Europe.

   歐洲七位反貪腐的高階**法官**呼籲全歐推行全面的**司法改革**。

3. China's **Supreme** _____ will have to help overcome such cronyism.

   中國的**最高人民法院**必須協助改革這種內舉不避親的陋習。

4. Ten long years later, we still await the conclusion of the **judicial** _____ of that crime.

   漫長的 10 年過去了，我們還在等待那件犯罪事件的**司法調查**結果。

解答：1. interpretation　2. judges, reforms　3. Court　4. investigation

暖身練習解答：②

crime/criminal

(n.) 罪行 / (adj.) 犯罪的；刑事上的

▶ 答案請見 p. 55

暖身練習

⚙ 請就以下中英譯文選出適當的搭配詞。

This age group is most likely to ① **make** ② **commit crimes**,
irrespective of nationality.
不論是什麼國籍，這個年齡層的人最容易**犯罪**。

crime 是可數名詞，前面常搭配動詞 commit 或 do 來表達「犯罪」
之意，但臺灣的學習者卻常搭配動詞 make 而產生錯誤，這可能跟表達
「犯錯」時使用 make a mistake 有關。同樣地，表達「犯錯」時也不能用
commit/do a mistake。此外，crime 的形容詞是 criminal（犯罪的），但
criminal 同時也可當名詞用，意指「罪犯」，如 convicted criminal 為「判
決有罪的犯人」。而動詞 criminalize 是指「制定法律使…成為非法行為」，
名詞 criminology 則為「犯罪學」。

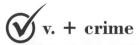 **v. + crime**

v.	crime	中譯
carry out / commit/do		犯罪
combat/fight/tackle	crime	打擊犯罪
confess		認罪
curb/deter		遏止犯罪

eradicate / wipe out		消滅犯罪
investigate		調查犯罪
report	crime	報案
solve		破案
witness		目擊犯罪

搭配詞例句

- The FBI reported that 1,207,704 violent crimes were committed in 2017, up 2.1% from 2016.

  聯邦調查局報告指出，2017 年暴力犯罪計有 1,207,704 件，比 2016 年多出 2.1%。

  說明 此句為被動語態，常用的 commit crimes 變成 crimes were committed。

- Local police no longer fight crime just on the streets, they fight it on computers, smartphones and tablets.

  地方警察不再只是在街頭打擊犯罪，還利用電腦、智慧型手機和平板電腦對付罪犯。

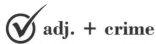 adj. + crime

adj.	crime	中譯
alleged		涉嫌犯罪，被指控（但尚未證實的）罪行
appalling/brutal/heinous/horrendous/horrible/horrific	crime	殘酷罪行
economic		經濟犯罪
grave/great/major/serious/terrible		嚴重罪行

juvenile		青少年犯罪
minor/petty		輕微罪行
non-violent		非暴力犯罪
organized	crime	組織犯罪
vicious/violent		暴力犯罪
white-collar		白領階級犯罪

搭配詞例句

- Human trafficking is a serious crime in Taiwan.
  販賣人口在臺灣是嚴重的罪行。

....

- Migrants may be responsible for most of a recent rise in violent crime in Germany, research commissioned by the government suggests.
  政府委託的研究指出，移民可能是導致德國近來暴力犯罪增加的主因。

....

 **crime + n.**

crime	n.	中譯
	prevention	防止犯罪
	rate/statistics	犯罪率
crime	scene	犯罪現場
	suspect	犯罪嫌疑人
	victim	犯罪受害人

搭配詞例句

- Memphis's violent crime rate of 1,740 incidents per 100,000 residents trails only three other U.S. cities.
  孟菲斯的暴力犯罪率在每 10 萬居民中有 1,740 件，在全美只低於其他三個城市。

  說明 此句中的 trails 是動詞，指「跟在⋯後面」。

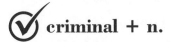 **criminal + n.**

criminal	n.	中譯
criminal	act/offence	犯罪行為
	charge	刑事指控，公訴
	court	刑事法庭
	investigation	犯罪調查
	record	犯罪紀錄，前科

搭配詞例句

- Having a criminal record can destroy your chances of getting employed.
  有前科可能會害你找不到工作。

相關詞彙之搭配使用

片語

... was suspected of fraud and embezzlement	⋯涉嫌詐欺與盜用公款
armed robbery	持械搶劫
be arrested or detained on a criminal charge	因刑事指控而被捕或遭拘留

carjacking / car hijacking	劫車
cocaine/drug/heroin smuggling	走私古柯鹼 / 毒品 / 海洛英
cocaine/drug/heroin trafficking	販售古柯鹼 / 毒品 / 海洛英
crime against humanity	危害人類罪，違反人道罪
document forgery	偽造文書
drug dealer	毒販
gun control	槍枝管制
involuntary manslaughter	過失殺人
juvenile delinquent	少年犯
premeditated murder	預謀殺人
sex abuse / sexual assault	性侵
sexually harass / sexual harassment	性騷擾
terror/terrorist attack	恐怖攻擊
to check the scene of the crime	勘查犯罪現場
to commit a criminal act to commit an offence	從事犯罪行為
to commit the offense of burglary/larceny/theft	犯下竊盜罪
to curb gang violence	遏止幫派暴力
to stand trial on sex abuse charges	因被控性侵而受審
vandalism and graffiti	毀損和塗鴉

句子

- Yasukuni Shrine is contentious for enshrining military figures <u>convicted of war crimes</u> by an international tribunal.
  靖國神社因祭祀被國際法庭判決爲戰犯的軍人而充滿爭議。

- Violent crimes are broken into four categories: <u>murder and nonnegligent manslaughter, rape, robbery, and aggravated assault</u>.
  暴力犯罪分爲四類：謀殺和非過失殺人、強姦、搶劫、加重的企圖傷害罪。

- <u>A spike in violent crime</u> in London saw more <u>murders committed</u> in the city in February and March than there were in New York, figures show.
  數據顯示，倫敦暴力犯罪遽增，二月和三月所發生的謀殺案比紐約還要多。

- <u>Religious hate crimes</u> on the railways, tubes and buses increased almost five-fold since 2013, while homophobic incidents saw a 200 percent rise.
  從 2013 年以來，在鐵路、地下鐵、公車上所發生的宗教仇恨罪行增加近五倍，而恐同的事件則增加 200%。

段落

At least 17 students at a Florida high school were killed after a gunman <u>opened fire on them with an automatic rifle</u>[①], in <u>one of the deadliest school shootings</u>[②] on record in the US. The suspect has been identified as 19-year-old former student Nikolas Cruz, who was arrested after a brief manhunt. Mr. Cruz had been expelled for "disciplinary reasons", while teachers said they had previously been warned that he could pose a danger to the campus. (*The Independent*)

一名槍手闖入佛羅里達州一所高中並以自動步槍掃射，造成至少 17 名學生喪生，是美國<u>死傷極為慘重</u>的校園槍擊案。嫌犯經指認為 19 歲的尼可拉斯‧克魯茲，曾就讀該校的他在警方短暫搜索後被逮捕。克魯茲曾因「行為不檢」遭學校退學，教師表示曾有人警告，該生可能會危害校園安全。（《獨立報》）

說明

① 「開火」的英文為 open fire，後面搭配介系詞 on 再接對象，表示「對…開火」，或是搭配 with 再接武器，表示「用…開火」，例如此處的 opened fire on them with an automatic rifle，就是「用自動步槍對他們開火」。

② school shooting 是「校園槍擊案」，也可說 campus shooting。shooting 前面可搭配形容詞 massive 或 mass（大規模的），如 massive/mass shooting 即表示「大規模槍擊案」。

搭配詞練習

⚙ 請從方格中挑選正確的搭配詞來完成以下的句子。

alleged	scenes	curb	juvenile	investigation

1. We must strengthen the rule of law in order to _____ **crime** in a sustainable manner.
   我們必須強化法治，持續遏止犯罪。

2. All the _____ **crimes** were committed on unknown dates between March 1 and December 31 last year.
   所有遭指控的罪行都發生在去年 3 月 1 日至 12 月 31 日之間，但確切日期不清楚。

3. **Crime** _____ contain physical evidence that is pertinent to a **criminal** _____.
   犯罪現場留有與犯罪調查相關的物證。

4. During the same time period _____ **violent crime rates** have grown almost twice as quickly as adult crime rates.
   在同一時期，青少年暴力犯罪率的成長幾乎是成人犯罪率的兩倍。

解答：1. curb　2. alleged　3. scenes, investigation　4. juvenile

暖身練習解答：②

55

election

(n.) 選舉，競選

暖身練習

⚙ 請就以下中英譯文選出適當的搭配詞。　　　　　　　　　▶ 答案請見 p. 62

That presidential candidate will not be able to retrieve the NT$15 million security deposit he submitted to ① **elect** ② **run for president**.

那位總統候選人將無法領回他**競選總統**時繳交的保證金新臺幣 1,500 萬元。

　　各國的「選舉制度」(electoral system) 不同，因此選舉相關詞彙也有差異。例如臺灣的「總統選舉」(presidential election) 是由每位民眾投票的「直接選舉」(direct election)，但美國的總統選舉分為「政黨初選」(primary election) 和「大選」(general election)，也就是由「民主黨」(the Democratic Party) 和「共和黨」(the Republican Party，或稱 the Grand Old Party, GOP) 兩個政黨先進行「總統初選」(presidential primaries)，並於「全國黨大會」(national party convention) 上選出參加大選的「總統候選人」(presidential candidate)。而且美國有「選舉人團」(electoral college) 制度，一般民眾並不能直接選舉總統，只能在各州選出承諾會支持某個候選人的「選舉人候選人」(elector candidate)，再由當選的「選舉人」(elector) 投票給總統候選人。另外，選民必須事先「登記」(register) 才能投票。

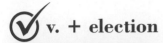 **v. + election**

v.	election	中譯
boycott		抵制選舉
contest/fight		在選舉中競爭
have/hold		舉行選舉
interfere/meddle in	election	干預選舉
lose		輸掉選舉，競選失利
monitor		觀察選舉
rig		操弄選舉
run for		投入選舉，競選

搭配詞例句

- Mr. Chen urged voters not to boycott the election.
  陳先生力勸選民不要抵制選舉。

- Mr. Lee lost the election and then retired from politics.
  李先生競選失利，隨後並退出政壇。

- He accused the ruling party of rigging the elections.
  他指控執政黨操弄選舉。

- The candidate ran for election after her husband died in a political assassination.
  她在丈夫死於政治暗殺後便投入選舉，成為候選人。

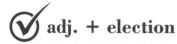 **adj. + election**

adj.	election	中譯
congressional/parliamentary		國會選舉
disputed		有爭議的選舉
fixed/fraudulent/rigged/tainted		舞弊的／腐敗的選舉
general	election	大選
heated		激烈的選舉
legislative		立法委員選舉
presidential		總統選舉
upcoming		即將到來的選舉

搭配詞例句

- Tens of thousands of middle-class urbanites gathered Saturday to vent their anger over tainted elections.
  成千上萬的中產階級都會居民在週六集結，發洩他們對於腐敗選舉的怒氣。

- The KMT's seats saw a significant drop in comparison to the number in the previous legislative election.
  國民黨的席次與前次立法委員選舉時相較減少許多。

- They knew they had little chance of winning the presidential election.
  他們知道要贏得總統選舉的機會渺茫。

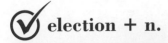 **election + n.**

election	n.	中譯
election	act	選舉法令
	boycott	抵制選舉
	campaign	選舉活動
	committee	選舉委員會
	fraud/manipulation/rigging	選舉舞弊 / 操弄
	subsidy	選舉補助金
	victory	勝選
	violation	選舉違法

搭配詞例句

- The opposition party challenged his election victory last year.
  反對黨質疑他去年的勝選結果。

相關詞彙之搭配使用

片語

... and ... are rivals in the party's leadership election	…與…在黨主席選舉是對手
a hotly contested election	競爭激烈的選舉
a landslide election victory	壓倒性勝選
campaign headquarters	競選總部
campaign rally	選舉造勢集會

campaign speech	競選演說
campaign strategy/tactic	競選策略
Civil Servants Election and Recall Act	公職人員選舉罷免法
election, recall, initiative and referendum	選舉、罷免、創制和複決
president-elect	總統當選人（尚未就任）
presidential campaign	總統大選競選活動
presidential debate	總統大選競選辯論
presidential nomination	總統候選人提名
running mate	競選夥伴
seeking re-election	尋求連任
smear campaign	選舉抹黑
the invalidation of the election results	選舉結果無效
to force a rigged presidential election to be rerun	迫使受到操弄的總統大選重新選舉
to quit the US presidential race	退出美國總統大選
to run for public office	競選公職

句子

- President Trump said that he believed President Vladimir V. Putin was sincere in his denials of interference in the 2016 presidential elections.
  川普總統表示，他相信普丁總統否認干預 2016 年總統大選是眞實的。

- The interim government promised free elections under the new Constitution.
  該過渡政府承諾將依據新憲法舉行自由選舉。

- There was <u>no immediate reaction</u> from Beijing <u>on the election results</u>.
  北京<u>對於選舉結果</u><u>沒有立即的回應</u>。

段落

Emmanuel Macron <u>was elected France's youngest head of state</u>[①] since Napoleon last night after beating his far-right rival Marine Le Pen in an emphatic result that will have <u>far-reaching consequences</u>[②] for <u>Brexit</u>[③] and Europe. Projections gave 39-year-old Mr. Macron almost two thirds of the vote, showing a clear path to <u>the Élysée Palace</u>[④] for the pro-EU centrist who was a political unknown until three years ago and has never <u>held elected office</u>[⑤]. (*The Daily Telegraph*)

馬克宏昨晚擊敗極右派的對手雷朋，<u>當選為自拿破崙以來法國最年輕的總統</u>，此重要結果將<u>對英國脫歐</u>和歐洲有<u>深遠影響</u>。39 歲的馬克宏據估計贏得近三分之二選票，可穩步邁向愛麗舍宮。馬克宏是支持歐盟的中間派，三年前在政壇還沒沒無聞，也從未<u>擔任經由選舉取得的官職</u>。(《每日電訊報》)

說明

① head of state 是「國家元首」，在法國為 President（總統）。
② 形容詞 far-reaching 意思是「影響深遠的」，常搭配 consequence（後果）、impact（衝擊）、effect（效果）、reform（改革）、decision（決定）等名詞使用。
③ Brexit 是 British（英國）和 exit（退場）兩字的混合字，指「英國要退出歐盟」。
④ Élysée Palace（愛麗舍宮）是法國的總統府和官邸，英文新聞喜用官邸來代表該國政府或政權，如美國的 White House（白宮）、英國的 10 Downing Street（唐寧街 10 號）、俄國的 Kremlin（克里姆林宮）、韓國的 Blue House（青瓦臺）等。
⑤ hold office 是「任職」的意思，相反的「停止職務」為 cease to hold office。此處的 hold elected office 是指「經由選舉而擔任某職務」。

搭配詞練習

⚙ 請從方格中挑選正確的搭配詞來完成以下的句子。

presidential	monitored	heated
subsidy	Act	legislative

1. More than 2,000 international observers _____ this **election**.
   超過兩千名國際觀察員來**觀察**這次**選舉**。

2. He defeated his rival in the _____ _____ **election**.
   他在競爭**激烈的總統大選**中擊敗對手。

3. According to the **Election** _____, candidates for presidential and
   _____ **elections** whose support reaches one-third of the overall
   vote are eligible to collect an **election** _____ of NT$30 per vote
   from the government.
   根據《**選舉法**》，總統和**立法委員選舉**候選人獲得選票達總票數三分之一者，
   可獲得政府的**選舉補助金**，每票新臺幣 30 元。

解答：1. monitored　2. heated, presidential　3. Act, legislative, subsidy

暖身練習解答：②

vote
(n.) 選票

暖身練習

⚙ 請就以下中英譯文選出適當的搭配詞。　　　　▶ 答案請見 p. 68

We have a secret ballot and so there is no way of knowing how someone has ① **cast** ② **dropped** his **vote**.
我們採用不記名投票方式，無法得知別人如何**投票**。

vote 當名詞時指「選票」，當動詞時則指「投票」，動詞 vote 常當不及物動詞使用，後面接介系詞 for 再接對象，指「投票給…」，或接 against 再接對象，指「投票反對…」，例如以下例句：

● The new legislature is set to take its oath of office on Feb. 1 and vote for a new speaker and vice speaker on the same day.
新當選的立法委員將於 2 月 1 日宣誓就職，並在同一天投票選出新的立法院院長和副院長。
　說明　句中的 speaker 並不是「講者」或「發言人」，而是「國會的議長」，在臺灣則等同於立法院院長。另外，「發言人」的英文為 spokesperson。

● A few Democrats will likely vote against President Obama's jobs bill.
部分民主黨議員可能會投票反對歐巴馬總統的就業法案。

因為 vote 當名詞時指「選票」，所以「投票」可說成 cast a vote。vote 字尾加 -r 變成 voter，即「投票者」，「有資格投票的人」稱為 eligible voter。在有些國家如美國必須「註冊登記才有資格投票的人」，就稱為 registered voter。

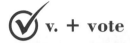 v. + vote

v.	vote	中譯
attract		吸引選票
canvass/court/solicit		爭取選票，遊說選民投票
capture/gain/garner/get/obtain/poll/receive/secure/win		獲得選票
cast	vote	投票
count/tally		計票
lose		輸掉選票
put to		投票表決
split		瓜分票源

搭配詞例句

- He attracted just 0.2% of the vote in May's local government elections.
  五月舉行的地方政府選舉，他只吸引到 0.2% 的選票。

- These political parties are making use of this opportunity to solicit votes.
  這些政黨利用此機會爭取選票。

- The incumbent garnered more than 6 million votes to win another four-year term.
  現任者獲得超過 600 萬票，贏得接下來四年的任期。

- The legislators who received the highest number of votes will be awarded the greatest number of subsidies.
  得到最多選票的立法委員將獲得最高額的補助金。

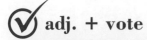 adj. + vote

adj.	vote	中譯
decisive		決定性的一票
dissenting		反對票
final		最後投票
invalid	vote	廢票
popular		普選
unanimous		一致投票通過

搭配詞例句

- The Senate voted 50 to 49 for the measure, with Vice President Biden casting the decisive vote.
  副總統拜登投下決定性的一票，使參議院對於該措施的票數是 50 比 49。

- A final vote on whether the United Nations authorizes war on Iraq is expected before Saturday.
  預計聯合國將於週六前就是否授權對伊拉克開戰作最後投票。

- By a unanimous vote, members of the UN Security Council voted to extend the mission.
  聯合國安全理事會成員國一致投票通過延長該任務的期限。

相關詞彙之搭配使用

片語	
ballot box	投票箱
exit poll	出口民調

first time voter	首次投票者
massive ballot fraud/rigging/tampering massive vote fraud/rigging/tampering	大規模選舉作票
overwhelming majority of votes	壓倒性過半多數票
plurality in the popular vote	普選的相對多數票
polling booth	圈票處
polling station	投票所
swing voter	搖擺不定的選民
to capture more than half of the votes	獲得逾半的選票
to cast an abstention vote	投棄權票
universal suffrage	普選權
vote of no confidence	不信任投票
voter turnout	投票率
widespread vote buying	大舉買票
women's suffrage	婦女投票權

句子

- Voting rules in the U.S. are different in every state.
  美國各州的投票規定都不相同。

....

- The 30 votes against were all cast by members of the right-wing Conservative Party.
  30 張反對票皆由右翼保守黨所投下。

  說明 上句中的 votes 為名詞，也可以用動詞片語 vote against... 表示「投票反對…」。

....

段落

President Donald Trump has signed an executive order today establishing a commission to review <u>alleged voter fraud and voter suppression</u>[①] in the American election system. In the aftermath of the 2016 election, Trump <u>claimed</u>[②] widespread voter fraud explained why former Secretary of State Hillary Clinton emerged with nearly 3 million more popular votes. To date, neither Trump nor his team has provided evidence to <u>substantiate the claims</u>[③], but they have promised an investigation. (*ABC*)

川普總統今日簽署一行政命令，將成立一委員會，審查美國選舉體系中<u>被指爲選民詐欺和選民壓制</u>的漏洞。川普在 2016 年總統大選過後<u>宣稱</u>，前國務卿希拉蕊所獲普選票數之所以比他多了近三百萬票，是因爲大規模的選民詐欺。不過截至目前爲止，川普和他的團隊都未能提出證據來<u>證實這項指控</u>，他們只承諾將調查此事。(《美國廣播公司》)

說明

① 此處 alleged 是形容詞，意指「被指控但未經證實的」，後接名詞片語 voter fraud（選民詐欺）和 voter suppression（選民壓制）。所謂的 voter suppression 是指制定讓選民無法或難以投票的規定，例如美國過去曾限制特定種族、性別和年齡才能投票。

② 此處 claimed 是動詞，意指「宣稱」，與 allege（斷言，宣稱）的意義接近，後面的 widespread voter fraud ... popular votes 是宣稱的內容。

③ 此處 claims 是名詞，意指「宣稱」，在此文境可譯為「指控」，前面常搭配動詞 make（做出）或 substantiate（證實）。而「證實這項指控」也可說成 substantiate the allegations（allegation 是 allege 的名詞）。

搭配詞練習

⚙ 請從方格中挑選正確的搭配詞來完成以下的句子。

nationwide	popular	canvass	invalid	captured

1. The parties have _____ close to 70 percent of the _____
   vote so far.
   這些政黨截止目前為止已**獲得全國**近 70% 的**選票**。

2. Opposition parties increased their share of the _____ **vote** from
   33% to almost 40%.
   反對黨的**普選得票數**從 33% 增加到近 40%。

3. He who could _____ sufficient **votes** would be elected.
   能夠**爭取**到足夠**票數**的人就能當選。

4. We investigate the role of ballot design in explaining the high rate of
   _____ **votes** in Colombia.
   我們調查選票設計所扮演的角色，來解釋哥倫比亞的高**廢票**率。

解答：1. captured, nationwide　2. popular　3. canvass　4. invalid

暖身練習解答：①

strike

(n.) 罷工

▶ 答案請見 p. 74

暖身練習

⚙ 請就以下中英譯文選出適當的搭配詞。

The company would close the *New York Daily News* within 60 days if it could not settle a ① **paralyzed** ② **crippling strike** at the newspaper.

該公司如果無法解決《紐約每日新聞報》員工發起的**癱瘓性罷工**，就會在 60 天內關閉該報社。

strike 當名詞用時可指「打擊」、「攻擊」，如 airstrike 即為「空襲」。strike 和 airstrike 前面可搭配動詞 launch（發動），後面搭配介系詞 against 或 on 再接對象，表示「對…發動攻擊」，例如以下例句：

- Tokyo said it is prepared to launch a military strike against North Korea.
  日本表示，已準備好對北韓發動軍事攻擊。

- America launched airstrikes on Syrian government-backed troops.
  美國對敘利亞政府軍發動空襲。

strike 當名詞用時也可指「罷工」，又可稱為 walkout 或 stoppage，在學校則是「罷課」，常用的句型為 go on strike，例如以下例句：

- Airport security officers were going on strike to protest staff cuts and demand pay hikes.
  機場安檢人員舉行罷工，抗議編制縮減並要求提高薪資。

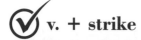 **v. + strike**

v.	strike	中譯
avert/avoid/prevent		避免罷工
ban		禁止罷工
begin / kick off		開始罷工
call/start		發起罷工
call off		取消罷工
end		結束罷工
escalate / step up	strike	擴大罷工
hold/stage		舉行罷工
join / take part in		加入罷工
orchestrate		精心策動罷工
prompt		激起罷工
settle		解決罷工問題

搭配詞例句

- The trade union group called the strike to protest last week's government decision to triple the cost of gasoline.
  該工會團體發起罷工，抗議政府上週將汽油價格調漲三倍的決定。

- The strike could be called off, but protesters have promised to halt production if they don't get the full, $8 billion subsidy restored.
  這場罷工可能會取消，但是抗議者表示如果沒有完全恢復 80 億美元的津貼，他們一定會停工。

- They were ending the strike for humanitarian reasons.
  他們基於人道理由而結束罷工。

- Plans to hold the strike had caused worries in the oil markets.
  舉行罷工的計畫引起原油市場的焦慮。

- The government accused the opposition of orchestrating the strike.
  政府指控反對黨精心策動了這場罷工。

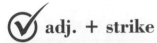 **adj. + strike**

adj.	strike	中譯
crippling		癱瘓性罷工
general/massive		全面／大規模罷工
nationwide	strike	全國性罷工
violent		激烈的罷工

搭配詞例句

- Negotiators reached a tentative agreement to end the crippling strike.
  談判代表達成暫定協議，結束此癱瘓性罷工。

- There were eight general strikes in Argentina in 2001.
  阿根廷於 2001 年發生過八次全面大罷工。

相關詞彙之搭配使用

片語

a violent six-week strike by railway workers	鐵路工人進行六週激烈的罷工
to conduct the strike authorization vote via telephone	透過電話進行罷工授權投票
to hold a strike vote	舉行罷工投票
to reach a settlement	達成協議
to volunteer to work under strike conditions	在罷工時志願工作

句子

- We are on strike until our demands are met.
  我們要罷工直到要求得到回應為止。

....

- Angry Greek workers kicked off a protest against new measures in a 48-hour-long general strike all across the country.
  憤怒的希臘工人開始 48 小時的全國大罷工以抗議新措施。

....

- Fifteen workers started a hunger strike to pressure authorities to step in and settle the dispute.
  15 名工人發起絕食罷工，要求當局介入並調解紛爭。

....

- Public school teachers across West Virginia staged walk-out protests to demand higher wages and better health benefits.
  西維吉尼亞州公立學校的教師舉行罷教抗議，要求較佳的薪資和醫療福利。

  說明 形容詞 walk-out 來自名詞 walkout（罷工），意為「罷工的」，修飾名詞 protests（抗議）。兩字分開的 walk out 則是動詞片語，如 to walk out indefinitely 為「無限期罷工」。

....

段落

Millions of Londoners endured a chaotic start to the week on Monday after a strike shut down most of the Underground network, including many city center stations. Clapham Junction, a major transport hub in the south of the capital, had to be evacuated in the morning rush hour due to overcrowding as passengers were forced onto packed overland trains to get to work. <u>Ten of the 11 Tube lines</u>[①] were disrupted by the <u>24-hour strike</u>[②] by members of the RMT union, who <u>walked out</u>[③] on Sunday evening <u>in a dispute over job cuts and staffing levels</u>. (*AFP*)

週一倫敦大部分地鐵線因罷工而停駛，殃及許多市中心的站點，使得數百萬民眾在新的一週開始就得忍受混亂情況。乘客被迫改搭滿載的地面火車上班，使得倫敦南部的主要交通樞紐克拉普罕站，在早晨尖峰時間即因過度擁擠不得不疏散乘客。倫敦地鐵工會 (RMT) 會員進行 24 小時罷工，11 條地鐵線中有 10 條受到影響。工會週日晚間因削減員工與人員編制的爭議而展開罷工。(《法新社》)

説明

① tube 一般指「管子」，也可指「電視機」，例如 YouTube 就有「你的電視」之意。而倫敦的地下鐵 (the Underground) 也稱作 the Tube（字首需大寫），倫敦的地鐵線即為 Tube line，地鐵站就可説 Tube station，跟美國常説的 subway station 不太一樣。

② 24-hour 是用連字號連結 24 和 hour 而成的形容詞，因此 hour 不能用複數形，也就是不能寫成 24-hours 來修飾後面的名詞 strike。

③ walk out 就字面上看是「走出去」的意思，在此指「勞資雙方會議談判破裂，勞方退席發動罷工」，也可將兩字合寫成一字變成名詞 walkout，例如 stage a walkout 就是「舉行罷工」。

搭配詞練習

⚙ 請從方格中挑選正確的搭配詞來完成以下的句子。

nationwide	general	staging	strike	averting

1. The government recently removed fuel subsidies, which has sent transportation costs soaring and **prompted** _____ **strikes**.
政府最近廢除了燃油津貼，造成運輸成本大增，並**激起全國性罷工**。

2. The opposition will continue _____ _____ **strikes**.
反對黨將持續**舉行大罷工**。

3. Most public transportation will be shut down thanks to the _____.
大部分的公共運輸系統將因**罷工**而停擺。

4. Macy's and the New York City union representing its retail workers have reached a tentative deal, _____ a **strike** that was set to begin Thursday.
梅西百貨與代表其零售工作者的紐約工會已達成暫定協議，**避免**了一場原訂於週四開始的**罷工**。

解答：1. nationwide　2. staging, general　3. strike　4. averting
暖身練習解答：②

74

protest

(n.) 抗議

▶ 答案請見 p. 80

暖身練習

⚙ 請就以下中英譯文選出適當的搭配詞。

Successive **protest** ① **rallies** ② **meetings** have yielded no result.
連續的**抗議集會**都沒有產生任何結果。

protest 可當名詞與動詞使用，都是表示「抗議」的意思，但是發音不一樣，當名詞時重音在第一音節，當動詞時則在第二音節。另外，動詞的 protest 有及物與不及物之分，當及物動詞時後面直接接抗議對象為受詞，例如以下例句：

- This organization's objective was to protest U.S. nuclear-weapons testing.
  這個組織的目標是抗議美國的核武試爆。

如果 protest 當不及物動詞，後面常接介系詞 against, about, at, over 等，再接抗議的對象，例如以下例句：

- Thousands of demonstrators gathered to protest against electoral fraud.
  數千名示威民眾集結，抗議選舉舞弊。

而 protest 字尾加 -er 成為 protester 是指「抗議者」，字尾加 -ant 變成 Protestant 則是指「新教徒」，兩者意義大不相同。其他與名詞 protest 搭配的詞彙如下。

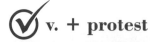 **v. + protest**

v.	protest	中譯
arouse/spark/trigger		引發抗議
continue		持續抗議活動
file/hold/lodge/make/stage	protest	提出抗議
join		加入抗議行列
organize		組織抗議活動

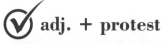

- That visit triggered a brief protest by several dozen Iraqi students.
  那次訪問引發了數十位伊拉克學生的短暫抗議。

....

- Student leaders vowed to continue anti-American protests.
  學生領袖誓言持續反美的抗議活動。

....

- Tens of thousands of people joined protests across the nation.
  全國各地成千上萬的民眾都加入抗議行列。

....

adj. + protest

adj.	protest	中譯
anti-government		反政府抗議
diplomatic		外交抗議
formal	protest	嚴正抗議
peaceful		和平抗議
public		公開抗議

strong/vigorous/violent	protest	強烈抗議
widespread		全面抗議

搭配詞例句

- The organization has made a formal protest against the nuclear testing.
  該組織已針對核子試爆一事提出嚴正抗議。

- Uganda's opposition called for peaceful protests against the government's huge election win last week.
  烏干達的反對黨呼籲對上週政府的選舉大勝採取和平抗議。

- It was the first public protest in Beijing since June.
  這是自六月以來在北京的第一起公開抗議事件。

✓ protest + n.

protest	n.	中譯
protest	demonstration	抗議示威
	march	抗議遊行
	movement	抗議運動
	rally	抗議集會

搭配詞例句

- Several labor unions are preparing to hold a protest march in Taipei.
  好幾個勞工工會正準備在臺北舉行抗議遊行。

- Union leaders lend their support to the protest movement.
  工會領袖支持該抗議運動。

....

- The Pakistani government stops a protest rally before it starts.
  巴基斯坦政府事先阻止了一場抗議集會。

....

相關詞彙之搭配使用

片語

a protest against government policies on education, health care and consumer prices	抗議政府的教育、健保和物價政策
riot police	鎮暴警察
rubber bullet	塑膠子彈
tear gas	催淚瓦斯
to break up a demonstration	驅散示威活動
to hit the streets to protest against...	走上街頭抗議…
to rally together to protest against...	一起集會抗議…
to stage a rally to protest...	舉行集會抗議…
water cannon	水砲，強力水柱

句子

- The protesters demanded early parliamentary elections.
  抗議群眾要求國會提前改選。

....

- Tens of thousands of people rallied to protest government reforms and cuts.
  成千上萬的民眾集會抗議政府的改革和撙節措施。

....

- Thousands of <u>pensioners marched on</u> the Legislative Yuan in Taipei <u>to protest proposed pension cuts.</u>
  數千名<u>退休人員上街遊行</u>至臺北立法院，<u>抗議年金給付縮減的提案</u>。

- At least 10 people were arrested as up to 2,000 demonstrators <u>began a sit-down protest</u> last night.
  昨晚多達 2,000 名示威民眾<u>開始靜坐抗議</u>，至少 10 人被逮捕。

段落

President Tsai Ing-wen said violence "would not slow the pace of reform," after protesters outside the Legislative Yuan physically attacked lawmakers prior to a review of two <u>pension</u>① reform bills. Protesters, many of whom <u>camped out on the streets</u>② Tuesday night, criticized the government's <u>use of barbed wire to barricade</u>③ the Legislative Yuan. (*China Post*)

立法院準備審查兩個年金改革草案前，院外的抗議群眾追打立法委員。蔡英文總統聞訊後表示，暴力「無法減緩改革的進程」。許多抗議者週二在街頭夜宿，他們批評政府使用鐵刺拒馬封鎖立法院。(《英文中國郵報》)

> **說明**
> ① pension 是「退休金」，而「領取退休金者」稱為 pensioner，在此新聞中是指抗議年金改革的「軍公教退休人員」，英文為 retired public-school teachers, civil servants and military personnel。
> ② camp out 為「野營」，加上 on the street 就變成「露宿街頭」。
> ③ barbed wire 是「帶刺鐵絲網」，在此新聞中是指立法院外的「拒馬」；barricade 當名詞時是「路障」，在此當動詞用，指「堵住」、「封鎖」。

搭配詞練習

⚙ **請從方格中挑選正確的搭配詞來完成以下的句子。**

lodge	Violent	sparked	protest	formal

1. _____ **protests** in Egypt have dominated international headlines of late.

   埃及**激烈的抗議活動**成為近日來的國際頭條新聞。

2. An accident in June, in which two Korean girls were killed by a U.S. military vehicle, _____ **widespread** anti-American **protests**.

   六月一場意外中兩名南韓女孩被美軍軍車撞死，**引發全面的**反美**抗議活動**。

3. The Ministry of Foreign Affairs summoned Philippine trade representatives to _____ a _____ **protest**.

   外交部召見菲律賓駐臺貿易代表並**提出嚴正抗議**。

4. Egyptian activists are taking to the streets to _____ the failure of the police to prevent violence at a soccer match.

   埃及的人權活動人士走上街頭，**抗議**警方無力阻止足球賽中發生的暴動。

解答：1. Violent　2. sparked　3. lodge, formal　4. protest

暖身練習解答：①

II. 財經商務類

economy/economic

(n.) 經濟 / (adj.) 經濟的

▶ 答案請見 p. 91

> **暖身練習**
>
> ⚙ 請就以下中英譯文選出適當的搭配詞。
>
> A ① **tiresome** ② **weak economy** keeps the U.S. unemployment stuck above 9 percent.
>
> 疲軟的經濟使得美國的失業率仍超過 9%。

economy 當名詞時除了抽象的「經濟」之意,也可表示「經濟體」,例如以下例句:

- China and Japan are the world's second and third largest economies.
  中國和日本是世界第二和第三大經濟體。

另外,形容詞 economic 是「經濟的」,而另一個相關字 economical 也是形容詞,但意思卻是「節儉的,節約的」,如 economical car 為「省油車」。如果 economic 字尾加了 -s 成為 economics,則詞性又轉為名詞,表示「經濟學」或「經濟情況」,如 behavioral economics 為「行為經濟學」,而「經濟學家」為 economist。

以下提供 economy 和 economic 的搭配詞彙。

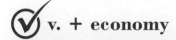 **v. + economy**

v.	economy	中譯
boost		提振經濟
build/develop/expand		發展經濟
control/regulate		管制經濟
harm/hurt		傷害經濟
rattle		撼動經濟
rebuild/reinvigorate/revitalize/revive	economy	重振經濟
stabilize		穩定經濟
stimulate		刺激經濟
strengthen		強化經濟
weaken		弱化經濟

搭配詞例句

- The disaster rattled global economy and prompted massive intervention in currency markets by the G7 industrial nations.
  這場災難撼動了全球經濟，並促使七大工業國大力介入貨幣市場。

- The U.S. is still struggling to revitalize an economy that for so many years was the envy of the world.
  美國仍在掙扎，企圖重振長年來舉世欣羨的經濟榮景。

- This would not only attract visitors, but also help stimulate the domestic economy.
  這不但能吸引遊客，也會幫助刺激國內經濟。

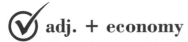 **adj. + economy**

adj.	economy	中譯
booming/dynamic/healthy/strong		欣欣向榮的 / 強健的經濟
distressed/down/feeble/flagging/ fragile/sagging/sluggish/stagnant/ struggling/troubled/weak		衰弱的 / 停滯的經濟
domestic		國內經濟
global/international/world		全球 / 國際經濟
growing	economy	成長的經濟
knowledge-based		知識經濟
local		地方經濟
red-hot		火紅的經濟
regional		區域經濟
state-dominated		國家主導的經濟
wobbly		搖擺的 / 不穩定經濟

搭配詞例句

- Free trade agreements can help the flagging international economy get back on its feet.
  自由貿易協定有助於提振疲軟的國際經濟。

- The euro zone makes up 20% of the global economy.
  歐元區占全球經濟的 20%。

- Income from tourism has made some contribution to the local economy.
  觀光業收入對當地經濟帶來一些貢獻。

- Demonstrators across the country began to show their anger over the wobbly economy.
  面對不穩定的經濟，全國各地的示威民眾開始表達憤怒。

 economy + v.

economy	v.	中譯
economy	collapse	經濟崩潰
	continue	經濟持續
	contract/languish/ slow down / weaken	經濟緊縮 / 衰退 / 萎靡
	develop/expand/grow/rise	經濟發展 / 成長
	flourish/thrive	經濟繁榮
	show	經濟呈現
	slide into	經濟陷入
	stagnate	經濟停滯

搭配詞例句

- The economy will continue in its sluggish state.
  經濟將持續在低迷的狀態。

- With Western economies languishing, emerging countries in Asia have become a primary engine of global growth in recent years.
近年來西方的經濟體萎靡不振，亞洲新興國家已成為全球經濟成長的主要動力。

- The economy is growing much more slowly than in a typical recovery.
此次經濟成長比典型的經濟復甦來得緩慢許多。

- The German economy rose only 0.1 percent in the second quarter of 2011 from the first quarter.
德國 2011 年第二季的經濟比起第一季僅成長 0.1%。

- For years the economy has thrived on state-run investment.
多年來經濟因國家主導的投資而繁榮。

- The economy is showing new signs of weakness.
經濟正呈現新的疲弱跡象。

- At the end of World War One, the American economy slid into depression.
第一次世界大戰結束後，美國經濟陷入衰退期。

 economic + n.

economic	n.	中譯
economic	affair	經濟事務
	agreement/pact	經濟協議
	aid	經濟援助
	blockade	經濟封鎖
	boom	經濟繁榮
	bubble	經濟泡沫

economic		
	circumstance/climate	經濟環境
	condition/situation	經濟情況
	crisis/disaster/trouble/upheaval	經濟危機 / 災難 / 動盪
	cycle	經濟循環
	decline/depression/downturn/ recession/slowdown	經濟衰退，不景 氣
	forecast	經濟預測
	hub	經濟中心
	interdependence	經濟相互依存
	liberalization	經濟自由化
	outlook/prospect	經濟前景
	recovery	經濟復甦
	sanction	經濟制裁
	stimulus/upturn	經濟振興

搭配詞例句

- Taiwan's fashion industry began with the economic boom of the 1970s.
  臺灣的時裝產業肇始於 1970 年代的經濟繁榮時期。

- Beijing has done a decent job of managing a threatening economic climate.
  北京政府身處險惡經濟環境中仍表現得當。

- Everlight's furlough plan was scheduled to begin next month as a means of coping with slow demand amid a global economic downturn.
  億光電子的休假計畫預計於下個月開始實施，以因應全球經濟衰退下產品需求減少的困境。

- The economic outlook for the movie industry is gloomy.
  電影產業的經濟前景暗淡。

- The US economic recovery has gradually stabilized.
  美國的經濟復甦漸趨穩定。

相關詞彙之搭配使用

片語	
a drag on global growth	拖緩全球經濟成長
a heavy blow to the economy	對經濟的嚴重打擊
a sign of improvement in South Korea's economy	南韓經濟改善的跡象
Economic Cooperation Framework Agreement (ECFA)	經濟合作架構協議
further economic tightening measure	進一步推動經濟緊縮的措施
Gross Domestic Product (GDP)	國內生產總值
socioeconomic status	社經地位
the era of knowledge economy	知識經濟的時代
the rapid urbanization and the emergence of a vibrant middle class	快速都市化並興起活躍的中產階級
to impose/initiate economic sanctions	實施經濟制裁

to lift economic sanctions	解除經濟制裁
to plunge/slide/slip into a serious recession	陷入嚴重的經濟衰退
to raise its economic growth forecast	提高其經濟成長預測
to recover and develop different segments of economy	復甦並發展經濟的不同產業
to recover from the aftermath of last year's economic crisis	從去年經濟危機的餘波中恢復生機
to trigger a serious economic downturn	引爆嚴重的經濟衰退

句子

- The euro-zone economy would grind to a halt in the final quarter of 2018.
  歐元區的經濟在 2018 年的最後一季將陷於停滯。

- India's economy has taken off, with growth forecast at 7.8% this year.
  印度的經濟起飛，預估今年的成長率為 7.8%。

- The financial crisis did not result in a worldwide Great Depression.
  此次金融危機沒有造成全球大蕭條。

- Her administration is willing to create a mutually beneficial economic partnership with Beijing, Tsai said.
  蔡英文總統表示，她的政府願意與北京創造一個互惠的經濟夥伴關係。

- China's economic growth remains solid and is expected to reach 6.7 percent this year.
  中國的經濟成長維持強健，預期今年的成長率將達 6.7%。

段落

South Africa's <u>economy contracted</u>[①] in the first quarter of this year, pushing the continent's largest economy into its first recession since 2009. <u>The manufacturing sector</u>[②] decreased by 3.7 percent as <u>unemployment climbed to a record</u>[③] 27.7 percent, the highest joblessness rate in 14 years. Only the mining and agriculture sectors posted growth rates of 12.8 percent and 22.2 percent respectively in the first quarter. South Africa's economy has been experiencing weak growth in recent years. (*AFP*)

南非今年第一季<u>經濟緊縮</u>，是這個非洲最大經濟體自 2009 年來首次衰退。<u>製造業</u>下跌 3.7%，同時<u>失業率攀升至</u> 27.7% 的<u>新紀錄</u>，為 14 年來最高點。只有礦業和農業在第一季各自成長 12.8% 和 22.2%。近年來南非的經濟成長相當疲軟。(《法新社》)

說明

① contract 當名詞是指「合約」，當動詞指「簽訂合約」，但還有另一個意思是「縮小，收縮」，與前面名詞 economy 搭配，就譯成「經濟緊縮」。

② sector 在此處是「產業」的意思，如 manufacturing sector 為「製造業」。sector 也可當「部門」解釋，如 public sector 是「公部門」，而 private sector 為「私部門」或「民營部門」。

③ record 通常當名詞用，意思是「紀錄」，也當動詞用，意思是「記錄」，但在此處是形容詞，意思是「創紀錄的」，等同於 record-breaking（破紀錄的），後面接名詞 percent。另外，此處 record 前的 climb to 要譯為「攀升至」，不能只譯「攀升」，因為「攀升至 27.7%」與「攀升 27.7%」意義大不相同。而 climb to 也可代換為 reach，如 reach a record high 可譯為「創下歷史新高」。

搭配詞練習

⚙ 請從方格中挑選正確的搭配詞來完成以下的句子。

revitalize	contracted	stagnant
stimulate	interdependence	recovery

1. The **economy** _____ by 0.2 percent in the previous quarter.
   上一季的**經濟衰退** 0.2%。

2. Supporters insist the budget will _____ a _____ U.S. **economy**.
   支持者堅稱，該預算將**重振**美國**停滯的經濟**。

3. To _____ **economic** _____, investment in public services is crucial.
   要**刺激經濟復甦**，公共投資非常重要。

4. Both Chinese and Americans view their **economic** _____ warily.
   中美兩國皆謹慎看待其**經濟的相互依存關係**。

解答：1. contracted　2. revitalize, stagnant　3. stimulate, recovery　4. interdependence

business

(n.) 商業；事業，生意；企業

暖身練習

⚙ 請就以下中英譯文選出適當的搭配詞。　　　　　　▶ 答案請見 p. 99

Investors remain reluctant to ① **do** ② **make business** in Haiti.
投資者仍然不願意在海地**做生意**。

business 除了指「生意買賣」、「公司企業」之外，也可以表示「個人的事務」，例如 mind your own business 或 none of your business 都是叫他人「不要管閒事」。以下僅介紹 business 在商業領域的搭配詞彙。

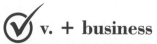 v. + business

v.	business	中譯
attract		吸引生意
boost/improve		提振生意
build/establish/ set up /start		創立事業
conduct/do/run		經營事業，做生意
develop/expand/grow/ promote	business	發展 / 擴張事業
get/go into		投入事業
go out of / shut down / shutter		退出 / 結束事業
invest in		投資事業

manage	business	管理事業
win		贏得生意

搭配詞例句

- You might be one of the 73 percent of Americans who want to start their own business.
  有 73% 的美國人想要創業，你也許是其中一個。

- They run their own business and employ seven staff members.
  他們經營自己的事業並雇用七名員工。

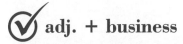 adj. + business

adj.	business	中譯
booming/brisk/thriving	business	蓬勃發展的事業
family-owned		家族事業
global/international		國際性的事業
struggling		陷入困境的事業

搭配詞例句

- Nearly five decades after its debut, San Diego Comic-Con is a booming business, complete with corporate sponsorships and tens of thousands of paying fans.
  從首次舉辦至今經過了約 50 年，聖地牙哥動漫展現在是一門蓬勃發展的生意，湧入大量企業贊助和成千上萬的付費粉絲。

- He had to work hard, long hours in a struggling family-owned business.
  他必須在陷入困境的家族事業中長時間努力工作。

 **business ＋ v.**

business	v.	中譯
business	boom/flourish	生意興隆
	expand/grow	事業擴展 / 成長
	fail/fold / go under	事業失敗 / 倒閉
	grow into	事業成長爲

搭配詞例句

- This company quickly discovered that there was a huge market for their low cost, high quality electronics and the business boomed.
  這家公司很快就發現，他們價廉物美的電子產品有龐大的市場，而且生意興隆。

- The business was growing very rapidly and expanding abroad.
  事業成長相當快速並向海外擴展。

- The business failed, and now he carries $2 million in related debts.
  事業失敗了，他現在背負 200 萬美元的相關債務。

- After the business grew into a lucrative export company, he moved to Taipei.
  事業成長爲開始賺錢的出口公司後，他就搬到臺北了。

 **business + n.**

business	n.	中譯
business	boom	生意興隆
	climate	商業氛圍
	cycle	景氣循環
	etiquette	商業禮儀
	expansion/growth	事業擴展 / 成長
	fluctuation	景氣起伏
	hours	營業時間
	indicator	景氣指標
	outlook/prospect	商業前景
	owner	企業主
	partner	生意夥伴
	school	商學院
	tie	商業關係

搭配詞例句

- Canada's business climate nurtures innovation and enhances economic growth.
  加拿大的商業氛圍有助於培養創新能力並促進經濟成長。

- Japanese business etiquette is not so different from that of Germany, France or the UK.
  日本的商業禮儀與德國、法國或英國並沒有太大不同。

- I look for another good year for the electronics industry despite the uncertainties in the business outlook generally.
  儘管整體的商業前景並不確定，但我看好電子產業仍會是豐收的一年。

相關詞彙之搭配使用

片語

a start-up business/company	新創 / 新興企業
board of directors	董事會
building customer loyalty	建立顧客忠誠度
chief shareholder of a company	公司主要股東
Corporate Social Responsibility (CSR)	企業社會責任
luxury brand	奢侈品牌，名牌
merger and acquisition deals	併購案
regional business hub	區域商業中心
to attract a million-dollar angel investment	吸引百萬美元的天使投資
to file for bankruptcy / to go bankrupt	聲請破產
to open up new possibilities for businesses	打開新市場的可能性
to reach/strike a deal	達成交易
to strengthen your customer relationship	強化你與顧客的關係
venture capital (VC)	創業投資
venture capitalist	風險投資家

- Business is business.
  公事公辦。

- Almost nine out of ten British businesses believe Britain should become a full member of the European Monetary System.
  英國近九成的企業認為英國應該成為歐洲貨幣體系的正式成員。

- Japan is trying to force inefficient firms to go out of business.
  日本正企圖使經營不善的公司倒閉。

段落

Small businesses in China have an acclaimed record of helping Alibaba lay a solid foundation for[①] a decade of rapid growth, and transform the e-commerce company into today's robust conglomerate that has 50,000 employees worldwide and has generated $547 billion in gross merchandise volume[②] as of March 2017. Having accumulated more than 800 flight hours last year by attending trade shows and expos worldwide to promote Alibaba's business solutions, Ma said he plans to fly longer hours, probably 1,000 or so this year, to help American SMEs[③] grow globally and sell to China. (*China Post*)

中國的小型企業為阿里巴巴奠下 10 年快速成長的穩固基礎,讓這間電子商務公司轉型成為今日強大的企業集團。阿里巴巴在全球擁有五萬名員工,截至 2017 年三月為止的商品交易總額更高達 5,470 億美元。馬雲去年到世界各地參加貿易商展,推廣阿里巴巴的商業解決方案,累積超過 800 個小時的飛行時數。他表示今年計畫飛行更多時數,可能高達 1,000 個小時,來協助美國中小企業在全球成長,並銷售商品至中國。(《英文中國郵報》)

說明

① lay a solid foundation for...（為…奠下穩固基礎）是常見的搭配詞組。名詞 foundation（基礎）前面搭配的動詞還有 build（建立）、form（形成）、create（創造）等。而 foundation 前面也可以搭配形容詞如 sound（健全的）、firm（堅固的）、strong（強健的）等，可以視需要代換。

② gross merchandise volume 是電子商務平台常用的術語，指線上的「商品交易總額」，但容易受虛報交易或假訂單影響而衝高金額。

③ SMEs 是 Small and Medium-sized Enterprises 的頭字詞，意指「中小型企業」，也可以用 Small and Medium-sized Businesses (SMBs)。

搭配詞練習

⚙ **請從方格中挑選正確的搭配詞來完成以下的句子。**

invest	owners	start
thriving	family-owned	businesses

1. In North America alone, there are more than twenty-five million **small-business _____**.
   光是在北美就有超過 2,500 萬個**小型企業主**。

2. Business immigrants can _____ **in** or _____ **businesses** in Canada.
   商業移民可在加拿大**投資**或**創業**。

3. After years of concentrated effort, he finally **established** a _____ _____ **business**.
   經過長年全力以赴的努力，他終於**建立了興旺的家庭事業**。

4. U.S. economic growth cooled in the first quarter as _____ **cut back on investment**.
   美國的**企業縮減投資**，導致第一季經濟成長下滑。

解答：1. owners　2. invest, start　3. thriving, family-owned　4. businesses

market

(n.) 市場

暖身練習

⚙ 請就以下中英譯文選出適當的搭配詞。　　　▶ 答案請見 p. 107

Prices have roared back to enter a ① **bear** ② **bull market**.
價格強勢回漲，進入**多頭市場**。

market 當名詞時指「市場」，當動詞則是指「行銷」，例如以下例句：

- She marketed the book heavily through bloggers.
  她透過部落客大力行銷這本書。

另外，「行銷」的名詞為 marketing，例如「行銷活動」為 marketing campaigns，「行銷策略」則為 marketing strategies。

以下列出 market 當名詞「市場」時的搭配用法。

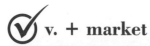 **v. + market**

v.	market	中譯
boost		振興市場
broaden/expand		擴展市場
control/regulate	market	管制市場
deregulate		解除市場管制
distort		扭曲市場

diversify		使市場多樣化
dominate		支配市場
enter / jump into		進入市場
manipulate	market	操控市場
monopolize		壟斷市場
saturate		滲透市場
target		以某市場爲目標

搭配詞例句

- The government attempted to boost the housing market.
  政府試圖振興房屋市場。

....

- New and ever-cheaper technology was broadening the market.
  新穎而價廉的科技不斷擴大市場。

....

- The company is targeting the growing market for children's cereals.
  該公司以愈來愈大的兒童穀類食品市場爲目標。

....

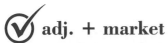 adj. + market

adj.	market	中譯
black		黑市
booming/bullish/rising		上漲的市場
buyer's	market	買方市場
deregulated		解除管制的 / 自由化的市場

domestic		國內市場
emerging		新興市場
fast-changing		快速變化的市場
fast-expanding/fast-growing		快速擴展／快速成長的市場
mature		成熟的市場
overcrowded	market	過度擁擠的市場
promising		有潛力的市場
saturated		飽和的市場
seller's		賣方市場
sluggish/stagnant		停滯的市場
volatile		多變的市場

搭配詞例句

- Some radioactive materials have reportedly been smuggled out of Russia and sold on the black market.
  據報導，部分放射性物料已被走私運出俄羅斯，並且在黑市中販售。

- Competition is intense in the deregulated financial markets.
  自由化的金融市場競爭非常激烈。

- GE is focusing on Russia as a key area for growth, as well as other emerging markets.
  奇異公司聚焦於俄羅斯以及其他新興市場，作為成長的重要區域。

✓ n. + market

n.	market	中譯
bear		熊市，空頭市場
bond		債券市場
bull		牛市，多頭市場
capital		資本市場
currency/money		貨幣市場
equity		股權市場
export	market	出口市場
foreign exchange		外匯市場
futures		期貨市場
labor		勞工市場
over-the-counter		店頭市場
securities		證券市場
stock		股票市場

搭配詞例句

- China is now Taiwan's largest export market.
  中國現在是臺灣最大的出口市場。

- Most worrisome is the anemic state of the labor market.
  勞工市場的停滯狀態最令人憂心。

 market + v.

market	v.	中譯
market	drop	市場下跌
	grow	市場成長
	plunge	市場急降
	reopen	重新開市

搭配詞例句

- Most Asian stock markets dropped on Thursday amid concerns over Europe's ability to come up with a credible fix to the euro-zone debt crisis.
因憂心歐洲能否提出有效方法來解決歐元區債務危機，週四亞洲大部分的股票市場都下跌。

 market + n.

market	n.	中譯
market	confidence	市場信心
	crash	市場崩盤
	economy	市場經濟
	potential	市場潛力
	research/survey	市場調查
	share	市場占有率
	value	市場價值

- Many are still feeling the impact of the stock market crash in 1987.
  許多人仍可感受到 1987 年股票市場崩盤所帶來的衝擊。

- We have to be flexible in our business approach in order to increase our market share.
  我們在經營方式上必須要有彈性，以擴大市場占有率。

相關詞彙之搭配使用

片語

rapid market share expansion	快速擴大的市場占有率
to anticipate/assess/evaluate market needs	評估市場需求
to compete on an equal footing in the market	在市場上基於公平的立足點競爭
to do/perform thorough market research	進行詳盡的市場調查
to free up restrictions on labor and product markets	放寬對勞工和商品市場的限制
to help bolster market confidence	有助於支撐市場信心
to stay competitive in the market	在市場上保有競爭力

句子

- Apple Inc. remains the leader in a global tablet computer market that has been in an extended slump for the past two years.
  過去兩年全球平板電腦市場買氣持續低迷，但蘋果公司仍穩坐該市場龍頭寶座。

段落

Since 2014, India has been the emerging-market world's most positive story. That's mainly because Prime Minister Narendra Modi and his Bharatiya Janata Party (BJP) <u>have cut red tape</u>[1] to make it easier to do business in this historically closed country. Modi's government <u>has lowered barriers to foreign investment</u>[2] and dramatically simplified the tax system. India's economy has taken off, with growth forecast at 7.8% this year. (*Time*)

從 2014 年開始，印度一直是全球新興市場最成功的典範。這主要歸功於總理莫迪和他所屬的印度人民黨刪減繁瑣的官僚程序，此舉有助於在這個向來封閉的國家做生意。莫迪的政府降低外國投資的障礙，並大幅簡化稅制。印度經濟因而起飛，預估今年的成長率為 7.8%。（《時代雜誌》）

說明

① cut red tape 是一固定搭配，red tape 字面上的意思是「紅色帶子」，據說是因為在 17 世紀的英國，政府的官方文件都是用紅色布帶綑綁，後來引申為「繁文縟節」、「官僚作風」等義，例如「太多的繁瑣規定或手續」就可說 too much red tape 或 a lot of red tape。而「剪斷這些紅色帶子」就是「刪減繁文縟節」的意思，搭配的動詞是 cut。

② barrier 的原義是「柵欄」，引申為「障礙」。此處 barrier 前面搭配的動詞是 lower（降低），也可以搭配其他動詞如 break down（破除）、go through（衝破）。另外，barrier 後面接 to 可形成「對⋯造成障礙」的句型，例如 a barrier to effective communication（有效溝通的障礙）、a barrier to the transfer of scientific knowledge（科學知識轉移的障礙）等。

搭配詞練習

⚙ 請從方格中挑選正確的搭配詞來完成以下的句子。

value	bond	economy	domestic

1. Weakness in the _____ **market** also helped pull down the Dow
   Jones and the Standard & Poor's 500-stock index.
   債券市場疲軟也拖垮了道瓊和標準普爾 500 的股價指數。

2. There's a **huge** _____ **market** for tea in India.
   在印度，茶的**國內市場**龐大。

3. A ticket's face value often has little to do with its true **market**
   _____.
   票券的面值通常不等於其**市值**。

4. The classical economists stressed the self-adjusting tendencies of a
   market _____.
   古典經濟學家強調，**市場經濟**有自行調整的趨勢。

stock

(n.) 股票

暖身練習

⚙ 請就以下中英譯文選出適當的搭配詞。　　　　　　　▶ 答案請見 p. 116

Apple Inc.'s **stock** ① **sank** ② **ended** on Tuesday because of missed iPhone expectations.

由於 iPhone 的表現不如預期，週二蘋果公司的**股票下挫**。

「股票」的英文除了用 stock 之外，也可用 share 表達，例如「每股收益」為 earnings per share (EPS)，又如下例：

● Shares of most local electronics makers fell Wednesday morning.
週三上午本地多數電子廠商的股票都下跌。

持有股票的人稱為「股東」，英文是 stockholder 或 shareholder，「股票經紀人」為 stockbroker，而反映股市行情高低的「股價指數」是 stock market index，全球常見股價指數的英文名稱如下：

● Dow Jones Industrial Average 道瓊工業指數（美國）
● Standard & Poor's 500-stock index 標準普爾 500 股價指數（美國）
● NASDAQ (National Association of Securities Dealers Automated Quotations) composite index 那斯達克綜合指數（美國）
● FTSE 100 index 金融時報 100／富時 100 指數（英國）
● CAC 40 index 巴黎券商公會 40 指數（法國）
● DAX index 法蘭克福 DAX 指數（德國）

- Stoxx Europe 600 index 斯托克斯歐洲 600 指數（歐洲）
- Nikkei stock average 日經股價指數（日本）
- Hang Seng index 恆生指數（香港）
- Shanghai Composite Index 上海證券綜合指數（中國）
- TAIEX (Taiwan Stock Exchange Capitalization Weighted Stock Index) 臺灣證券交易所發行量加權股價指數（臺灣）

描述股價指數行情的例句如下：

- The Standard & Poor's 500-stock index closed up 0.1 percent to 1,315.38, and the Dow Jones Industrial Average added 0.8 percent or 96.50 points to 12,720.48.
  標準普爾 500 股價指數收盤下跌 0.1%，達 1,315.38 點；道瓊工業指數上漲 0.8% 或 96.50 點，收在 12,720.48 點。

- The NASDAQ composite index fell slightly, down 0.1 percent, to end at 2,786.78.
  那斯達克綜合指數小降 0.1%，收盤為 2,786.78 點。

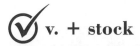 **v. + stock**

v.	stock	中譯
acquire		獲得股票
boost / push up		推升股價
buy/purchase		買進股票
cash in / liquidate	stock	股票變現
hold		持有股票
invest in		投資股票
issue		發行股票

	stock	
manipulate		操縱股市
sell / sell off		賣出股票
subscribe for		認購股票
trade		交易股票

搭配詞例句

- In pursuit of overnight wealth, many people mortgaged their property to buy stocks.
  為了一夜致富，很多人抵押房地產來買股票。

- The Dutch East India Company was the first public company to issue stock.
  荷蘭東印度公司是第一家發行股票的上市公司。

- We can trade stocks, buy insurance and book air-tickets online.
  我們可以在線上交易股票、購買保險和訂購機票。

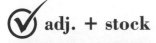 adj. + stock

adj.	stock	中譯
blue-chip		績優股，藍籌股
common		普通股
financial	stock	金融股
listed		上市股票
lower-priced		低價股
preferred		優先股

搭配詞例句

- Blue-chip stocks are stocks in well established companies, often companies that have been profitable and paying dividends for many years.
  績優股是信譽卓著公司所發行的股票，這些公司通常多年來獲利良好並支付股息。

....

- Financial stocks were hardest hit, falling about 3.3 percent.
  金融股受創最深，下跌約 3.3%。

....

 stock + v.

stock	v.	中譯
stock	advance/climb/ edge up / gain / go up / move up / rise	股市上漲 / 攀升
	close/end	股市收盤
	collapse/crash/crumble/dive/ nosedive/plummet/plunge/slump/ tumble	股市急跌 / 重挫
	decline/drop / edge down / fall / go down / lose/retreat/shed/sink/ slide/slip	股市下跌 / 下挫
	open	開盤
	rebound/recover/regain	股市行情反彈 / 翻轉
	roar up / rocket / shoot up / skyrocket/soar/surge	股市高漲 / 飆升

搭配詞例句

• Bank stocks rose more than 4 percent by the close of the trading session.
收盤時銀行股上漲超過 4%。

• The stock ended at NT$661 per share after pulling back from an intraday high of NT$698.
盤中高點曾達到每股新臺幣 698 元，股市收盤時則拉回到每股 661 元。

• Stocks plunged about 5 percent across Europe and in Hong Kong and more than 3 percent in the United States.
歐洲各地和香港的股市急跌約 5%，在美國則下跌超過 3%。

 stock + n.

stock	n.	中譯
stock	acquisition	股權收購
	certificate	股票
	dividend	股息
	exchange/trading	股票／證券交易
	holder	股票持有人
	index	股價指數
	market	股市
	option	股票選擇權
	price	股價
	split	股票分割
	volatility	股市波動

搭配詞例句

- The stock market crashed as the Dow Jones Industrial Average plunged 508 points.
  道瓊工業指數慘跌 508 點，造成股市崩盤。

- Kodak's stock price has declined nearly 70 percent since the start of the year.
  柯達公司的股價從年初至今已大跌近 70%。

相關詞彙之搭配使用

片語

... has brought uncertainty to the stock market	…為股市帶來不確定因素
a stock listed firm	股票上市公司
a stock market struggling with falling volumes	受交易量下跌所苦的股市
counterfeit/fake/phony stock certificate	假股票
hedge fund	避險基金
individual investor	散戶投資人
Initial Public Offering (IPO)	首次公開募股
institutional investors	法人投資人
mutual fund	共同基金
Securities and Exchange Commission (SEC)	證券交易委員會
selling pressures	賣壓
stock gains tax	證券交易所得稅

stock index futures	股票指數期貨
stock market stabilization fund	股市穩定基金
stock transaction tax	證券交易稅
the 200-day moving average	200 日移動平均線
the best/largest single-day rise	單日最高漲幅

句子

- The stock market has been in a slump.
  股市一直積弱不振。

- The market closed at a historic peak of 2,841.43.
  股市收盤達到歷史高峰的 2,841.43 點。

- The market was mixed at the start and trading was sluggish for a while.
  股市開盤時漲跌互見，而且有一陣子交易清淡。

- The stocks fell amid a broad market decline. Losses accelerated late in the session and indexes ended near session lows.
  各股均隨著大盤跌勢下滑。尾盤跌勢加劇，收盤時股價指數接近盤中的低點。

- Trade is expected to remain thin in the coming weeks.
  接下來幾週的交易預期仍將維持冷清。

- In a short two years the number of stock-holders has increased 5-fold, the stock market index has increased 10-fold, and the daily trading volume has also increased 20-fold.
  短短兩年內股民增加五倍，股價指數成長 10 倍，而每日成交總值更提升了 20 倍。

段落

The TAIEX closed[1] above the 10,000-point level on May 11 for the first time in 17 years. It surpassed the level again on May 23 and has stayed there since, reinforcing investors' confidence in the market. On Friday, the TAIEX closed at 10,156.73 as investors shrugged off concerns[2] over high valuations of many large-cap high-tech stocks[3]. The benchmark index has gained 9.76 percent since the beginning of this year. (*Taipei Times*)

臺股加權股價指數 5 月 11 日收盤突破一萬點大關,是過去 17 年來首見。5 月 23 日再度站上關卡,並維持強勁態勢,因而強化市場投資人信心。週五因投資人不在乎許多大型科技股的高估價位,臺股加權股價指數收在 10,156.73 點。從今年年初以來,加權股價指數已成長 9.76%。(《臺北時報》)

說明

① TAIEX 的全名是 Taiwan Stock Exchange Capitalization Weighted Stock Index(臺灣證券交易所發行量加權股價指數),簡稱「臺股加權股價指數」。此外,股市收盤的動詞用 close,開盤則用 open。

② 動詞 shrug 是「聳肩」的意思,shrug off... 則表示「對⋯不予理會」,引申為「不在乎⋯」,其後搭配的名詞 concern 是指「擔心」。

③ large-cap stock(大型股)的 cap 是 capitalization(資本額)的縮寫,而依資本額不同所產生的類似詞彙還有 small-cap stock(小型股)、mid-cap stock(中型股)、micro-cap stock(微型股)、penny stock(低價股)等。

搭配詞練習

⚙ 請從方格中挑選正確的搭配詞來完成以下的句子。

Exchange	opened	volatility	blue-chip

1. **Stock** _____ will be unlikely this week as investors take a wait-and-see attitude.

   由於投資者採取觀望態度，本週**股市波動**不至於太大。

2. He has been trading on the floor of NYSE, the New York **Stock** _____ for 40 years.

   他在紐約**證券交易所**從事交易已經 40 年了。

3. Investing your money in _____ **stocks** is probably about as safe as you can get when investing in the stock market.

   投資**績優股**可能是你投資股市最安全的作法了。

4. **Stocks** _____ **lower** after data showed China's economy expanded at its slowest pace in three years last quarter.

   股市開盤走低，肇因於資料顯示，中國上一季經濟成長是近三年來最緩慢的一季。

解答：1. volatility 2. Exchange 3. blue-chip 4. opened

暖身練習解答：①

currency

(n.) 貨幣

▶ 答案請見 p. 123

暖身練習

⚙ 請就以下中英譯文選出適當的搭配詞。

China's **currency** has ① **valued up** ② **appreciated** 2.3 percent against the dollar over the past six months.

過去六個月來，中國的**貨幣**兌美元已經**升值** 2.3%。

currency 指「貨幣」，各國貨幣的英文名稱不盡相同，例如臺灣用「新臺幣」(New Taiwan Dollar, NTD)，中國用「人民幣」(Renminbi, RMB)，單位是「元」(Chinese Yuan)，美國用「美元」(US Dollar, USD)，歐洲多國用「歐元」(Euro, EUR)，英國用「英鎊」(British Pound, GBP)，日本用「日圓」(Japanese Yen, JPY)，韓國用「韓元」(Korean Won, KRW)，印度用「盧比」(Indian Rupee, INR)，泰國用「泰銖」(Thai Baht, THB) 等。描述貨幣市場行情的例句如下：

- The Indian rupee yesterday hit a record low against the US dollar as fears about euro zone debt and the global economy, as well as falling local stock markets, provoked further selling of the currency.
  昨日印度盧比兌美元創下歷史新低，肇因於市場擔心歐元區債務和全球經濟問題，而當地股市下挫也造成盧比進一步的賣壓。

- The local currency dropped NT$0.086 to close at NT$30.395 against the US dollar yesterday.
  昨日新臺幣兌美元下跌 0.086 元，收在 30.395 元。

　　貨幣在國際市場交易時稱為「外匯」，英文是 foreign currency，而「匯率」為 exchange rate，例如「外匯存款利率」就是 foreign currency deposit rate，「外匯存底」則是 foreign exchange reserves。貨幣的「升值」稱為 appreciation（動詞為 appreciate），「貶值」稱為 depreciation（動詞為 depreciate）或 devaluation（動詞為 devaluate 或 devalue）。美國一直認為中國政府有操控人民幣之嫌，使得人民幣升值幅度過慢，有利中國商品出口，卻使中美間的「貿易逆差」(trade deficit) 不斷擴大。

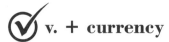 **v. + currency**

v.	currency	中譯
appreciate		使貨幣升值
buy/purchase		購買貨幣
defend		保衛幣值
depreciate/depress/devaluate/ devalue/ drive down		壓低幣值，使貨幣貶值
exchange	currency	買賣貨幣
float		浮動幣值
issue/print		發行貨幣
manipulate		操控貨幣
stabilize		穩定幣值

搭配詞例句

- Costs of purchasing foreign currency vary considerably.
  購買外幣的價格變化非常大。

- Countries would move to drive down their own currency to hang on to what advantage they have in exporting.
  各國會採取行動壓低幣值，使其保持在有利出口的水準。

- -

- Estonia was the first of the former Soviet republics to issue its own currency.
  愛沙尼亞是前蘇聯各共和國中第一個自行發行貨幣的國家。

- -

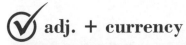 adj. + currency

adj.	currency	中譯
foreign		外匯
global/international		國際貨幣
hard/strong		強勢貨幣
inflated	currency	膨脹的通貨
overvalued		高估的貨幣
single		單一貨幣
undervalued		低估的貨幣

搭配詞例句

- A strong currency would help control inflation.
  強勢貨幣有助於控制通貨膨脹。

- -

- Among the ten non-euro states of the EU there are countries such as Britain and Denmark that have no intention of joining the single currency.
  在歐盟 10 個非歐元國家中，有些國家如英國和丹麥都無意加入此單一貨幣。

- -

- The entire world joined in on jawboning China to level the playing field and let its undervalued currency, the renminbi, appreciate.
全世界聯手向中國施壓，要求中國創造公平的競爭環境，並讓其低估的貨幣人民幣升值。

 **currency + n.**

currency	n.	中譯
currency	crisis	貨幣危機
	fluctuation	幣值波動
	loss	貨幣損失
	manipulation	貨幣操控
	stability/stabilization	貨幣穩定性
	swap	貨幣交換
	trading	貨幣交易
	value	幣值

搭配詞例句

- Oracle has attributed the poor results to currency fluctuations that weakened the value of its European and Asian sales.
甲骨文公司將表現不佳歸因於幣值波動，表示幣值波動導致其在歐洲和亞洲的銷售數字欠佳。

- The monetary authority was weighing action to curb currency losses.
金融當局在考慮實施遏止貨幣損失的措施。

相關詞彙之搭配使用

片語

a 3 percent upward revaluation of its currency	其貨幣升值 3%
the diversification of the country's foreign exchange reserves	國家外匯存底的多元化
the single-currency bloc	單一貨幣集團（即歐元區）
the yen's sharp rise against the U.S. dollar	日圓兌美元急劇上升
tight grip on the yuan	嚴格管制人民幣
to adopt market-based exchange rates	採用市場匯率
to devalue its currency by 1 percent	使其貨幣貶值 1%
to hike the value of its currency against the dollar	調升其貨幣兌美元的價值

句子

- Japan has recently intervened in the currency market.
  日本近來干預貨幣市場。

- The United States chided Japan for stepping into the currency market to stem the yen's rise.
  美國指責日本介入貨幣市場，阻止日圓升值。

- Other emerging market currencies have fallen against the strengthening dollar.
  其他新興市場貨幣兌增強的美元皆呈下跌狀態。

段落

The Trump administration declined Friday to label China a currency manipulator[①]. Instead, the administration's twice-yearly currency review singled out China and five other countries as needing to be monitored for their currency practices. In its report to Congress, the Treasury Department noted that Beijing had intervened in currency markets for about a decade to depress the value of its currency[②], the renminbi. Keeping the renminbi low gave its exporters a competitive edge[③] by making Chinese goods more affordable overseas and other nations' products costlier for Chinese buyers. (*AP*)

川普政府週五並未將中國列為貨幣操縱國，而是在半年一次的外匯評估報告中將中國與其他五個國家並列為貨幣操作的必須觀察名單。在這份提交給國會的報告中，美國財政部指出北京過去十年來干預貨幣市場，壓低人民幣幣值。讓人民幣保持在低點可壓低中國商品在海外的價格，使中國的出口商保有競爭優勢，同時也可使其他國家的商品在中國變得更貴。（《美聯社》）

① currency manipulator 是「貨幣操縱者」，相關的搭配詞彙還有 currency manipulation（貨幣操縱）、to manipulate currency markets（操縱貨幣市場）、to manipulate currency rates（操縱匯率）等。

② 動詞 depress 原是「使沮喪」之意，然而在此處的意義與 depreciate、devalue 等字相同，depress the value 是指「使貶值」。

③ give ... a competitive edge 是常見搭配形式，表示「給…帶來競爭優勢」，其他搭配還有 gain competitive edge（獲得競爭優勢）、maintain competitive edge（維持競爭優勢）等。此外，competitive edge 也可代換成 competitive advantage。

搭配詞練習

⚙ 請從方格中挑選正確的搭配詞來完成以下的句子。

foreign	undervalued	manipulates	defend

1. With high tariffs and an _____ **currency**, the prices for foreign goods were naturally high.

   高關稅加上**低估的貨幣**，進口商品的價格自然就高。

2. Poor nations are under great pressure to earn _____ **currency**.

   貧窮國家面臨賺取**外匯**的龐大壓力。

3. The U.S. Treasury said that China's yuan is still significantly undervalued, although it refrained from saying Beijing _____ the **currency**.

   儘管美國財政部自我克制，未指責北京**操控貨幣**，但仍表示中國人民幣的幣值被嚴重低估。

4. The Nigerian central bank's interventions to _____ its **currency** have reduced its FX reserves to $36,697 billion.

   奈及利亞央行介入**保衛**其**貨幣**，導致其外匯存底大減至 366.97 億美元。

解答：1. undervalued 2. foreign 3. manipulates 4. defend

暖身練習解答：②

trade

(n.) 貿易，交易

▶ 答案請見 p. 130

暖身練習

⚙ 請就以下中英譯文選出適當的搭配詞。

China and the U.S. have been involved in a **trade** ① **argument**
② **dispute** over steel products for more than a decade.
中國和美國捲入鋼鐵製品的**貿易爭端**已有十多年。

trade 當動詞時表示「交易」、「買賣」等意思，例如以下例句：

- Six different polluting gases are traded on the CCX (Chicago
  Climate Exchange).
  六種不同的汙染氣體在芝加哥氣候交易所買賣。

trade 當名詞時表示「貿易」、「交易」，例如監督、管理世界各經濟體
間貿易之協議與執行的國際組織「世界貿易組織」（簡稱世貿組織）就叫
作 World Trade Organization (WTO)。trade 後面加 -r 成為 trader，意
思是「交易員」，工作內容包括股市、外幣、黃金、期貨等的買賣。其他
trade 的搭配形式如下。

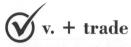 **v. + trade**

v.	trade	中譯
conduct/do	trade	從事交易
expand		擴展貿易

forbid		禁止交易
promote	trade	促進貿易
restrict		限制交易

搭配詞例句

- The new Taiwanese government continues to expand trade with Mainland China.
  臺灣新上任的政府持續擴展與中國大陸的貿易。

- The attempt to forbid the trade of rum, brandy, and other hard liquor was fruitless.
  想要禁止蘭姆酒、白蘭地和其他烈酒的交易是徒勞無功的。

- The construction of a railway will promote prosperous trade and commerce.
  興建鐵路將促進繁榮的貿易和商業活動。

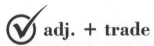 **adj. + trade**

adj.	trade	中譯
bilateral		雙邊貿易
illegal		非法交易
legitimate	trade	合法交易
multilateral		多邊貿易
profitable		獲利的交易

搭配詞例句

● The new round of discussions would focus on bilateral trade issues of mutual concern.
新一回合的討論將聚焦在共同關切的雙邊貿易議題上。

 **trade + n.**

trade	n.	中譯
trade	accord/agreement/deal/pact	貿易協定
	balance	貿易平衡
	barrier	貿易障礙
	bill	貿易法案
	bloc	貿易集團
	conflict	貿易衝突
	cooperation	貿易合作
	deficit	貿易逆差 / 赤字
	dispute	貿易爭端
	embargo	貿易禁運
	friction	貿易摩擦
	imbalance	貿易不平衡 / 失衡
	negotiation/talks	貿易談判
	partner	貿易夥伴
	protectionism	貿易保護主義
	retaliation	貿易報復

trade	surplus	貿易順差 / 盈餘
	tariff	貿易關稅

搭配詞例句

- South Korea's trade deficit with Japan sharply fell last year as the powerful earthquake and the appreciating yen pushed up the island country's imports.
  去年南韓對日本的貿易逆差劇減，這是強烈地震和日圓升值造成日本增加進口所致。

....

- It is widely understood that the Renminbi exchange rate is not the cause of China-U.S. trade imbalances.
  一般認為人民幣匯率並不是中美貿易失衡的原因。

....

- Trade protectionism is a type of policy that limits unfair competition from foreign industries.
  貿易保護主義是一種限制外國企業不得不當競爭的政策。

....

相關詞彙之搭配使用

片語

a new round of multilateral trade negotiation	新一回合的多邊貿易談判
a source of potential trade conflict	潛在貿易衝突的來源
carbon trading	碳交易（溫室氣體二氧化碳排放權交易）
free trade area	自由貿易區
strategic trading partner	戰略貿易夥伴

Taipei World Trade Center	臺北世貿中心
to change the balance of trade	改變貿易差額
to promote bilateral trade cooperation	促進雙邊貿易合作
to reduce global trade barriers	減少全球的貿易障礙
to retaliate against trade agreement violation	報復違反貿易協定
under-the-table deals between private and state corporations	私人企業與國家企業在檯面下的交易

句子

● Singapore is a heavily trade-reliant economy.
新加坡是一個高度依賴貿易的經濟體。

● Technical barriers to trade arise from differing national product regulations and standards.
貿易的技術性障礙起因於不同國家的產品規範和標準。

段落

Investments in Indonesia[①] have grown rapidly as the New Southbound Policy begins to take hold[②], the Ministry of Economic Affairs said yesterday. Investments in the first quarter of this year alone reached US$224 million, outpacing last year's annual total. The Ministry of Economic Affairs attributed the rise to[③] more frequent investment forums and discussion events, which has helped companies on both sides overcome a variety of barriers. Indonesia is the nation's second-most popular investment destination in Southeast Asia, with inflows creating more than 100,000 jobs there. (*Taipei Times*)

經濟部昨日表示，新南向政策開始展現成果，我國在印尼的投資成長快速。今年光是第一季的投資金額就高達 2 億 2 千 4 百萬美元，超過去年全年投資總額。經濟部表示，投資成長要歸功於舉辦了更多投資論壇和研討活動，協助兩國的企業克服各種障礙。印尼是我國在東南亞第二受歡迎的投資國家，流入的資金為當地創造超過 10 萬個工作機會。（《臺北時報》）

說明

① 名詞 investment 後面搭配的介系詞常用 in，動詞 invest 則同時可當及物和不及物動詞使用。當及物動詞時先接受詞，再接介系詞 in，如 invest time and energy in my study（投注時間和精力在我的學業上）；當不及物動詞時則常接介系詞 in 再接受詞，如 invest in technology stocks（投資科技股）。

② take hold 有「站穩」、「開展」之意，在此文境中是指新南向政策的努力已開始產生效果。

③ attribute 當動詞時要與 to 搭配，句型為 attribute A to B，表達出「把 A 歸因於 B」的因果關係。attribute 當名詞時則有「特質」之意，例如 ideal attributes of a teacher 為「理想教師的特質」。

搭配詞練習

⚙ 請從方格中挑選正確的搭配詞來完成以下的句子。

surplus	agreement	deals	partners	deficit

1. An agricultural product procurement delegation from Taiwan signed a total of 22 **trade** _____ during its two-week visit to the US.
   臺灣的農產品採購團在訪美兩週期間共簽署了 22 項**交易案**。

2. The widening of China's **trade** _____ might fuel strains with the United States and other **trade** _____.
   中國**貿易盈餘**擴增，可能讓其與美國以及其他**貿易夥伴**間的關係更加緊張。

3. Mexico has had a free **trade** _____ with Canada and the U.S. since 1994.
   墨西哥從 1994 年起就與加拿大和美國簽訂了自由**貿易協定**。

4. Concern over the mounting **trade** _____ has spooked investors, pushing the Indian rupee to record lows.
   憂慮高漲的**貿易逆差**讓投資人恐慌不已，這也使得印度盧比貶值至史上最低點。

解答：1. deals   2. surplus, partners   3. agreement   4. deficit

暖身練習解答：②

sale
(n.) 銷售，出售

暖身練習

⚙ 請就以下中英譯文選出適當的搭配詞。　　▶ 答案請見 p. 136

Despite ① **handsome** ② **bright sales**, the album wasn't a universal hit.
這張專輯雖然**銷售成績亮眼**，但還算不上全面走紅。

「銷售」、「出售」可用名詞 sale 來表達，如 on sale 是「拍賣」，而 clearance sale 是規模更大的「清倉大拍賣」。另外，for sale 是「出售」，而 wholesale 是「批發」。sale 字尾加 -s 變成 sales，通常是指「銷售額」或「業務」，而 salesman, salesperson, saleswoman 則是「業務員」。

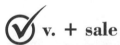 **v. + sale**

v.	sale	中譯
ban/forbid/prohibit		禁止出售
block/stop		阻止出售
boost/increase/promote		增加銷售
call off	sale	取消銷售
limit		限制銷售
lose		失去生意
make		做成生意

搭配詞例句

- Heated debate is expected today when state House tackles a bill that would ban sale of assault weapons.
  今天州議會將討論一禁止販售攻擊性武器的法案，預期將有熱烈的爭辯。

- Expanding into the Chinese market will continue to boost the sale of agricultural products and improve the lives of our farmers.
  擴展中國市場將持續增加農產品的銷售，並改善我們農民的生活。

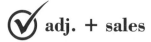 adj. + sales

adj.	sales	中譯
brisk/good/handsome/heated/massive/strong/surging	sales	銷售成績亮眼
global/international/overseas/worldwide		國際銷售
inaugural		首度開賣
limited-time		限時特賣
poor/slipping/sluggish		銷售成績欠佳

搭配詞例句

- Hotel operators garnered handsome sales from the first day of this year's Taipei International Travel Fair.
  今年臺北國際旅遊展才開幕第一天，飯店業者的業績就相當亮眼。

- Apple sets strict regulations on the inaugural sales and promotion of its products.
  蘋果對旗下產品的首度開賣和促銷都訂下嚴格的規範。

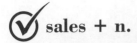 **sales + n.**

sales	n.	中譯
	campaign/promotion	促銷活動
	clerk	營業員
	department/office	業務部
sales	force/staff/team	銷售團隊
	pitch/talk	推銷商品的說詞
	rep/representative	業務代表
	revenue	銷售收入
	target	銷售目標
	tax	營業稅

搭配詞例句

- The hotel operator said both online and physical travel fairs have surpassed a sales target of NT$40 million.
  飯店業者表示,線上和實體的旅遊展都已超越新臺幣四千萬元的銷售目標。

- New Jersey slashes its 6% sales tax in half for shoppers in Newark.
  紐澤西州將 6% 的營業稅削減一半,以嘉惠紐華克的購物者。

相關詞彙之搭配使用

片語	
a decline in sales	銷售額下降
clearance sale on clothing for men and women	男女裝清倉大拍賣

going-out-of-business sale	結束營業大拍賣
suffering a dramatic drop in retail sales	深受零售業績慘跌之苦
to garner/generate/post NT$15 million in sales	獲得／產出／達到新臺幣 1,500 萬元的銷售額
to stop illegal drug sales	阻止非法藥品販售

句子

- Sales of beauty products are climbing/growing.
  美容產品的銷售額上揚。

. . . .

- The PC business, including desktop and notebook computers, still accounted for 76 percent of Acer's total sales.
  個人電腦的事業，包括桌上型和筆記型電腦，仍占宏碁公司總銷售額的 76%。

. . . .

段落

Harley-Davidson shares plunged Tuesday when the iconic U.S. motorcycle maker warned about a steep drop[①] in sales this year. The company said it now expects deliveries for the year to decline 6% to 8%. It had previously expected sales for the year to be flat or down only modestly. Global sales were down 7% in the second quarter and expected to decline more in the current period. The problem is U.S. sales, which fell 9% in the quarter, which was far worse than expected. Foreign sales, which make up[②] nearly 40% of its sales worldwide, slipped 2% in the quarter but are expected to be higher in the second half the year. Despite the sales problems[③], Harley's profits only dipped 1% thanks to cost-cutting efforts[④]. (CNN)

哈雷這家美國代表性的機車廠發出警告，表示今年銷售額將<u>陡降</u>，此舉導致週二哈雷公司股價重挫。該公司表示，預估今年交車數將下跌 6% 至 8%，原本預估今年銷售額將持平或小幅下滑。全球第二季銷售額下跌 7%，本季降幅預計將會擴大。歸咎其原因在於美國本季銷售額跌幅達 9%，遠高於之前的評估。而<u>占</u>全球銷售額近 40% 的國外銷售額本季則小跌 2%，不過預期下半年買氣將可回升。<u>儘管銷售遲緩</u>，但<u>由於</u>哈雷公司<u>致力削減成本</u>，使其利潤僅小跌 1%。(《有線電視新聞網》)

> **說明**
>
> ① 此段新聞提供許多與「下降」有關的表達方式，除了此處的 a steep drop（陡降）之外，還有 plunge（急降）、decline（下降）、be down modestly（小幅小滑）、be down（下降）、fall（下跌）、slip（小跌）、dip（小跌）等不同程度的「下降」。
>
> ② make up 這個搭配可以表示許多意思，例如 make up an excuse（編織藉口）、make up my mind（我下定決心）、make up for lost time（彌補失去的時光）、I will make it up to you.（我會補償你。）make 和 up 用連字號連接成為名詞 make-up，意思是「化妝品」，put on make-up 和 wear make-up 就是「化妝」。而此處的 make up 表示「組成」。
>
> ③ despite（儘管）是介系詞，後面接名詞，例如此處的 Despite the sales problems，如果要接子句，必須用 despite the fact that 接子句。同學常將 despite 作為連接詞接子句，或是用 despite of 接名詞，都是不對的搭配。
>
> ④ thanks to 不宜譯為「感謝」，應譯成較為中性的「由於」。另外，形容詞 cost-cutting 後面搭配名詞 efforts，表示「為削減成本所做的努力」，也可用 cost-cutting measures（削減成本的措施）表示。

搭配詞練習

⚙ 請從方格中挑選正確的搭配詞來完成以下的句子。

brisk	limited-time	pitch	strong

1. The production value of vehicles in Taiwan is expected to grow by 13.2 percent this year thanks to _____ **sales** in the domestic automobile market.
   由於國內汽車市場**買氣暢旺**，今年臺灣汽車的產值預計成長 13.2%。

2. They can find _____ **sales** on specific flight tickets.
   他們可以找到特定航班**限時特賣**的機票。

3. Apple had reported a 50% increase in quarterly profit thanks to _____ **sales** of iPhones and Mac computers.
   蘋果表示，由於 iPhone 和 Mac 電腦**熱賣**，其季利潤成長了 50%。

4. Entrepreneurs cannot forget the importance of crafting a well-thought-out **sales** _____ when planning their business.
   創業人士不可忘記，在規劃自己的事業時，打造一套思慮周詳的**銷售說法**相當重要。

解答：1. brisk　2. limited-time　3. strong　4. pitch

暖身練習解答：①

price

(n.) 價格

▶ 答案請見 p. 144

暖身練習

⚙ 請就以下中英譯文選出適當的搭配詞。

Most companies do not ① **rise up** ② **jack up** the **price** of their goods for no reason.
大多數公司不會無緣無故**提高**商品的**價格**。

　　price 大多當名詞用，意思是「價格」，後面接否定字尾 -less 的 priceless 則是形容詞，意思是「無價的」、「貴重的」，如 priceless asset（寶貴的資產）。而 price 也可以當動詞用，意指「定價」，且常用被動語態，例如以下例句：

- Analysts had expected Amazon's tablet to be priced around US$250, roughly half the price of Apple's iPad.
  分析師預測亞馬遜的平板電腦將定在 250 美元左右，大概是蘋果 iPad 價格的一半。
  說明 此句中 be priced 是被動語態，後面接介系詞 around 表大概的價格，若需表達確切的價格可接介系詞 at。句中第二個 price 則是名詞，half the price of... 表示「…一半的價格」。

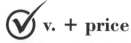 **v. + price**

v.	price	中譯
afford		負擔得起價格
boost/increase/ jack up / push up / raise		提高價格
bring down / cut/decrease/drop/ lower/ push down / reduce/slash		調降價格
charge		收取費用
control		控制價格
discount	price	價格打折
freeze		凍結價格
halve		將價格減少一半
liberalize		讓價格自由化
rig		操控價格
set		訂定價格
stabilize		穩定物價

搭配詞例句

- The firm decided to lower fuel prices by NT$0.2 per liter based on its pricing mechanism.

  該公司決定調降燃油價格，根據其油價計算公式每公升調降新臺幣 0.2 元。

- They could be forced to discount their prices very heavily.

  他們可能被迫對價格打很大的折扣。

- The world's largest maker of AIDS drugs has almost halved the price of its Combivir medicine in developing countries.
  這家世界最大的愛滋病藥廠，在發展中國家將其藥品卡貝滋的價格減少近一半。

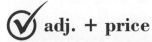 adj. + price

adj.	price	中譯
affordable		負擔得起的價格
average		平均價格
competitive		有競爭力的價格
discounted		折扣價
escalating/hiking/rising/soaring		攀升的價格
exorbitant/heavy/high/steep		高昂的價格
fair/reasonable/right	price	合理的價格
falling		滑落的價格
half		半價
low		低廉的價格
original		原價
retail		零售價
wholesale		批發價

搭配詞例句

- The opening of Zara and its competitive price could boost daily traffic at the mall by 5 percent.
  Zara 的開幕及其有競爭力的價格，可爲這家商場增加每日 5% 的來客量。

- The recent privatization of bus services has led to escalating prices and a lowering of standards.
  最近公車民營化已造成價格攀升以及服務品質低落。

- While such policies have led to soaring stock markets and real-estate prices, they have done little to help the real economy.
  這些政策雖助長股市和房市價格高漲，但對實質經濟卻沒有什麼幫助。

 price + n.

price	n.	中譯
price	competition	價格競爭
	cut/decrease/reduction	價格下降
	fixing	價格操縱
	fluctuation	價格波動
	freeze	價格凍結
	hike/increase	價格上漲
	index	物價指數
	setting	價格設定
	tag	標價，價格
	war	價格戰

搭配詞例句

- The IC designer has been under great pressure from price competition in the Chinese market.
  IC 設計公司向來必須面對中國市場價格競爭所帶來的龐大壓力。

- Food price fluctuations driven by local demand and supply conditions have been an important factor in China's overall inflation trends.
  由當地供需所驅動的食品價格波動，一直是影響中國整體通膨趨勢的重要因素。

- The onslaught of a tropical storm has led the government to order a price freeze on all basic commodities for the next 60 days.
  熱帶風暴帶來嚴重災情，迫使政府下令在接下來 60 天內凍結所有民生基本物資的價格。

- Growth in the Consumer Price Index and Personal Consumption Expenditures Price Index remained close to zero between 2001 and 2005.
  消費者物價指數與個人消費支出價格指數在 2001 至 2005 年間的成長仍趨近於零。

相關詞彙之搭配使用

片語

a hike in the price of milk	鮮乳價格上漲
above the market price	高於市價
at a bargain price	以便宜價格
be worth the price	值得這個價格
Consumer Price Index (CPI)	消費者物價指數
declines in international crude oil prices	國際原油價格下跌
maintaining stable electricity prices	維持穩定的供電價格
prices for pre-sale housing	預售屋價格
to counter hoarding and soaring prices on the market	抑制囤積和市場物價飆漲

to impose ceilings on the prices of a wide range of goods	限制許多商品的價格
to negotiate a purchase price	議價
to price out of the market	訂價過高導致無人購買（有行無市）

句子

- Housing prices in Taipei jumped to a record high.
  臺北的房價飆漲至歷史新高。

....

- Prices cannot remain at this level for long.
  價格無法長期維持在這個水準。

  說明 prices remain（價格維持）後面還可搭配 low（低的）、high（高的）、stable（穩定的）、steady（平穩的）、fixed（固定的）、unstable（不穩定的）、volatile（易變的）、weak（疲弱的）、competitive（有競爭力的）等形容詞。

....

段落

Prices for real estate in Paris are set to reach new records this summer, as buyers scramble to get their hands on flats[1] in the French capital's most well-heeled districts[2]. Demand was outstripping supply[3], particularly for the most select properties. While Italians were the biggest group of foreign homebuyers in Paris, snapping up[4] 17 percent of properties sold to non-French buyers, Britons came second, accounting for[5] 10 percent of such transactions. Already in the first three months of this year, prices for existing apartments in Paris rose by 5.5 percent to 8,450 euros per square meter. (*AFP*)

巴黎今夏房地產價格將創下新高，眾多買家<u>蜂擁至</u>法國首都<u>最富有的區域</u>搶購<u>樓房</u>。買方需求<u>遠超過</u>市場供應，特別是某些精選房產。義大利人是巴黎最大的外國買家，<u>搶購</u>了 17% 賣給非法國人的房產。英國人排名第二，<u>占</u>此類交易的 10%。今年前三個月巴黎現有公寓房價已上漲 5.5%，達每平方公尺 8,450 歐元。（《法新社》）

說明

① scramble 當動詞時有「爭搶」之意，另一有趣搭配 scrambled eggs 是「炒蛋」。而 get their hands on... 也可代換成 lay/put their hands on...，表示「把…弄到手」。另外，flat 在此不是形容詞「平坦的」，而是名詞「公寓」，如 a third-floor flat 是「位於三樓的公寓」，不過這是英式英文的說法，美式英文用 apartment。

② well-heeled 是口語說法，意思是「富有的」，除了此處搭配 districts（區域）之外，也可用來形容人，例如 a well-heeled man（有錢人），或 He is well-heeled.（他很有錢。）

③ 動詞 outstrip 的意思是「超過」，而 demand outstrips supply 就是「供不應求」，反過來 supply outstrips demand 就變成「供過於求」。此外，the balance between supply and demand 則是「供需平衡」。

④ snap up 指「搶購」，可搭配如 bargain（特價商品）、souvenir（紀念品）等名詞。

⑤ account for 有幾個不同意義，此處為「占…比例」，其他還有「解釋」、「說明」之意，例如 to account for the error（解釋這個錯誤）。

搭配詞練習

⚙ **請從方格中挑選正確的搭配詞來完成以下的句子。**

discounted	afford	control
cut	average	tag

1. Pharmaceutical companies promised to _____ **prices** and to increase their spending on research into new drugs.

   製藥公司承諾將會**控制**藥品**價格**,並增加研發新藥的經費。

2. A friend told him about a demonstration model available at a heavily _____ **price**.

   朋友告訴他,有個展示品以非常低的**折扣價**出售。

3. The idea of supporting American creativity is an appealing one — most of us know that the quality is better, but we can not always _____ what's on the **price** _____.

   支持美國創造力這個構想很吸引人,我們多數人都知道美國貨品質較高,但我們並不一定**負擔**得起其**價格**。

4. Formosa Petrochemical Corp said it would _____ gasoline and diesel **prices** by NT$0.2 per liter.

   台塑石化表示將**調降**汽油和柴油**價格**,每公升調降新臺幣 0.2 元。

5. The _____ **price** of a new house in Taipei rose to a record NT$800,000 per ping compared with an average of NT$550,000 a year earlier.

   臺北新屋的**平均價格**上漲至每坪新臺幣 80 萬元的新高,高於去年每坪均價 55 萬元。

解答:1. control　2. discounted　3. afford, tag　4. cut　5. average

暖身練習解答:②

profit

(n.) 利潤，盈利，收益

▶ 答案請見 p. 150

暖身練習

⚙ 請就以下中英譯文選出適當的搭配詞。

Tesla has never had a ① **pure** ② **net profit** for a single year in its brief history.

特斯拉汽車在其短暫的歷史中未曾有過單年營收出現**淨利潤**的紀錄。

profit 指的是企業經營所獲得的「利潤」或「盈利」，也常用 earning, income, revenue 等字表示，其搭配形式也差不多，例如以下例句：

- EBay reported that its net income grew sharply in the fourth quarter.
  EBay 表示其第四季淨收益成長幅度驚人。

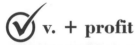 **v. + profit**

v.	profit	中譯
cut/eliminate		削減利潤
earn/generate/get/make/produce/reap	profit	賺取 / 產生 / 創造利潤
increase		增加利潤

- The companies on the S&P 500 generate 46% of their profits outside of the U.S.
  標準普爾 500 指數公司所產生的利潤有 46% 來自於美國境外。

- After a short while, they began to make a profit.
  沒多久他們就開始賺錢了。

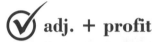 **adj. + profit**

adj.	profit	中譯
after-tax/post-tax		稅後利潤
corporate		企業利潤
enormous/hefty/huge/substantial		龐大利潤
gross		總利潤
net	profit	淨利潤
pretax		稅前利潤
quarterly		季利潤
shrinking		縮減的利潤
soaring		高漲的利潤

- In fact, taxes on corporate profits make up only a small part of federal revenue.
  針對企業利潤所課的稅事實上只占聯邦稅收的一小部分。

- China Steel Corp said its third-quarter pretax profit fell 45.92 percent to NT$5.4 billion from the previous quarter.
  中鋼公司表示第三季稅前利潤與前季相較下降 45.92%，跌至新臺幣 54 億元。

- IBM reported solid quarterly profits on Monday.
  IBM 公司於週一公布亮眼的季利潤。

 **profit + v.**

profit	v.	中譯
profit	climb/gain/generate/grow/increase/jump/rise	利潤成長 / 增加
	decline/decrease/dip/drop/fall/slump	利潤下滑 / 減少
	plummet/plunge/tumble	利潤急降
	soar/surge	利潤高漲

搭配詞例句

- UBS reported that second-quarter profit increased 28 percent over the same period last year.
  瑞銀公布第二季利潤與去年同期相比成長 28%。

- Uni-President Enterprises Corp yesterday reported that net profits for the first nine months of the year fell 21.7 percent from a year earlier.
  統一企業昨日公布，今年前九個月的淨利潤比去年同期下滑 21.7%。

相關詞彙之搭配使用

片語

a 14 percent fall in quarterly profits	季利潤下降 14%
a ballooning net profit in 2018	2018 年高升的淨利潤
a stronger-than-expected profit margin	超乎預期的利潤率
to eke out a little profit	勉力維持低額的利潤

句子

- This company's <u>net profit rose</u> 10.3 percent <u>to</u> 2.97 billion Euros during its 2016 fiscal year.

  這家公司於 2016 會計年度的<u>淨利潤成長</u> 10.3%，達 29.7 億歐元。

段落

General Motors Co on Tuesday reported a better-than-expected quarterly net profit, helped by <u>cost cuts</u>[①], and promised to cut production in the second half to curtail its burgeoning U.S. inventory of unsold vehicles. The No. 1 U.S. automaker also maintained its earnings outlook for 2017 despite falling revenue. GM <u>Chief Financial Officer</u>[②] Chuck Stevens cautioned in a call with analysts that production of its profitable large <u>pickup trucks</u>[③] in North America could fall by 10 percent in 2018 as a new generation of trucks is launched. However, Stevens said GM could maintain 10 percent pre-tax profit margins in North America if overall sales remain close to 17 million vehicles a year. (*New York Times*)

通用汽車公司週二公布超乎預期的季淨利潤，這都要歸功於降低成本，並承諾下半年將減產以降低其於美國快速增長的未售汽車庫存量。這個全美最大汽車製造商儘管營收下滑，但仍看好 2017 年的獲利前景。通用汽車財務長史蒂文斯在跟分析師通電話時審慎提出，由於新一代貨卡上市，該公司在北美獲利頗豐的大型皮卡車 (pickup truck) 在 2018 年可能減產 10%。然而史蒂文斯表示，如果每年整體銷售量仍接近 1,700 萬輛車，通用公司可在北美維持 10% 的稅前利潤率。（《紐約時報》）

說明

① 「降低成本」在臺灣近年來都講成 cost down，這其實是中式英文，正確說法可用此處的名詞片語 cost cuts，或是用動詞 cut 搭配名詞 cost。另外，「降低產量」就可說 cut production。

② Chief Financial Officer（財務長）在英文新聞中也常用其頭字詞 CFO。其他企業高階主管的英文職稱還有 Chief Executive Officer (CEO)（執行長）、Chief Technology Officer (CTO)（技術長）、Chief Procurement Officer (CPO)（採購長）等。

③ pickup truck 的特色是車後有敞篷貨台，常譯為「小貨卡」、「敞篷小卡車」等，但這些譯名並不清楚，跟一般貨車難以區分。目前國內愈來愈多媒體譯成「皮卡車」，再加上圓括號中用英文 (pickup truck) 說明，兼具音譯和意譯效果。

搭配詞練習

⚙ 請從方格中挑選正確的搭配詞來完成以下的句子。

net	made	fell	grew	quarterly

1. TSMC yesterday reported its weakest _____ _____ **profit** in two years.

   台積電昨日公布兩年來最低的**季淨利潤**。

2. The firm _____ NT$24.44 billion **profit**.

   該公司**創造**了新臺幣 244.4 億元的**利潤**。

3. Toyota said that its **profit** _____ 19 percent to 80.4 billion yen in the July-September quarter.

   豐田汽車表示,在七至九月這一季的**利潤下滑** 19%,為 804 億日圓。

4. This company's **net profit** _____ from US$1.14m to US$6.26m in the second quarter of its 2018 fiscal year.

   這家公司 2018 會計年度第二季的**淨利潤**從 114 萬美元**成長**至 626 萬美元。

tariff

(n.) 關稅

▶ 答案請見 p. 156

暖身練習

⚙ 請就以下中英譯文選出適當的搭配詞。

The European Union has escalated its ① **revengeful** ② **retaliatory tariffs** on U.S. corn, spectacle frames and women's jeans from 0.45 percent up to 4.3 percent.
歐盟已提高對美國的**報復性關稅**，將玉米、眼鏡鏡框和女性牛仔褲的稅率從 0.45% 調高至 4.3%。

tariff 是「關稅」，也可稱為 customs duties。其他表示「稅」的單字還有 duty 和 tax。如 duty 一字，在機場就常會看到 duty-free shop（免稅商店）。而 tax 的常見搭配有 consumption tax（消費稅）、sales tax（營業稅）、value-added tax（加值稅）、personal income tax（個人所得稅）、tax payer（納稅人）、tax evasion（逃稅）、tax cut（減稅）等，例句如下：

- Countries use a variety of strategies to protect their trade. One way is to enact tariffs that tax imports.
  各國政府使用各種策略來保護本國貿易，其中一種就是制定關稅，對進口商品課稅。

  說明 此句同時出現 tariffs 和 tax 兩字，tariffs 是名詞「關稅」，與前面動詞 enact 搭配，意為「制定關稅」；但 tax 當動詞用，表示「對⋯課稅」，與後面的名詞 imports（進口商品）搭配。

以下為 tariff 的搭配形式。

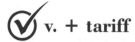 **v. + tariff**

v.	tariff	中譯
abolish		廢除關稅
adjust		調整關稅
boost/increase/raise		提高關稅
cut/lower/reduce		降低關稅
enact	tariff	制定關稅
freeze		凍結關稅
impose/levy/slap		徵收關稅
stabilize		穩定關稅

搭配詞例句

- China would retaliate by boosting tariffs on U.S. products.
  中國將提高對美國商品所課的關稅，作為報復。

- The trade deal lowers tariffs on a range of goods.
  此貿易協定降低某一範圍商品的關稅。

- China will reduce its import tariff on autos from 25% to 15% starting July 1 in a concession to U.S. trade complaints.
  中國將降低汽車進口關稅，從 7 月 1 日起由 25% 降至 15%，作為對美國抱怨貿易不公的讓步。

- The consequences of imposing higher tariffs on Chinese goods are hard to predict.
  對中國商品課徵更高的關稅所帶來的後果很難預測。

 **adj. + tariff**

adj.	tariff	中譯
anti-dumping		反傾銷關稅
declining		降低的關稅
high	tariff	高關稅
protective		保護性關稅
punitive		懲罰性關稅
retaliatory		報復性關稅

搭配詞例句

- Anti-dumping tariffs are a useful means of shielding domestic firms and workers from the unfair pricing practices of foreign firms.
  反傾銷關稅是種利器，可保護本國企業和員工免受外國企業不公平削價手法的影響。

- The trade agreement is separated into four stages, including 15 successive years of declining tariffs between the member nations.
  此貿易協定分為四個階段，包括以 15 年時間陸續降低會員國之間的關稅。

- America should place punitive tariffs on China if it continues to maintain an artificially weak currency.
  如果中國持續操控人民幣走軟，美國應該對中國實施懲罰性關稅。

- The Chinese government announced it will slap a 25 percent retaliatory tariff on $16 billion worth of U.S. imports.
  中國政府宣布，將對美國進口、價值 160 億美元的商品課徵 25% 的報復性關稅。

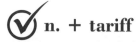 **n. + tariff**

n.	tariff	中譯
export		出口關稅
import		進口關稅
trade	tariff	貿易關稅
transit		過境關稅

搭配詞例句

- Import tariffs have provided the federal government with much of its revenue.
  進口關稅提供聯邦政府許多稅收。

相關詞彙之搭配使用

片語

to implement both welfare and tax reforms	實施福利和稅制改革
to impose a tax on the wealthy to make taxes fairer	對富人徵稅以增進賦稅公平
to raise the tariff to 20 percent on manufactured goods, to between 25 and 30 percent on luxury goods and to 33 percent on chemicals and a wide range of other goods	把對工業製品課徵的關稅提高至 20%，奢侈品關稅提高到 25% 至 30%，化學製品以及其他多種商品則提高為 33%

- Japan has rejected that criticism, saying it <u>does not impose tariffs on US auto imports nor put up discriminatory non-tariff barriers</u>.
  日本駁斥該批評，表示<u>不會對美國進口汽車徵收關稅</u>，也<u>不會提出歧視性的非關稅障礙</u>。

段落

President Donald Trump is considering <u>putting tariffs and quotas on</u>[①] steel imported from foreign countries. The president says that China and other unnamed countries are <u>dumping</u>[②] steel in the U.S. market. That hurts U.S. steelmakers by reducing prices, he told reporters. The Commerce Department is reviewing at his request whether to impose a tariff on steel imports for national security reasons. The U.S. imports 30 percent of the steel it consumes. Only 3 percent of steel imports come from China. (*AP*)

川普總統考慮<u>對</u>外國進口鋼鐵<u>徵收關稅</u>並設定限額，他表示中國和其他國家在美國市場傾銷鋼鐵。川普告訴記者，如此削價會傷害美國鋼鐵製造業。在川普的要求下，美國商業部正在研究是否要以國家安全為由，對進口鋼鐵徵收關稅。美國所消費的鋼鐵有 30% 依賴進口，其中只有 3% 來自中國。(《美聯社》)

說明

① 「對…徵收關稅」的搭配詞組為 put/impose tariffs on...，而「對…設定限額」為 put/impose quotas on...，此處將兩者結合，成為 putting tariffs and quotas on...。

② dump 當名詞時為「垃圾場」，當動詞時才有「傾倒」之意，在此處則指「傾銷」，它常是被徵收高關稅的理由。而 anti-dumping tariff 就是「反傾銷關稅」。

搭配詞練習

⚙ **請從方格中挑選正確的搭配詞來完成以下的句子。**

impose	Punitive	protective	high

1. _____ **tariffs** on Chinese imports would hurt U.S. consumers and multinational companies.
   對中國進口商品課徵**懲罰性關稅**終將傷害美國消費者和跨國企業。

2. The United States unfairly calculates penalties for dumping, resulting in _____ **tariffs** on European imports.
   美國對傾銷採取不公平的罰款，造成歐洲進口商品的**高關稅**。

3. The USA could _____ **anti-dumping tariffs** of up to 100 percent on Chinese exports.
   美國可能對中國出口的商品**課徵**高達 100% 的**反傾銷關稅**。

4. U.S. President Donald Trump has **imposed** _____ **tariffs** on imported PV cells and washing machines, targeting those from China and South Korea.
   美國總統川普對來自中國和南韓的太陽能電池以及洗衣機**課徵保護性關稅**。

解答：1. Punitive 2. high 3. impose 4. protective
暖身練習解答：②

job

(n.) 工作，職業

答案請見 p. 166

暖身練習

請就以下中英譯文選出適當的搭配詞。

Senior high ranking managers are not likely to ① **lose** ② **lost** their **jobs**.
資深高階經理人較不容易**失去工作**。

與 job 意義接近的字彙有 employment（就業），「就業率」即為 employment rate，例如以下例句：

- The total employment rate for people aged 15-64 in the EU27 rose steadily from 53.2% in 2006 to 66.9% in 2010, but fell to 65.2% in 2016.
  歐盟 27 國中 15 至 64 歲人口的總就業率，從 2006 年的 53.2% 穩定成長至 2010 年的 66.9%，但於 2016 年下滑至 65.2%。

而與「就業」相反的詞彙「失業」可用 jobless 或 unemployment 來表示，如「失業救濟金」為 jobless/unemployment benefit，而「失業率」為 jobless/unemployment rate，例句如下：

- The number of Americans filing for **unemployment benefits** unexpectedly fell last week, dropping to its lowest level in nearly 45 years.
  美國上週申請**失業救濟金**的人數出乎意料減少，降至近 45 年來的最低水準。

- The unemployment rate in the United States was last reported at 8.1 percent in September of 2017.
  美國失業率最新數據是 2017 年九月所公布的 8.1%。

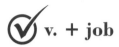 **v. + job**

v.	job	中譯
accept/acquire/get/land/receive/secure/take		獲得工作
apply for		申請工作
create		創造工作機會
cut/eliminate/shed/slash		削減工作機會
find / look for	job	找工作
leave		離職
lose		失去工作
offer		提供工作
quit/resign		辭掉工作
tackle/undertake		處理工作

搭配詞例句

- He has landed the job he always wanted.
  他得到夢寐以求的工作。

- They need bilingual skills to secure jobs in sectors such as public relations, bilingual editing and education.
  他們需要雙語技能來取得像公關、雙語編輯和教育領域的工作。

- The vital first step when you apply for jobs is to complete an application form.
  申請工作時重要的第一步是填寫申請表。

- The U.S. economy created 103,000 jobs in September.
  美國九月份經濟創造了 10 萬 3 千個工作機會。

- Retail trade lost 6,100 jobs overall, according to data from the Bureau of Labor Statistics.
  根據勞工統計局的資料，零售業總共失去 6,100 個工作。
  說明 lost 在此是動詞 lose 的過去式，因和形容詞 lost（失去的；迷路的）拼字相同，容易混淆。例如「失去的時間」為 lost time，「迷路的小孩」為 lost child。

- Tom had been offered a job at Northwestern University as an instructor in the English Department.
  西北大學提供湯姆一個工作，在英文系擔任教師。
  說明 此句中的 had been offered 是過去完成式的被動語態。

- He regularly tackles the most difficult jobs with calm confidence.
  他經常以平穩的信心來處理最困難的工作。

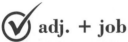 **adj. + job**

adj.	job	中譯
blue-collar		藍領工作
dead-end		沒有前景的工作
decent/good	job	不錯的工作
demanding		要求很高的工作
dream/ideal		理想的工作

entry-level		入門的 / 基本的工作
full-time		全職工作
lousy/menial		卑下的工作
low-paid/low-wage		低薪的工作
low-skilled/lower-skilled/unskilled		低技能的 / 無需技能的工作
manual		勞力的工作
middle-class		中產階級的工作
nine-to-five	job	朝九晚五的工作
odd		零工
part-time		兼職工作
permanent		永久的工作
routine		例行性工作
skilled		需要技能的工作
temporary		臨時的工作
well-paid		高薪的工作
white-collar		白領工作

搭配詞例句

- Millions of blue-collar jobs in manufacturing, construction and transportation disappear, subject to offshoring and automation.
  受制於產業外包和自動化，數百萬計的製造業、營建業和交通業的藍領工作都消失了。

- It seemed indeed that the numbers of low-paid unskilled jobs were growing with the advance of mechanization.
  隨著機械化的進展，低薪且無需技能的工作似乎真的愈來愈多。

- Less than half of all employees now have manual jobs.
  目前所有雇員中不到一半從事勞力的工作。

- The jobs that once kept the city prosperous are being replaced by skilled jobs in service sectors such as health care, finance and information technology.
  過去使這個城市繁榮的工作，正被健康照護、金融和資訊科技等服務業的技能工作所取代。

- The most important reason for taking a temporary job was that a permanent job was not available.
  人們之所以會接受臨時工作，最主要的原因是缺乏永久工作的機會。

 **job + n.**

job	n.	中譯
job	applicant	申請工作者
	application	申請工作
	creation	創造工作
	crisis	工作危機
	cut	裁員
	hunter/seeker	求職者
	hunting	找工作
	loss	失去工作

	market	就業市場
	offer	提供工作
job	opening/vacancy	工作職缺
	prospect	工作前景
	satisfaction	工作滿意度

搭配詞例句

- He stressed the importance of increasing U.S. exports as a key driver of economic growth and job creation.
  他強調增加美國出口的重要性，以作為經濟成長和創造工作的重要驅動力。

- High CEO pay is not the cause of America's job crisis or weak economic growth.
  執行長的高薪並不是美國工作危機或疲軟經濟成長的元凶。

- A series of major investment banks have announced job cuts.
  連續幾家大型投資銀行都宣布裁員。

- The number of job vacancies increased to 350,000 in July.
  七月份的工作職缺增加到 35 萬個。

- Young workers are discovering that their job prospects remain bleak.
  年輕的工作者發現他們的工作前景仍是黯淡無光。

- Job satisfaction is dependent on a variety of factors, many of which are within your control.
  工作滿意度取決於各種因素，其中有許多因素是你可以掌控的。

相關詞彙之搭配使用

片語

a lack of skilled labor a shortage of seasoned manpower	缺乏有技能的人力／缺乏 有經驗的人力
a strong work ethic	敬業，極佳的職場倫理
blue-collar worker	藍領工作者
career/job fair	就業博覽會，人才招募會
current hiring trends in the job market	目前就業市場的雇用趨勢
curriculum vitae (CV) /resume	履歷表
cyclical unemployment	循環性失業，週期性失業
difficult for youths to land good jobs	年輕人很難找到好工作
discrimination at work	職場歧視
freelance worker	自由接案工作者
high level of unemployment high unemployment rate	高失業率
in-service/on-the-job training	在職訓練
internship program	實習計畫
labor force	勞動力
Labor Standards Act	勞動基準法（臺灣）
massive layoffs	大舉裁員
meager salaries and few benefits	微薄的薪資與福利
minimum wage	最低薪資，基本工資
paid parental leave	帶薪育嬰假
pre-service training	職前訓練

the recent abatement of heavy layoffs	近來大量裁員情勢減緩
the rise in employment	就業人數增加
to get fired/sacked/ to get the pink slip	被解雇
to give someone the sack	開除某人
to invest in job-creating export markets	投資創造就業的出口市場
white-collar professional/worker	白領專業人士 / 工作者
young people embarking on their career	開展職涯的年輕人

句子

- Those jobs do not <u>offer basic benefits</u> like health insurance.
  那些工作並沒有提供像醫療保險之類的<u>基本福利</u>。

  說明 benefits 又稱為 employee/fringe benefits 或 perks，也就是除了「薪資」(salaries/wages) 以外，員工能從雇主所獲得的附加福利，通常包括醫療保險、休假、退休金、住宿或交通津貼等。

- <u>Hourly employees</u> will see their wages increase to $11 per hour from $9 per hour, effective April 2018.
  <u>時薪雇員</u>的薪資將從每小時九美元調高至 11 美元，從 2018 年四月起生效。

- Often women feel they have to prove themselves even though they know they <u>are highly qualified for the job</u>.
  儘管女性自知<u>在工作上可勝任愉快</u>，她們通常還是覺得必須證明自己的能力。

- Hiring a <u>headhunter</u> might benefit your company in <u>recruiting highly qualified talents</u>.
  雇用<u>獵才顧問</u>對你的公司在<u>招募高階專業人才</u>上可能有幫助。

- As <u>automation disrupts the labor market</u> and good middle-class jobs <u>disappear,</u> schools are struggling to equip students with <u>future-proof skills.</u>
  <u>自動化破壞勞動市場，好的中產階級工作消失，學校正努力讓學生學習未來可用的技能。</u>

....

> **段落**

The U.S. <u>unemployment rate</u>[1] in November fell to its lowest level since August 2007 as the economy continued to add new jobs. The jobless rate fell an unusually large <u>three-tenths</u>[2] to a surprising 4.6 percent, the Labor Department reported Friday. A solid 178,000 net new positions were created, <u>in line with</u>[3] analysts' expectations. The economy has added jobs at an average rate of 180,000 a month so far this year, a healthy pace but below the 229,000 rate in 2015. (*AFP*)

美國經濟成長，新職缺持續增加，使得 11 月失業率下降至 2007 年八月以來最低點。美國勞工部週五表示，失業率不尋常地大幅下降 0.3 個百分點，達到令人驚訝的 4.6%。此次共創造 17 萬 8 千個新工作，符合分析師預期。從年初至今，美國經濟成長使得每月平均新增 18 萬個工作，以合理步調成長，不過仍低於 2015 年的每月 22 萬 9 千個新工作。（《法新社》）

> **說明**
> ① unemployment rate（失業率）等同於下文的 jobless rate，可交替使用。
> ② three-tenths（10 分之 3）是英文分數 (fraction) 的寫法，其中 three 是分子 (numerator)，用基數表示；tenths 是分母 (denominator)，用序數表示。當分子的數字超過 1 時，分母的序數要用複數形，因此 three-tenths 就是「10 分之 3」。譯成中文新聞時不妨換算成小數點 (decimal)，約為 0.3，便於國內讀者理解。
> ③ in line with...（符合…）也可代換成 consistent with...。

搭配詞練習

⚙ **請從方格中挑選正確的搭配詞來完成以下的句子。**

market	leaving	openings	receiving	loss

1. It will take years for the U.S. **job** _____ to return to its pre-recession glory.

   美國的**就業市場**需要好幾年時間才能恢復衰退前的榮景。

2. About 14 million Americans are unemployed, yet 3 million **job** _____ remain unfilled.

   雖然有高達約 1,400 萬美國人失業，但有 300 萬個**工作職缺**仍乏人問津。

3. The number of people _____ or _____ **jobs** picked up in September.

   九月份**離職**或**就職**的人數逐漸增加。

4. Some allege that the **job** _____ in the first two years of the FTA was over 200,000 in Ontario alone.

   部分人士宣稱，簽訂自由貿易協定後頭兩年，光是在安大略就**流失**了超過 20 萬個**工作機會**。

解答：1. market　2. openings　3. leaving, receiving　4. loss

暖身練習解答：①

III. 軍事戰爭類

military

(n.) 軍事，軍隊 (adj.) 軍事的，軍隊的

▶ 答案請見 p. 175

暖身練習

請就以下中英譯文選出適當的搭配詞。

Chinese President Xi Jinping is overseeing a large-scale **military** ① **parade** ② **inspection** in a show of China's fighting prowess.
中國國家主席習近平主持大規模**閱兵儀式**，展現中國強大武力。

military 可當名詞用，指「軍事」、「軍隊」，通常是指由國家組織訓練的武力，包括 army（陸軍）、navy（海軍）、air force（空軍）、Marine Corps（海軍陸戰隊）等。如果是由民眾自行組織的武裝組織則稱為 militia（民兵）、guerrilla（游擊隊）等。另外也有受雇的 mercenary（傭兵），其中最為有名的是法國的 Foreign Legion（外籍兵團）。至於陸軍編制常見中英文名稱如下：

- army corps：軍（軍長 commanding general）
- division：師（師長 commanding general）
- brigade：旅（旅長 brigade commander）
- regiment：團（團長 regiment commander）
- battalion：營（營長 battalion commander）
- company：連（連長 company commander）
- platoon：排（排長 platoon leader）
- squad：班（班長 squad leader）

　　military 也可以當形容詞用，意思是「軍事的」、「軍隊的」。以下列出 military 的名詞和形容詞兩種詞性之搭配。

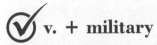 **v. + military**

v.	military	中譯
build up		建立軍隊
debilitate	military	削弱軍力
disband		解散軍隊
maintain		維持軍力

搭配詞例句

- Republican presidential candidates are charging that President Obama is debilitating the military.
  共和黨總統候選人一直指控歐巴馬總統在削弱軍力。

- The United States would still maintain the strongest military in the world.
  美國仍會維持全球最強大的軍力。

 **military + n.**

military	n.	中譯
military	academy	軍事院校
	action/mission/operation	軍事行動
	balance	軍力平衡

military	capability/capacity/force/might/muscle/power/prowess/strength	軍事力量
	coup	軍事政變
	crackdown	軍事鎮壓
	drill/exercise	軍事演習
	hotline	軍事熱線
	intervention	軍事介入 / 干預
	junta/regime	軍事政權
	mutiny	軍事叛變
	parade	閱兵儀式
	police	憲兵
	retiree/veteran	退伍軍人
	service	兵役
	stalemate	軍事僵局
	tension	軍事緊張
	upgrading	軍力升級

搭配詞例句

- Congress authorized military action through a series of statutes.
  國會透過一系列的法令授權軍事行動。

....

- China is developing the military might to go along with its economic strength.
  中國正配合其經濟實力來發展軍事力量。

....

- Norway hit one of its own submarines with a dummy torpedo during a joint military exercise.
  挪威在一場聯合軍事演習中，一枚假魚雷擊中了自家的潛艇。

- The two sides are now talking about setting up a military hotline.
  雙方目前正在討論設置一條軍事熱線。

- While the United States did not have a vital interest at stake in Libya, a limited military intervention solely on humanitarian grounds could be justified.
  雖然美國在利比亞沒有重大利益受到威脅，僅只基於人道立場所做有限度的軍事介入是可以接受的。

- President Trump has been impressed with how other countries put on their military parades.
  川普總統向來對其他國家舉辦的閱兵大典印象深刻。

  說明 本句「舉辦閱兵大典」的英文為 put on military parades，動詞「舉辦」也可用 hold。而「閱兵」的目的通常是為了「炫耀軍力」，英文為 flaunt/showcase military power 或 show off military power。

相關詞彙之搭配使用

片語	
a show of military force/strength	軍力展示
combat operations overseas	海外戰鬥任務
combat troops	戰鬥部隊
compulsory military service	義務兵役
demilitarized zone (DMZ/DZ)	非軍事區
military contingency plan	軍事應變計劃

People's Liberation Army (PLA)	中國人民解放軍
poorly equipped and disorganized rebel forces	裝備簡陋、缺乏組織的反叛軍
security forces	安全部隊
special (opertations) forces	特種部隊（如美國海軍的「海豹」(SEALs)、陸軍的「綠扁帽」(Green Berets)、「遊騎兵」(Rangers) 和「三角洲部隊」(Delta Force) 等）
state-of-the-art military equipment	先進的軍事裝備
the 38th parallel between North and South Korea	南北韓邊界的北緯 38 度線
the Pentagon	五角大廈（美國國防部）
to end in a military stalemate	陷入軍事僵局
to flex military muscle	展現軍事實力

句子

- Israel launched strikes on Syrian military positions.
  以色列對敘利亞的軍事據點發動攻擊。

....

- German Chancellor Angela Merkel vowed to boost security and improve counterterrorism measures following three attacks allegedly carried out by refugees.
  歷經三起據稱是難民所發動的攻擊事件後，德國總理梅克爾宣示將加強安全工作並提升反恐措施。

....

- The US military has a presence of several hundred troops in Somalia to carry out special operations and to train government forces.
  美國軍方在索馬利亞駐有數百名士兵，負責執行特別任務和訓練該國部隊。

....

- The annual Han Kuang live-fire military drills were launched in Taiwan to test and boost the country's defense capabilities, focusing on joint anti-airborne operations at Ching Chuan Kang air base in Taichung.
臺灣舉行年度漢光實彈演習，用以檢視並提升國防能力，重點項目是在臺中清泉崗基地進行的「聯合反空降作戰」。

段落

Russia's defense minister says the military received an array of[1] new weapons last year, including 41 intercontinental ballistic missiles[2]. Sergei Shoigu told lawmakers Wednesday that the sweeping military modernization program will continue at a high pace this year. Amid tensions with the West, the Kremlin has continued to spend big on new weapons despite Russia's economic downturn. He said Russia has now deployed new long-range early warning radars[3] to survey the airspace along the entire length of its borders. (*AP*)

俄羅斯國防部長紹伊古表示，該國軍隊去年配置大量新式武器，其中包括 41 枚洲際彈道飛彈。他於週三告訴國會議員，全面軍隊現代化計畫今年將持續快速進行。在與西方對峙的緊張氛圍中，儘管經濟衰退，俄羅斯仍繼續耗費巨資添購新武器。紹伊古說，俄羅斯目前已部署新式長程預警雷達系統，監看全幅邊境沿線的空域。(《美聯社》)

說明

① an array of... 表示「大量的…」，如 an array of heavily armed troops（大量重裝部隊）。

② intercontinental ballistic missile（洲際彈道飛彈）在英文新聞中也常用其頭字詞 ICBM 表示，是射程達 5,500 公里以上的導彈。依射程不同還有 medium-range ballistic missile (MRBM)（中程彈道飛彈）、short-range ballistic missile (SRBM)（短程彈道飛彈）等。

③ deploy 是動詞，意為「部署」，後面可以搭配名詞 troops（部隊）、weapons（武器）或此處的 early warning radars（預警雷達系統），也可用名詞 deployment 來表達相同意思，如 deployment of troops（部署部隊）、deployment of weapons（部署武器）等。另外，radar（雷達）其實是 RAdio Detection And Ranging（無線電偵查與測距）的頭字詞，在軍事領域中常用這種簡短術語。

搭配詞練習

⚙ **請從方格中挑選正確的搭配詞來完成以下的句子。**

capabilities	build	action	stalemate	balances

1. Italy and Germany would have to _____ **up** their own **military forces** and provide for their own security.

   義大利和德國必須**建立**他們的**軍隊**並保衛自己的安全。

2. China's expanding **military** _____ are a major factor in altering **military** _____ in East Asia.

   中國持續擴張的**軍力**是改變東亞地區**軍力平衡**的重要因素。

3. The polls continue to say that 70 percent of Americans support **military** _____ against Iraq.

   民調持續顯示，70% 的美國民眾支持對伊拉克採取**軍事行動**。

4. The **military** _____ is less a reflection of opposition strength than of the weakness of the Transitional Federal Government.

   此次**軍事僵局**與其說是反映出反對勢力的強大，不如說是反映出過渡聯邦政府的軟弱無能。

解答：1. build　2. capabilities, balances　3. action　4. stalemate

暖身練習解答：①

arms

(n.) 武器

暖身練習

⚙ 請就以下中英譯文選出適當的搭配詞。　　　　　▶ 答案請見 p. 182

The Ministry of National Defense stressed the **arms** ① **sell** ② **sale** was proposed based on actual needs.

國防部強調是基於實際需求提出**軍售案**。

單數名詞 arm 是指「手臂」，複數名詞 arms 可指「雙臂」、「懷中」，例如以下例句：

- We welcome you with open arms.
  我們張開雙臂熱誠歡迎你。

- She jumped into his arms.
  她躍入他的懷中。

而複數的 arms 還可以指「武器」，例如 side arms 是指如刀或手槍的「隨身武器」。arm 還可以當動詞用，指「提供武器」，相反詞 disarm 就是「解除武裝」、「繳械」，例句如下：

- Poorly equipped rebel fighters have armed themselves with anything they can find.
  裝備簡陋的反叛軍以所有他們能找到的東西來武裝自己。

- The Democratic Republic of Congo wants to disarm and disband rebels on its territory.
  剛果民主共和國有意解除境內叛亂組織的武裝並令其解散。

另外，arm 字尾加 -ed 成爲 armed 就可當形容詞用，意指「武裝的」，如 armed force 就是「武裝部隊」。以下是名詞 arms 的搭配。

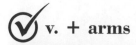 **v. + arms**

v.	arms	中譯
bear/carry		攜帶武器
control		管制武器
decommission		解除武裝
keep		擁有武器
lay down	arms	放下武器
provide/supply		提供武器
reduce		削減武器
sell		販售武器
take up		拿起武器

搭配詞例句

- The federal government has to honor an individual's right to keep and bear arms under the Second Amendment.
  根據《美國憲法第二條修正案》，聯邦政府必須允許個人履行擁有和攜帶武器的權利。

- At the summit in Istanbul, the President and 54 other world leaders signed a treaty to reduce arms in Europe.
  在伊斯坦堡的高峰會上，總統與其他 54 位世界領袖簽署了一項協議，削減在歐洲的武器。

- The United States was again selling arms to the Middle East on a massive scale.
  美國再度大規模販售武器給中東國家。

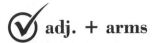 **adj. ＋ arms**

adj.	arms	中譯
conventional		傳統武器
nuclear	arms	核子武器
small		小型武器

搭配詞例句

- We are working vigorously to reduce the global traffic in conventional arms sales.
  我們正致力於減少全球傳統武器的交易。

- Iran is pursuing the development of its nuclear arms.
  伊朗正熱衷於發展自己的核子武器。

 **arms ＋ n.**

arms	n.	中譯
arms	control	武器管制

arms	deal/sale/trade	軍售交易
	dealer/merchant	軍火商
	embargo	武器禁運
	limitation	軍備限制
	proliferation	武器擴散
	provider/supplier	軍火供應者
	race	軍備競賽
	reduction	武器削減
	trafficking	軍火走私販賣

搭配詞例句

- The Obama administration this week approved a $5 billion arms deal to Taiwan.
  本週歐巴馬政府批准了對臺灣 50 億美元的軍售交易。

- Our allies are enforcing the no-fly zone over Libya and the arms embargo at sea.
  我們的盟友正在利比亞的領空實施禁航區，在海上則實施武器禁運。

- In 1972, the United States and the Soviet Union signed the first arms limitation treaty, aiming at the reduction of nuclear weapons.
  1972 年美國和蘇聯簽定第一次限武條約，旨在削減核武數量。

- The Vietnam War and the arms race greatly weakened the United States.
  越戰和軍備競賽大幅削弱了美國的國力。

相關詞彙之搭配使用

片語

armored car/vehicle	裝甲車輛
calling for more transfers of defense technology to the local military	要求轉移更多國防科技給當地軍方
chemical and biological weapons	生化武器
Strategic Arms Limitation Talks (SALT)	戰略武器限制談判
to assist the recovery of war-torn Europe	協助飽受戰火蹂躪的歐洲走上復興之路
to halt the proliferation of nuclear weapons	停止核子武器的擴散
to lower the price of arms sale	降低軍售價格
to sell arms to terrorists	把武器賣給恐怖分子
unarmed protesters	沒有武裝的抗議者
Weapons of Mass Destruction (WMD)	大規模毀滅性武器

句子

- Russia is in talks with Iran over a $10 billion arms deal in which Moscow would provide advanced tanks, artillery systems, planes and helicopters to the Islamic republic.

  俄羅斯正與伊朗商討價值逾 100 億美元的軍售交易，莫斯科將提供先進的坦克、火砲系統、飛機和直昇機給這個伊斯蘭共和國。

  說明 英文新聞較不喜歡重複使用相同的字彙，傾向用不同方式來指稱同一個事物或概念，同時也可增添訊息。如此句中的 Russia，在第二次提及時就改用 Moscow，而 Iran 在句子最後就用 the Islamic republic 代替。

段落

China launched a new domestically developed destroyer[①] in Shanghai on Wednesday, according to the People's Liberation Army Navy. The launch ceremony was held at the Jiangnan Shipyard of the China State Shipbuilding Corp. The ship is the first of China's new-generation guided-missile destroyer class, with a full displacement of around 10,000 metric tons[②]. It will be equipped with new types of air defense, missile defense, and anti-ship and anti-submarine weapons. Though the Navy has yet to[③] reveal which class the new destroyer belongs to, observers believe it is the Type 055 class and call it one of the largest and mightiest of its kind in the world. (*China Post*)

中國人民解放軍海軍表示，中國自製的新型驅逐艦週三在上海首度下水。下水儀式在中國船舶工業集團公司旗下的江南造船廠舉行。該艦是中國首艘新一代導彈驅逐艦，滿載排水量約一萬公噸，艦上將配備新式防空、反飛彈、反艦和反潛武器。雖然中國海軍尚未公布該艦所屬級別，但觀察家相信是 055 級驅逐艦，稱之為全球同級艦中最強大的一種驅逐艦。(《英文中國郵報》)

說明

① destroy 原為「毀滅」之意，字尾加 -er 形成 destroyer 就變成「驅逐艦」。新聞中常見的海軍艦種還有 aircraft carrier（航空母艦）、cruiser（巡洋艦）、battleship（戰艦）、corvette（護衛艦）等。

② displacement 字面上的意思為「移位」，在船舶術語中則為「排水量」，是指船舶的總重量，通常以 metric ton（公噸）為單位。

③ yet 通常用於否定句，表示「還沒」，例如 Just don't get too excited yet.（還不能太過興奮。）但此處 has/have yet to 是固定搭配，看起來雖是肯定句，但也有「尚未」的意思。

搭配詞練習

⚙ 請從方格中挑選正確的搭配詞來完成以下的句子。

control	trade	supplier	embargo	small

1. The global **arms** _____ has contracted.
   全球的**軍火交易**有縮減跡象。

2. China has threatened to withdraw from United Nations **arms** _____ **talks**.
   中國威脅要退出聯合國的**武器管制談判**。

3. Iran has repeatedly violated a U.N. **arms** _____ with exports to Syria.
   伊朗一再違反聯合國**武器禁運**的規定,將武器出口至敘利亞。

4. Military and intelligence officials say that Iran has recently flown into Syria _____ **arms**, chiefly rocket-propelled grenades.
   軍事和情報官員表示,伊朗最近將**小型武器**空運至敘利亞,主要是火箭推進式榴彈。

5. Russia is a leading **arms** _____ to Syria.
   俄羅斯是敘利亞重要的**軍火供應者**。

解答:1. trade　2. control　3. embargo　4. small　5. supplier

暖身練習解答:②

war

(n.) 戰爭

▶ 答案請見 p. 189

暖身練習

⚙ 請就以下中英譯文選出適當的搭配詞。

The hunt for German Nazi **war** ① **prisoners** ② **criminals** still goes on today.
直至今日仍在追捕德國納粹**戰犯**。

　　一場「戰爭」(war) 中通常會有許多場「戰役」(battles)，有句英文說 Someone has lost the battle, but won the war.，指「某人雖然輸掉戰役，但最後卻贏得戰爭。」可引申為人生的過程中雖有挫敗，但持續奮戰終能達至最終的理想，這才是最重要的。但也可以倒過來說成 win the battle but lose the war，也就是「贏得戰役卻輸掉戰爭」，那就是我們想要避免的狀況。

　　除了大型的戰爭或戰役之外，小型的軍事對抗還有「戰鬥」如 fighting, combat 和「衝突」如 clash, conflict, skirmish, strife 等，搭配的形容詞可用 intense（激烈的）、heavy（嚴重的）、sporadic（零星的）等，例如以下例句：

- The evidence of intense fighting could be seen everywhere.
  激烈戰鬥的痕跡處處可見。

　　另外，war 也可以用來表示對抗非軍事事物，如 trade war（貿易戰）或 Taiwan's war on drugs（臺灣對毒品宣戰）。

✅ v. + war

v.	war	中譯
avert/avoid/prevent		避免／防止戰爭
declare		宣戰
fight		戰鬥，參戰
go to		上戰場
launch/wage	war	發動戰爭
lose		戰敗
prepare for		備戰
win		戰勝

搭配詞例句

- On the morning of Dec. 11, the Government of Germany, pursuing its course of world conquest, declared war against the United States.
  12 月 11 日早晨，德國政府為遂行征服世界的野心，向美國宣戰。

- The report is expected to include a recommendation that the United States abandon its long-held goal of being able to fight and win two wars simultaneously.
  該報告預期會建議美國放棄長期抱持的目標：可同時參與兩場戰爭並贏得勝利。

✅ adj. + war

adj.	war	中譯
civil		內戰
cold	war	冷戰

continuing		持續的戰爭
conventional		傳統戰爭
economic		經濟戰
full-scale	war	大規模戰爭
guerrilla		游擊戰
violent		激烈的戰爭

搭配詞例句

● The end of the Cold War did not bring peace to the world.
冷戰結束並未為世界帶來和平。

....

● The continuing war in Afghanistan is one reason why that country leads all others in infant mortality rates.
連年戰亂是阿富汗嬰兒夭折率居全球之冠的原因之一。

....

● The Vietnam War started as a guerrilla war and then escalated into a conventional war.
越戰一開始只是游擊戰，之後逐步升高為傳統戰爭。

....

相關詞彙之搭配使用

片語

an act of war	戰爭行為
anti-war demonstration	反戰示威
clashes with government forces	與政府軍的衝突
Cold War-era psychological warfare	冷戰時期的心理戰

escalating tension to the brink of war	緊張局勢升高，戰爭一觸即發
heavy casualties/losses	死傷慘重
in an assault on... / in attacks on...	攻擊…
missing in action (MIA)	作戰中失蹤
outbreak of war	戰爭爆發
prisoner of war (POW)	戰俘
The Art of War	孫子兵法
the surviving veterans of the Vietnam War	越戰倖存的退伍軍人
to launch a relentless assault/attack on...	對…發動無情的攻擊
to launch an immediate counter attack against...	對…發動立即的反擊
to risk a full-scale trade war	冒著大規模貿易戰爭的風險
to seek a diplomatic solution through dialogue	通過對話尋求外交解決
to stage military exercise/drills to stage war games	舉行軍事演習
to teeter on the brink of war	瀕臨戰爭邊緣
war of attrition / attrition warfare	消耗戰

句子

- During World War II, many events helped to turn the tide of war in favor of the Allies.

  在第二次世界大戰期間，許多事件扭轉了戰爭的局勢，情勢轉而對盟軍有利。

- The great challenge facing both countries was that of <u>reducing the risk of nuclear war</u>.
  兩個國家所面臨的極大挑戰就是<u>降低核子戰爭的風險</u>。

- The <u>computer-aided war games</u> section of this year's <u>Han Kuang military exercises</u> kicked off Monday with <u>a simulation of an invasion by Chinese forces</u>.
  今年漢光軍事演習的電腦兵推於週一登場，<u>模擬中國武力進犯</u>。

段落

Syrian government <u>warplanes</u>① <u>broke a cease-fire agreement</u>② Monday for the second consecutive day with airstrikes on districts in rebel-held Eastern Ghouta near the country's capital, Damascus. A bombing raid Monday on the town of Arbin left eight civilians dead and at least 30 wounded. On Sunday, government warplanes <u>launched half-a-dozen airstrikes</u>③ on the towns of Douma and Ain Terma, breaking the so-called Cairo agreement sponsored by Egypt and Russia, which officially <u>went into effect</u>④ at noon Saturday. (*VOA*)

敘利亞政府的<u>戰機</u>週一<u>打破停火協議</u>，連續第二天空襲叛軍所占據的東古達，該地區鄰近首都大馬士革。週一亞賓鎮遭轟炸，造成八個平民喪生和至少30人受傷。週日政府戰機對杜瑪和艾特瑪兩個城鎮<u>發動六次空襲</u>，打破由埃及和俄羅斯發起的所謂開羅協議，該協議剛於週六中午正式<u>生效</u>。（《美國之音》）

說明

① warplanes（戰機）是總稱，更具體區分有 fighter（戰鬥機）、bomber（轟炸機）、attack aircraft（攻擊機）、electronic-warfare aircraft（電子作戰機）等。

② 與 cease-fire（停火）近似的詞有 truce（停戰）、cessation of hostilities（結束敵對狀態）、armistice（休戰）等，在英文新聞中經常交替使用，

但語義仍有細微差異。truce 屬於非正式的停戰，期間較短；cessation of hostilities 是較概括性的用語，對交戰方沒有約束性，隨時可能恢復戰事；cease-fire 需要協商和簽署協議，但通常也無法維持太久就會被打破；只有 armistice 是正式簽署協議要求交戰方終止戰爭，但之後仍需簽署 peace treaty（和平條約）才能維持和平，例如目前南北韓就是簽定 armistice agreement（休戰協議）。而「打破協議」的英文搭配為 break agreement。

③ airstrike（空襲）也可以說 air strike, air raid, air attack, bombing raid 等，前面可搭配動詞 launch（發動）。

④ go into effect 是「生效」的意思，類似說法還有 come into effect, take effect, become effective, come into force 等。

搭配詞練習

⚙ 請從方格中挑選正確的搭配詞來完成以下的句子。

economic	launched	civil	won	waging

1. The head of the Arab League warned that Syria may be sliding toward
   _____ **war**.
   阿拉伯聯盟領袖警告說敘利亞可能會陷入**內戰**。

2. Iran said the West was _____ "an _____ **war**" through
   sanctions.
   伊朗表示，西方國家透過制裁**發動**一場「**經濟戰**」。

3. President Bush _____ and _____ the first Gulf **War**.
   布希總統**發動**並**打贏**第一次波斯灣**戰爭**。

peace

(n.) 和平

暖身練習

⚙ 請就以下中英譯文選出適當的搭配詞。　　　　　　　　▶ 答案請見 p. 196

The **peace** ① **exercise** ② **movement** has been focused on global issues of nuclear disarmament, land mines, cluster bombs, and war.
和平運動向來聚焦於裁減核武、地雷、集束炸彈和戰爭的全球議題。

　　有戰爭的同時就會有人追求「和平」(peace)，此時就需要「調停戰爭者」(peacemaker) 來達成「停戰」(truce)，也需要「維持和平的部隊」(peacekeepers / peacekeeping force)，從事「維持和平的任務」(peacekeeping mission/operation)。其中最有名的就是「聯合國維和部隊」(UN peacekeeping force)，也因其成員都是戴藍色頭盔，又稱之為 Blue Helmets（藍盔軍）。

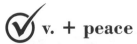 **v. + peace**

v.	peace	中譯
achieve/secure		達成和平
defend		保衛和平
disturb	peace	破壞和平
establish/forge/make		建立和平
keep/maintain/sustain		維持和平

promote		促進和平
reject		拒絕和平
restore	peace	恢復和平
seek		尋求和平
threaten		威脅和平

搭配詞例句

- Palestinians and Israelis believe that only through negotiations can real peace be achieved.
  巴勒斯坦人與以色列人都相信，唯有透過協商才能達成真正的和平。
  說明 that 引導的子句因為有 only，所以主詞 real peace 放在助動詞 can 後面，是倒裝用法，而且動詞 be achieved 是被動語態。

- America and our allies are called upon once again to defend the peace against an aggressive tyrant.
  美國和我們的盟友再次被請求前去保衛和平，對抗好戰的暴君。

- An international force should be sent to Liberia to maintain peace.
  應該派遣一支國際部隊到賴比瑞亞維持和平。

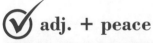 **adj. + peace**

adj.	peace	中譯
fragile		脆弱的和平
lasting/permanent	peace	持久的 / 永久的和平
regional		區域和平

搭配詞例句

• Ivory Coast's fragile peace is under threat by feuding warlords.
軍閥長期爭鬥，威脅象牙海岸脆弱的和平。

• Myanmar is negotiating peace with major rebel groups and is determined to achieve a permanent peace with them in three to four years.
緬甸正與各主要叛亂組織談判，並決心在三至四年內與他們達成永久和平。

 peace + n.

peace	n.	中譯
peace	accord/agreement/pact/treaty	和平協議 / 條約
	activist	和平運動者
	Corps	和平工作團
	envoy	和平特使
	mission	和平任務
	movement	和平運動
	negotiation/talks	和平談判
	rally	和平集會
	summit	和平高峰會
	troops	維和部隊

- After nearly three years of negotiations, Sudan's government and main rebel group have signed comprehensive peace accords to end more than 21 years of civil war.

  經過將近三年的協議，蘇丹政府與主要叛亂組織簽定了全面性的和平條約，終結逾 21 年的內戰。

- He had just returned from two years as a Peace Corps volunteer in Ecuador.

  他在厄瓜多擔任兩年和平工作團的志工才剛回來。

- Tony Blair, the United Nations' Middle East peace envoy, has broken his silence on the tense situation in Libya.

  聯合國中東和平特使布萊爾對利比亞的緊張局勢打破沉默。

- The last round of peace talks between Israel and the Palestinians broke down a year ago.

  以色列與巴勒斯坦上一回合的和平談判在一年前破局。

相關詞彙之搭配使用

片語

a heavy blow to hopes of peace talks	對和平談判曙光的重大打擊
a key step to securing peace	達成和平的重要步驟
a peaceful solution to the crisis	和平處理此危機的方式
bringing peace and stability to the region	為該地區帶來和平與穩定
fallen soldiers soldiers who make the ultimate sacrifice	為國捐軀的士兵

government's top peace negotiator	政府最高和平談判代表
resumption of direct peace talks	重新恢復直接和平談判
to break the cease-fire agreement	打破停火協議
to call for an eventual cessation of hostilities	呼籲最終結束敵對狀態
to call for an immediate humanitarian cease-fire	以人道理由呼籲立即停火
to rest in peace (RIP)	願逝者安息

句子

● The United States and Britain called on Sunday for an immediate and unconditional cease-fire in Yemen.
美英兩國於週日呼籲葉門立即無條件停火。

段落

Colombia opens peace talks[①] with its last active rebel group[②], the ELN, seeking to replicate its historic accord with the FARC guerrillas and deliver "complete peace" after 53 years of war. But experts warn the ELN will be a tougher negotiating partner than the FARC, and say no deal is likely before President Juan Manuel Santos leaves office next year. Santos, who won the Nobel Peace Prize[③] in October, was nevertheless full of optimism heading into the talks. (AFP)

哥倫比亞與境內最後一個武裝叛亂組織「哥倫比亞民族解放軍」(ELN) 展開和平談判。在經過 53 年內戰後，該國有意複製之前與「哥倫比亞革命武裝力量」(FARC) 達成歷史性協議的模式，以達成「完全的和平」。不過專家警

告，ELN 將會是比 FARC 更難纏的談判對手，在桑托斯總統明年下台前可能都無法達成協議。然而 10 月<u>榮獲諾貝爾和平獎</u>的桑托斯總統對進行談判充滿樂觀。(《法新社》)

說明

① open peace talks（展開和平談判）的 talks 要用複數形，才有「談判」的意思，即使是只有「展開新一回合的和平談判」，也要說 open a new round/session of peace talks。而 talks 在此也可代換成 negotiations。

② rebel group 和下文的 guerrillas 都是指反政府的「武裝叛亂組織」，也可稱為 rebel forces/fighters/soldiers/troops（叛軍）。英文新聞中經常報導的 rebel groups 還有中東地區的 Al-Qaeda（蓋達組織，基地組織）、ISIS (Islamic State of Iraq and al-Sham)（伊斯蘭國）等。

③ win the Nobel Peace Prize 是「榮獲諾貝爾和平獎」，而「諾貝爾和平獎得主」則是 Nobel Peace Prize winner 或 Nobel Peace Prize laureate。laureate（獲得殊榮者）來自名詞 laurel（月桂樹），laurel wreath 是「桂冠」，「桂冠詩人」稱為 Poet Laureate。

搭配詞練習

⚙ 請從方格中挑選正確的搭配詞來完成以下的句子。

lasting	summit	agreement	promote	regional

1. Israeli Prime Minister Netanyahu said he remains committed to making every effort to achieve a _____ **peace** with the Palestinians.
以色列總理納坦雅胡表示，他仍會致力於與巴勒斯坦達成**持久的和平**。

2. A NATO-centric security system can not **ensure** _____ **peace**.
以北大西洋公約為中心的安全系統無法**保證區域和平**。

3. Pope Francis has called for a **peace** _____ among religious leaders to discuss how they can _____ **peace**.
教宗方濟各呼籲各宗教領袖舉行**和平高峰會**，討論如何**促進和平**。

4. Yasser Arafat, the leader of the Palestine Liberation Organization, said today that he had won the support of his mainstream Fatah movement for a proposed **peace** _____ with Israel and that it could be signed within days.
巴勒斯坦解放組織領導人阿拉法特今日表示，他已獲得主流派法塔組織的支持，向以色列提議**和平協議**，並且在幾天內即可簽署。

解答：1. lasting 2. regional 3. summit, promote 4. agreement

暖身練習解答：②

IV. 科技電腦類

technology

(n.) 技術，科技

暖身練習

⚙ 請就以下中英譯文選出適當的搭配詞。　　　　　　▶ 答案請見 p. 204

Some of these ① **water-saving** ② **saving-water technologies** are brilliant.
這些**節水技術**中有一部分非常出色。

　　technology 可簡寫成 tech，方便造出新字，如 hi-tech（高科技，即 high technology）、info-tech（資訊科技，即 information technology）、bio-tech（生物科技，即 biology technology）、nano-tech（奈米科技，即 nanotechnology）、fin tech（金融科技，即 financial technology）等；或是將 tech 置前的 tech obsession（科技成癮）、tech company（科技公司）等。用連字號與 tech 合成的形容詞則有 tech-savvy（熟練科技的），如 a tech-savvy worker（嫻熟技術的工人）；tech-laden（搭載高科技的），如 an all-new, tech-laden vehicle（搭載高科技的新車）等。其他衍生字還有 technician（技師）、technical（技術性的）如 technical problem/glitch（技術問題）、technological（科技的）如 technological advance/change/breakthrough（科技進步／改變／突破）等。

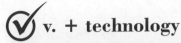 **v. + technology**

v.	technology	中譯
adopt/apply/employ/use/utilize		使用科技
create/develop		研發技術
import/introduce	technology	引進技術
promote		推廣技術
transfer		轉移技術

搭配詞例句

- While IT is morally neutral, the manner in which people apply technology can have moral implications.
  雖然資訊科技是道德中立的，但是人們使用科技的方式卻有道德上的影響。

- Record companies have developed a technology that disables computer devices from sharing copyrighted music.
  唱片公司研發出一種技術，可以使電腦裝置無法分享有版權的音樂。

- The primary reason for introducing new technology such as robots is to reduce costs and improve product quality.
  引進如機器人等新技術的主要原因，是為了削減成本和改進產品品質。

adj. + technology

adj.	technology	中譯
advanced/cutting-edge/leading/ leading-edge/state-of-the-art		先進技術
current/existing/present-day	technology	現有技術

digital		數位科技
emerging		新興科技
energy-saving		節能技術
green		綠色／環保科技
hybrid	technology	油電混合動力科技
innovative		創新技術
latest/up-to-date		最新技術
manufacturing		製造技術

搭配詞例句

- Engineers at two NASA centers are hard at work developing futuristic robots with cutting-edge technology.
  美國太空總署兩個中心的工程師正致力以先進技術開發未來的機器人。

- Continual advances in digital technology are opening new channels for teaching and learning.
  數位科技的持續進步開啟了教學與學習的新管道。

- Industries in developed countries are competing with each other to produce new products using energy-saving technology.
  已開發國家的廠商競相製造使用節能技術的新產品。

- As hybrid technology evolves, hybrid car owners will reap the benefits of lower emissions and fuel consumption.
  油電混合動力科技的進步，將使油電車的車主因低排氣和低油耗而受惠。

- These measures would encourage the private sector to invest more in innovative technology that will lessen demand for fossil energy.
這些措施將會鼓勵民間企業投資更多在降低化石能源需求的創新技術上。

....

相關詞彙之搭配使用

片語

artificial neural network	人工神經網路
Augmented Reality (AR)	擴增實境（如精靈寶可夢 Pokémon Go）
autonomous/driverless/self-driving car	自動駕駛車輛
big data	大數據
cloud computing	雲端計算
electric car/vehicle	電動車輛
facial recognition technology	臉部辨識技術
high-speed railway	高速鐵路
International Space Station (ISS)	國際太空站
machine learning	機器學習
mobile payment	行動支付
renewable energy	再生能源
solar/photovoltaic/PV cell	太陽能電池
solar panel	太陽能板
solar power station	太陽能電廠
sustainable energy	永續能源
technological leaps in solar and wind energy	太陽能和風力能源科技的快速成長

technology transfer from the public to the private sector	從公部門技術轉移到民間企業
through the use of sophisticated technology	透過使用精密技術
to improve core technology	改進核心技術
Virtual Reality (VR)	虛擬實境
wind power station	風力發電廠

句子

- In Asia, the birthplace of the selfie stick and the emoji, smartphone addiction is fast on the rise.
  在發明自拍棒和表情符號的亞洲，手機成癮的人數正快速增加。

- Government funding of technology has grown rapidly.
  政府對於科技的補助成長快速。

- As emerging technologies rapidly and thoroughly transform the workplace, some experts predict that by 2030, 400 million to 800 million people worldwide could be displaced and need to find new jobs.
  新興科技快速而徹底地改變職場型態，部分專家預測，在 2030 年前，全球將有四至八億人被迫離職，必需另尋新的工作。

段落

Microsoft released a new app[1] for iOS devices[2] called Seeing AI. The app uses computer vision to provide verbal description for users who are blind or visually impaired[3]. The Seeing AI app is very simple to use. Once the app is open, users will first have to select which channel they want to use. After that, users will just have to point their iPhone camera in their desired direction. Point the iPhone's camera to an object, and the app will be able to describe to the user what it is. Pointing it at a product's bar code will have the app describing what it is, and even provide additional information about how to use it.

(*International Business Times*)

微軟推出一款 iOS 裝置使用的全新應用程式 Seeing AI，該程式利用電腦視覺技術提供口語描述給視障人士聆聽。Seeing AI 非常容易使用，打開後首先選擇想使用的頻道，再將 iPhone 相機鏡頭朝著想看的方向即可。把 iPhone 相機指向一個物體，應用程式就會向使用者描述這個物體是什麼。而將 iPhone 相機指向一個產品的條碼，應用程式就會描述這個產品，甚至提供額外的訊息，告知如何使用。(《國際財經時報》)

說明

① app 是 application 的簡寫，一般譯為「應用程式」，但也可以不譯，而以英文 app 表示，有時反而讓讀者更容易理解。這種直接以原文表現的翻譯策略稱為「零翻譯」(zero translation)，包括文中的 iOS, Seeing AI, iPhone，以及新聞中常見的 YouTube, Wi-Fi, Google, Xbox 等都是。另外，app 前面搭配表示「推出」、「發行」之意的動詞 release，也可代換為另一動詞 launch，如「推出新產品」就是 launch a new product。

② iOS 是蘋果公司開發的行動作業系統 (mobile operation system)，只適用該公司的產品如 iPhone, iPad, iPod 等，也就是此處所說的 iOS devices。另外一個許多人使用的行動作業系統是 Android，通常譯為「安卓」或直接以英文呈現。

③ 此處 visually impaired（視力受損的）是副詞與形容詞的搭配，另一常用的搭配詞組是形容詞與名詞 visual impairment，中譯為「視障」，依視力傷殘程度區分，最嚴重者為 blindness（失明）。另外，「聽障」是 hearing impairment。

搭配詞練習

⚙ **請從方格中挑選正確的搭配詞來完成以下的句子。**

use	information	develop	existing	core

1. We _____ video **technology** to create an interactive training environment.

   我們**使用**錄影**技術**打造互動式的訓練環境。

2. We adapt _____ **technology** or _____ new **technology** based on needs.

   我們基於需求改造**現有技術**或**研發**新**技術**。

3. The Hsinchu Science-based Industrial Park is one of the major _____ **technology** manufacturing bases in the world.

   新竹科學園區是全球主要的**資訊科技**製造基地。

4. Huawei still relies on _____ US **technology**—as does every company in the world that uses silicon in its products.

   華為就和全世界所有在產品中使用矽的企業一樣，仍需仰賴美國的**核心技術**。

解答：1. use　2. existing, develop　3. information　4. core

暖身練習解答：①

computer

(n.) 電腦

▶ 答案請見 p. 211

暖身練習

⚙ 請就以下中英譯文選出適當的搭配詞。

You could ① **reopen** ② **reboot** your **computer** by powering it off and on.

要**重開電腦**，你可以把電源關掉後再打開。

　　computer 在臺灣譯為「電腦」，在中國譯為「計算機」，應該是從 compute 的譯名「計算」再加譯「機」一字而來。但臺灣人看到「計算機」常是想到另一個英文字 calculator，因此容易產生誤解。以下為 computer 的搭配詞彙。

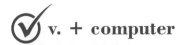 **v. + computer**

v.	computer	中譯
assemble		組裝電腦
build/manufacture		製造電腦
connect		連接電腦
hack into	computer	駭入電腦
operate		操作電腦
power up / switch on / turn on		電腦開機
program		設計電腦程式

reboot/restart		重開電腦
set up	computer	設定電腦
shut down / switch off / turn off		電腦關機
work on		使用電腦工作

搭配詞例句

- The Internet is a system for connecting computers together.
  網際網路是一個把許多電腦連接在一起的系統。

- I regularly switch on my computer when I enter my office in the morning.
  我習慣早上一進辦公室就打開電腦。

- He is programming his computer to recognize the shapes of strokes in the hands of various writers.
  他正在設計電腦程式，好辨識不同寫作者所寫的筆畫形狀。

- The poor designs of office furniture would lead to muscle and tendon troubles for employees working on the computer for long hours.
  設計不良的辦公桌椅，會使得長時間使用電腦工作的員工產生肌肉和肌腱問題。

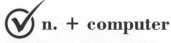 n. + computer

n.	computer	中譯
desktop		桌上型電腦
laptop/notebook	computer	膝上型 / 筆記型電腦
palmtop		掌上型電腦

tablet	computer	平板電腦
touch-screen		觸控式電腦

搭配詞例句

- In comparison, building a laptop computer is much easier than building a desktop computer from scratch.
  相對來說，組製膝上型電腦比從頭打造桌上型電腦簡單多了。

- Quanta shipped 55.8 million notebook computers last year, compared with 52.1 million units shipped in 2010.
  廣達電腦去年的筆記型電腦出貨量為 5,580 萬台，高於 2010 年的 5,210 萬台。

- Through the self-service touch-screen computers installed at Job Centers, job seekers can have quick access to information displayed in Chinese or English.
  透過安裝在職訓中心的自助觸控式電腦，求職者可以很快找到以中文或英文顯示的資訊。

 **computer + n.**

computer	n.	中譯
computer	chip	電腦晶片
	consultant	電腦顧問
	crash/failure/glitch	電腦故障
	freeze/lockup	電腦當機
	geek	電腦玩家
	hacker	電腦駭客

	programmer	電腦程式設計師
computer	system	電腦系統
	virus	電腦病毒

搭配詞例句

- Computer crashes affected all areas of the health system, including patient care, billing, and even the calendars of department managers.
  電腦故障影響醫療體系各個層面，包括病人照護、帳單資料，甚至是部門經理人的行事曆。

- A computer freeze or lockup occurs when all activity on the screen stops.
  電腦當機是指螢幕上所有的活動都靜止不動。

- In garages across the country, computer geeks are starting up ever more Internet companies.
  在全國各地的車庫裡，許多電腦玩家正開創出愈來愈多的網路公司。

相關詞彙之搭配使用

片語

a plastic card with a computer chip embedded in it	嵌入電腦晶片的塑膠卡片
electronic sports / esports professional video gaming	電子競技（電競）
mobile communication and media devices	移動通訊和媒體裝置
playing computer games for three consecutive days	連續三天玩電腦遊戲

portable digital music players	可攜式數位音樂播放器
to download files to your computer	下載檔案到你的電腦裡
to sit down at the computer	坐在電腦前

句子

- Before you can use a program, you must first <u>install it on your computer</u>.

  你得先<u>把程式安裝在電腦裡</u>，才能使用該程式。

- With technological advancements, the incidence of <u>cyber warfare is increasing daily</u>.

  隨著科技突飛猛進，<u>網路資訊戰爭</u>事件<u>與日俱增</u>。

段落

Google's <u>computer program AlphaGo</u>[①] defeated its human opponent, South Korean Go champion Lee Sedol. AlphaGo's victory in the ancient Chinese <u>board game</u>[②] is a breakthrough for <u>artificial intelligence</u>[③], showing the program developed by Google DeepMind has mastered one of the most creative and complex games ever devised. Computers conquered chess in 1997 in a match between IBM's Deep Blue and chess champion Garry Kasparov. (*AP*)

Google 的電腦程式 AlphaGo 擊敗人類對手：南韓的圍棋棋王李世乭。AlphaGo 在這項中國古代棋盤遊戲獲得勝利，是<u>人工智能</u>的一大突破，顯示這個由 Google 的 DeepMind 公司所研發的程式已精通這種極具創意和高度複雜的遊戲。1997 年電腦曾征服西洋棋，由 IBM 的深藍 (Deep Blue) 電腦擊敗西洋棋冠軍卡斯帕羅夫。(《美聯社》)

説明

① AlphaGo 是由 Alpha 和 Go 兩字合成，Alpha 是希臘文第一個字母讀音（大寫 A、小寫 α），有「起始」之意；而 Go 指「圍棋」，是西方人從日文中表示圍棋的漢字「碁」（ご）之發音音譯而來。

② board game 的概念很廣泛，Go（圍棋）、chess（西洋棋）、Chinese chess（象棋）等「棋盤遊戲」只是其中一種，其他如使用圖板的 Monopoly（大富翁）也是 board game。另外，臺灣近來流行「桌遊」(tabletop game)，而 board game 就是一種桌遊。

③ artificial intelligence 譯為「人工智能」或「人工智慧」，英文新聞也常用其頭字詞 AI 來表示。

搭配詞練習

⚙ 請從方格中挑選正確的搭配詞來完成以下的句子。

virus	personal	systems	hacker	operate

1. The students are fully conversant with the principles of word processing and have the computer skills needed to _____ a _____ **computer** effectively.
   學生都嫻熟文字處理原理，並具備有效**操作個人電腦**所需的電腦技能。

2. A **computer** _____ has accessed the data of 40 million credit card accounts.
   有個**電腦駭客**取得四千萬份信用卡帳戶資料。

3. The **computer** _____ is believed to have hit the internal **computer** _____ at Iran's oil ministry and its national oil company.
   據信這個**電腦病毒**攻擊了伊朗石油部及其國營石油企業內部的**電腦系統**。

解答：1. operate, personal　2. hacker　3. virus, systems

Internet

(n.) 網際網路

▶ 答案請見 p. 218

暖身練習

⚙ 請就以下中英譯文選出適當的搭配詞。

People on any wireless device will no longer have to pop into **Internet** ① **coffee** ② **cafés** to check e-mail or get stock updates.
攜帶無線裝置的人再也不用光顧**網咖**收閱電子郵件或股市最新行情了。

　　Internet 在臺灣譯爲「網際網路」或簡稱「網路」(net)，在中國則是音譯爲「因特網」或意譯爲「互聯網」。在英文拼寫上大多是字首大寫的 Internet，但也可用小寫的 internet，而且前面還常加上定冠詞 the，成爲 the Internet；如果 Internet 後面接另一個名詞時，Internet 前面不用加 the，如 Internet café（網咖）。而有些網路使用者被稱爲「網路鄉民」，英文爲 netizen，是由 net 和 citizen（公民）所組成。

　　另外，表示「網路中斷」時，動詞用 disconnect，常用被動語態，例如以下例句：

- Equipment at the plants has been disconnected from the net.
  工廠設備的網路都已中斷。

✅ v. + Internet

v.	Internet	中譯
appear on		出現在網路上
browse/surf		瀏覽網路
censor		審查網路
connect to		連上網路
download from	Internet	從網路上下載
go viral on		在網路上大量流傳而爆紅
publish on		公布在網路上
shop on		在網路上購物
spread over		在網路上散播

搭配詞例句

- A funny new video appeared on the Internet.
  一部有趣的新影片出現在網路上。

- New technology now allows passengers to surf the Internet 10,000 meters above the ground.
  新科技目前已能使乘客在一萬公尺的高空上瀏覽網路。

- Videos on hot and interesting topics are most likely to go viral on the Internet.
  主題熱門又有趣的影片最有可能在網路上大量流傳而爆紅。

- News-sharing arrangements have already linked the websites of most major news organizations, allowing news to spread over the Internet.
  新聞分享機制已連結多數主要新聞機構的網站,讓新聞能夠在網路上散播。

 Internet + n.

Internet	n.	中譯
Internet	access/connection	網路連接使用
	ad/advertisement	網路廣告
	browsing/surfing	瀏覽網路
	celebrity/personality	網路名人，網紅
	censorship	網路審查
	fraud/scam	網路詐騙
	security	網路安全
	service	網路服務
	surfer/user	網路使用者

搭配詞例句

- Some governments clamped down on Internet access in an attempt to quell the protesters.
  有些政府關閉網路連接，企圖壓制抗議者。

....

- Slow Internet connections can be infuriating.
  龜速的網路連接真是令人為之氣結。

....

相關詞彙之搭配使用

片語

a wireless internet access/connection	無線上網
access to the Internet	可使用網路

broadcast live video over the Internet	在網路上直播
cyber attack / cyberattack	網路攻擊
Integrated Services Digital Network (ISDN)	整合服務數位網路
Internet of Things (IoT)	物聯網
Internet Service Provider (ISP)	網路服務供應商
search engine	搜尋引擎（如 Google, Yahoo 等）
to cause a stir on the Internet	在網路上引起騷動
to install free Wi-Fi wireless hot spots	設置免費的 Wi-Fi 熱點
to jeopardize the freedom of the Internet	危及網路自由
to lift some restrictions on the media and the Internet	解除對媒體和網路的部分限制
to prompt furious discussions on the Internet	在網路上引起熱烈討論
to provide a high-speed Internet connection and data transmission	提供高速網路連結和資料傳輸
to spread quickly over the Internet	在網路上快速傳播
traveling via the Internet	透過網路流傳
unlimited access to the Internet	無限上網吃到飽

句子

- The videos, posted Sunday night, <u>were taken off the Internet</u> on Monday.
  在週日晚間上傳的影片，週一就從網路上下架了。

- People <u>say and do things in cyberspace</u> that they would not ordinarily say or do in the face-to-face world.
  人們<u>在網路世界的所說所爲</u>常與他們在現實世界中的言行舉止大不相同。

- <u>A quick search on the Internet</u> will result in a number of very useful online tutorials.
  <u>在網路上快速搜尋一下</u>就可得到許多有用的線上課程。

- Most <u>cybercrimes are committed by</u> individuals.
  大多數的<u>網路犯罪都是</u>個人<u>所爲</u>。

- <u>Crowdsourcing is the process of connecting with large groups of people via the Internet</u> who are tapped for their knowledge, expertise, time or resources.
  <u>群眾外包是透過網際網路連結許多群人</u>，獲取其知識、專業、時間或資源。

段落

China's Ministry of Industry and Information Technology has announced a 14-month "clean up" of <u>internet access services</u>[1], which includes a crackdown on virtual private networks, or VPNs. VPNs use encryption to disguise internet traffic, allowing users in China to <u>bypass the Great Firewall</u>[2] to access censored and restricted websites. The services typically cost around $10 a month. China's vast censorship apparatus—known as the Great Firewall—<u>prevents the country's 730 million internet users from accessing information</u>[3] on sensitive subjects like Tibet or the deadly 1989 crackdown on Tiananmen Square protests. (*CNN*)

中國工業和信息化部宣布將進行為期 14 個月的「清理」<u>網路通路服務</u>，其中包括掃蕩虛擬私人網絡 (VPN)。VPN 是使用加密技術來掩飾其在網路上的流量，讓中國的使用者可以<u>翻越防火牆</u>，連結遭審查或封鎖的網站。這種服務通常每月收費約 10 美元。中國龐大的審查機制，號稱防火長城，<u>可防堵該國 7 億 3 千萬網路使用者取得敏感議題的資訊</u>，例如西藏或 1989 年天安門血腥鎮壓抗議者的事件。（《有線電視新聞網》）

說明

① internet access services 為「網路通路服務」，其中 access 在此當名詞用，表示「通道」或「使用」，如 free Internet access 為「免費使用網路」。不過 access 也可當動詞用，表示「進入」或「取得」，如下文的 to access censored and restricted websites（連結遭審查或封鎖的網站）和 accessing information on sensitive subjects（取得敏感議題的資訊）。

② bypass 在此當動詞用，意思是「越過」，其後的 firewall（防火牆）是控制網路資料傳輸的安全系統，bypass firewall 就是俗稱的「翻牆」。而在此處 the Great Firewall 是西方媒體針對中國政府設置的防火牆所給的英文名稱，由 the Great Wall（長城）和 firewall 組合而成，中文也可譯作「防火長城」。

③ prevent ... from... 為「阻止…（人）做…（事）」，此處的「人」是 the country's 730 million internet users（該國 7 億 3 千萬網路使用者），而且 from 後面的 access 是動詞，要改成動名詞 accessing。

搭配詞練習

⚙ 請從方格中挑選正確的搭配詞來完成以下的句子。

users	service	wireless	access

1. The number of **Internet** _____ in China has surged past 500 million.
   中國的**網路使用者**爆增到五億人以上。

2. Residents and visitors to Taipei City are now able to take advantage of free **wireless Internet** _____. The service is available at a number of locations, including city hall, hospitals and MRT stations.
   臺北市居民和遊客現在可免費**享用無線網路**，提供服務的地點包括市政府、醫院和捷運站。

3. It gives a false impression of China's heavily regulated **Internet** _____.
   這造成中國嚴格控管**網路服務**的錯誤印象。

4. By 2018, when 80 percent of the residents are expected to carry smartphones or tablet PCs, _____ **connectivity** will be almost as free as it is ubiquitous.
   預計在 2018 年之前，將有 80% 的居民隨身攜帶智慧型手機或平板電腦，屆時幾乎到處皆可免費**無線上網**。

解答：1. users 2. access 3. service 4. wireless

暖身練習解答：②

online

(adj.) 線上的，網上的

暖身練習

⚙ 請就以下中英譯文選出適當的搭配詞。　　　　　▶ 答案請見 p. 223

Online ① **famous people** ② **celebrities** are a fairly new concept to Chinese culture, but they've gained traction quickly.

網路名人對中國文化而言還是相當新奇的觀念，但已快速吸引大眾注意。

online 在臺灣譯為「線上」，中國則直譯為「在線」，相反詞是 offline（離線的）。online 是由 on 和 line 兩字合成，早期在兩字間加連字號如 on-line，但經長期使用後，許多人就略去連字號而成為 online。online 常當形容詞用，但也可當副詞，例如以下例句：

- Taiwan's Internet users like to watch short films online.
  臺灣的網路使用者喜歡在線上觀賞短片。

以下為形容詞 online 搭配名詞的形式。

 online + n.

online	n.	中譯
online	ad/advertisement/advertising	線上廣告
	auction	線上拍賣
	celebrity	網路名人，網紅
	chat/messaging	線上聊天

	course/education	線上課程 / 教育
	dating	線上約會，線上交友
	forum	線上論壇
	gambling	線上賭博
	game/gaming	線上遊戲
	payment	線上付款
online	piracy	線上盜版
	poll/survey	線上投票 / 調查
	privacy	線上隱私
	retailer	線上零售商
	server	線上伺服器
	shopper	線上購物者

搭配詞例句

- Google has an incentive to ensure online ads remain as effective as possible because those commercial messages generate most of its revenue.
  Google 必須確保線上廣告保持最好的效果，因為那些廣告訊息是他們最主要的收入來源。

- With many single people trying to meet their perfect match, even online dating is susceptible to fraud and scams.
  許多單身族渴望覓得完美對象，甚至連線上約會都容易成為詐騙的溫床。

- States considering plans to legalize online gambling could collide with Congress.
許多州政府考慮將線上賭博合法化，但這可能與國會的立場相衝突。

- Big online retailers had a 19 percent jump in revenue over the holidays.
大型線上零售商在假期的營收大漲 19%。

相關詞彙之搭配使用

片語

a breach of online privacy an invasion of online privacy	侵犯線上隱私
a Facebook post with 10,000 shares	臉書貼文有一萬次的分享
a YouTube video with 5 million views	YouTube 影片有五百萬次的觀看次數
making online purchases	在線上購物
online video users	線上影片使用者
spread of messages on Twitter	在推特上散播訊息
target of online abuse/harassment	線上騷擾的對象
to protect online account passwords	保護線上帳號密碼
to submit another round of resume online	在線上再上傳一次履歷表

句子

- Constant attention switching online has a lasting negative effect on your brain.
在線上經常轉換注意力會對你的腦部造成永久性的負面影響。

> **段落**
>
> YouTube has become <u>the de facto launchpad</u>^① for the next generation of celebrities. These stars <u>rack up</u>^② millions of subscribers and have a direct relationship with fans. From comedians to gamers to <u>beauty vloggers</u>^③, <u>YouTubers</u>^④ have generally built their followings outside of the control of media giants, even if they are signing big deals with those companies. And there is power and independence in having that huge fan base. (*Business Insider*)
>
> YouTube 已成爲下一個世代的名人製造機。這些明星吸引數以百萬計的訂閱者，並與粉絲直接互動。不論是喜劇演員、遊戲玩家或美妝影音部落客，這些 YouTubers 儘管與大型媒體公司簽下鉅額合約，但他們通常會累積自己的鐵粉而不受這些公司控制。而擁有龐大粉絲團就擁有力量和自主性。
> 《《商業內幕》》

> **說明**
>
> ① de facto 是拉丁文，意思是「實質上」，用來修飾 launchpad（發射台）；而 launchpad 也可寫成 launch pad 或 launching pad。在此處 launchpad 引申為網路名人藉以發跡成名的「起步平台」，可譯成國內常用的「製造機」一詞。
>
> ② rack 當名詞用是指「置物架」，此處當動詞用，搭配 up，就有「大量累積」之意，引申為「吸引」。
>
> ③ beauty vlogger 是「美妝影音部落客」，比較特別的是 vlogger 這個新造字，是由 video（影音）和 blogger（部落客）兩字組合而成。有別於傳統的 blogger 以撰寫、發布文章為主，vlogger 是以上傳影音內容為主。至於 beauty vlogger 是專門分享或示範彩妝美髮的影片的部落客，目的在吸引大批粉絲觀賞。另外，「影音部落格」的英文是 vlog。
>
> ④ YouTuber 是在 YouTube 後面加 -r，主要是指「拍攝影音內容上傳 YouTube 的人」，一般並未譯成中文而直接使用 YouTuber，屬於零翻譯。YouTuber 通常靠廣告拆帳為所得，如果擁有超高點閱率，就可獲得非常可觀的收入。

搭配詞練習

⚙ 請從方格中挑選正確的搭配詞來完成以下的句子。

courses	shoppers	online	piracy	education

1. Some analysts of **online** _____ believe that the proliferation of
   online _____ will encourage quality instruction.
   部分**線上教育**分析家相信，**線上課程**增加將有助於提升教學品質。

2. She has been selling designer fashion to **online** _____ since 2010.
   從 2010 年起，她就一直販售設計師的流行商品給**線上購物者**。

3. **Online** _____ leads to U.S. job losses because it deprives content
   creators of income.
   線上盜版會剝奪內容創造者的收入，導致美國的工作流失。

4. The **survey**, **conducted** _____, collected 6,034 valid samples
   from respondents aged 12 to 54.
   這份**在線上所作的調查**從 12 至 54 歲的受訪者中取得 6,034 份有效樣本。

解答：1. education, courses 2. shoppers 3. piracy 4. online

暖身練習解答：②

website
(n.) 網站

▶ 答案請見 p. 229

暖身練習

✿ 請就以下中英譯文選出適當的搭配詞。

When you ① **renew** ② **update** your **website**, you are working to ensure that all of your links are working properly.
更新網站時，要確認所有的連結都能正常使用。

    website 指「網站」，也可分為兩字寫成 web site，其他相關字還有 web address（網址）、webcast（網路廣播，由 web 和 broadcast 組成）、webinar（網路研討會，由 web 和 seminar 組成）、webmaster（網站站長，由 web 和 master 組成）、web page（網頁）、web traffic（網路流量）、webzine（網路雜誌，由 web 和 magazine 組成）等。另外還有 web blog（網誌，簡稱 blog 或 weblog），臺灣將 blog 譯為「部落格」，中國譯為「博客」，大多是用文字與圖片呈現，而現在更發展出 video blog（影音部落格），簡稱 vlog。

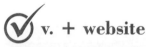
v. + website

v.	website	中譯
access		進入網站
block	website	封鎖網站
build/create/develop		建置網站

check out		看看網站內容
customize		客製化網站
cut off / shut down		關閉網站
design		設計網站
launch		推出網站
log into/onto		登入網站
maintain	website	維護網站
operate/run		經營網站
post on		公布在網站上
unblock		解除網站封鎖
update		更新網站
visit		造訪網站

搭配詞例句

- If your children have access to a home computer, blocking specific websites is important.
  如果你的小孩能夠使用家中的電腦，封鎖特定網站是很重要的。

- -

- For years, regulators have tried to come up with an effective way to shut down websites that contain pirated content.
  多年來當局不斷嘗試各種方法，希望能有效關閉侵害智慧財產權的網站。

- -

- Cigarette maker Altria Group has launched a website called Citizens for Tobacco Rights.
  香菸製造商奧馳亞集團推出一個名為「公民吸菸權」的網站。

- -

- At lunch, log onto a dream-interpretation website and figure out what the symbols from last night's fantasy say about you.

  午餐時登入一個解夢網站，了解一下昨晚幻夢中的象徵透露出什麼與你有關的訊息。

- In an article posted on Apple's website, Jobs defended Apple's decision, saying the stance is based on technology issues.

  賈伯斯在蘋果網站上所公布的一篇文章中為該公司的決定辯護，表示其立場是基於技術因素。

- The company estimates thirty million people visited the website of their local library.

  該公司估計有 3,000 萬人曾造訪過他們當地圖書館的網站。

✅ adj. + website

adj.	website	中譯
commercial		商業網站
fast-growing		快速成長的網站
fee-based		付費網站
malicious		惡意的網站
official	website	官方網站
personal		個人網站
social		社群網站
unsafe		不安全的網站

- The handbook can be downloaded for free from the university official website.
  該手冊可從大學的官方網站免費下載。

- A personal website can act as your online CV.
  個人網站可作為你的線上履歷表。

  說明 CV 為拉丁文 Curriculum Vitae 的頭字詞，和 resume 都是「履歷表」的意思，通常 CV 會比 resume 正式，提供的經歷資訊也比較詳實。

相關詞彙之搭配使用

片語

crowdfunding platform/website	群眾募資平台／網站
digital footprint	數位足跡
live online auction website	直播的線上拍賣網站
to search the website to find the information	搜尋網站找資料
to type in the web address	鍵入網址
video streaming website	影音串流網站

句子

- You can get information from its website at...
  你可從它的網站……獲得資訊。

- For more information, please visit our website at...
  欲知詳情，請造訪我們的網站……。

段落

Carding is a popular type of cybercrime. Thieves will steal credit card data from insecure databases, by <u>hacking into companies</u>[①] or just buying it <u>on the dark web you wouldn't find with a Google search</u>[②]. Criminals can also take emails and passwords leaked from other <u>data breaches</u>[③], and test them on banking websites. For instance, <u>credentials</u>[④] from LinkedIn, Dropbox, and Adobe have previously been leaked online. (*CNN*)

信用卡詐欺是常見的網路犯罪型態。小偷會駭入企業的電腦系統，從不安全的資料庫中竊取信用卡資訊，或是直接在 Google 上搜尋不到的暗網購買資訊。他們也可以從其他資料外洩管道擷取電子郵件和密碼，再拿到銀行網頁上測試。像是 LinkedIn, Dropbox, Adobe 的個人資料都曾在線上外洩。(《有線電視新聞網》)

說明

① 「駭客」(hacker)「入侵」或「駭入」別人電腦系統的動詞為 hack，可當及物和不及物動詞用，此處是當不及物動詞使用，後面搭配介系詞 into 再接受詞，如 hack into a computer（駭入電腦）。

② dark web（暗網）是指不會被一般搜尋引擎如 Google, Yahoo 等收錄的網站，其中有許多交易毒品、槍枝和違禁品的犯罪網站，有人也稱之為 deep web（深網）。

③ breach 在此為名詞，表示「違反」，如 breach of agreement/contract 為「違約」、breach of trust 為「背信」等，而此處 data breach 則是「資料外洩」。

④ credentials 通常用複數形，指個人的「資歷」或「證書」，但在此指「個人資料」，如登入網站所需的 usernames and passwords（使用者名稱和密碼）。credentials 可搭配動詞 leak（洩漏）使用。

搭配詞練習

⚙ 請從方格中挑選正確的搭配詞來完成以下的句子。

fastest-growing	launched	customize	design	run

1. He _____ a new **website**.
   他**推出**一個新的**網站**。

2. They _____ the _____ **website** on the planet.
   他們**經營**全球**成長最快速**的**網站**。

3. You can create and _____ your **website** with a few simple clicks.
   只要簡單點按幾個連結，你就可以打造並**客製化**你的**網站**。

4. Teaching your kids how to _____ a **website** can also be a learning experience for you.
   教導你的小孩如何**設計網站**，對你而言也是一種學習經驗。

解答：1. launched　2. run, fastest-growing　3. customize　4. design

暖身練習解答：②

software

(n.) 軟體

暖身練習

⚙ 請就以下中英譯文選出適當的搭配詞。 ▶ 答案請見 p. 236

The ① **safe** ② **security software** market continued to show resilience at a time of IT budget restrictions.
儘管資訊科技產業的預算受限，**安全軟體**市場仍能持續保持活力。

電腦「軟體」(software) 指的是讓電腦執行工作的「程式」(programs)；至於電腦「硬體」(hardware)，則是指組裝成電腦的「零組件裝置」(component devices)，例如 motherboard（主機板）、central processing unit (CPU)（中央處理器）、dynamic random access memory (DRAM)（動態隨機存取記憶體）、hard drive disk（硬碟）、keyboard（鍵盤）、mouse（滑鼠）等。

另外，security software 譯為「安全軟體」或「防毒軟體」，具備 antivirus（防病毒）、firewall（防火牆）、encryption（加密）等功能。另一方面，malicious software 譯成「惡意程式／軟體」，通常簡寫成 malware，由字首 mal-（不良的）加上字幹 ware（器皿）所組成，例如 ransomware（勒索軟體）就是一種 malicious software，例句如下：

● Iran has been forced to disconnect key oil facilities after suffering a malware attack.
伊朗的重要石油設施遭到惡意程式攻擊，因而被迫切斷網路連線。

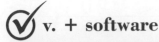 **v. + software**

v.	software	中譯
develop		開發軟體
issue/release		發行軟體
legalize	software	讓軟體合法化
run / run on		執行軟體
write		寫軟體

搭配詞例句

- He sounded a skeptical note about China's promise to legalize software at the local and provincial government levels.
  中國承諾會要求地方和省級政府使用合法軟體，對此他抱持懷疑的態度。

- Consumers begin to shift to buying tablet computers that do not run on Microsoft software.
  消費者開始轉而購買不需要執行微軟軟體的平板電腦。

- In learning how to write software, the first step is to decide what type of computer programming language you want to become proficient in.
  學習寫軟體的第一步，是決定要熟悉哪一種電腦程式語言。

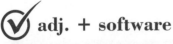 **adj. + software**

adj.	software	中譯
antivirus		防毒軟體
legal	software	合法軟體
obsolete/outdated		過時的軟體

specialized		專業軟體
unauthorized/unlicensed	software	未經授權的軟體
word-processing		文字處理軟體

搭配詞例句

- Microsoft is still a powerhouse supplier of the specialized software that meets the complex needs of large corporations.
  微軟仍是專業軟體的主要供應者，可符合大型企業的複雜需求。

- Chinese officials have not provided sufficient technical evidence proving the central government has reduced use of unlicensed software.
  中國官員尚未提出足夠的技術性證據，證明中央政府已經減少使用未經授權的軟體。

 software + n.

software	n.	中譯
software	application	軟體應用
	bug	軟體瑕疵，程式錯誤
	developer	軟體開發者
	engineer	軟體工程師
	legalization	軟體合法化
	piracy	軟體盜版
	update	軟體更新

搭配詞例句

- Apple has finally broken its silence on the battery life of its latest iPhone, the 4S, saying software bugs in its latest operating system are causing the issues.
  蘋果針對最新的 iPhone 4S 電池壽命問題終於打破沉默，表示其最新的作業系統出現程式錯誤才會導致此問題。

- The central government has completed its software legalization efforts.
  中央政府已經完成軟體合法化的工作。

- Software piracy in China isn't going away anytime soon.
  中國的軟體盜版問題短期內仍無法解決。

相關詞彙之搭配使用

片語

3D graphics software application	3D 繪圖軟體應用
Computer Generated Imagery (CGI)	電腦成像
illegitimate copies of software	非法軟體
the use of unauthorized copies of software by government agencies and state-owned enterprises	政府機關和國營企業使用未經授權的軟體
mobile app mobile software application	行動應用程式
to issue a software update to fix a number of minor problems	發行軟體更新來解決幾個小問題

句子

- In order to keep your Mac secure and operating efficiently it is important that you always <u>install software updates</u>.
  爲確保你的蘋果電腦安全無虞且操作順暢，一定要時常<u>安裝更新軟體</u>。

- <u>App developers</u> are competing with one another to create ever more addictive products.
  <u>應用程式開發者</u>競相創造更多令人上癮的產品。

段落

<u>The WannaCry ransomware</u>[①] <u>swept the globe</u>[②], infecting over 300,000 computers in 150 countries and regions. According to a survey, a total of 5,500 <u>cases of infection</u>[③] were reported in Taiwan—the fourth highest in the world—including a suspension of <u>the CPC Corporation's</u>[④] website and mobile payment services for a day. Amid an increasing threat to information security, Trend Micro pointed out in a 2016 information security assessment that the number of ransomware viruses had increased by 752 percent last year, causing global businesses to lose up to US$1 billion. (*China Post*)

<u>WannaCry 勒索軟體橫掃全球</u>，入侵 150 個國家、區域逾 30 萬台電腦。根據調查，臺灣共有 5,500 <u>起中毒事件</u>，爲全球第四位，其中包括<u>中油公司</u>暫時關閉其網站和行動支付服務一天。趨勢科技公司在一份 2016 年資訊安全評估報告中指出，在資安威脅日漸嚴重的情況下，去年勒索軟體病毒的數量爆增 752%，導致全球企業損失高達 10 億美元。(《英文中國郵報》)

說明

① ransomware（勒索軟體）是由 ransom（勒索）和 software（軟體）所組成。文中的勒索軟體名稱叫 WannaCry，其中 wanna 是 want to 的口語連音表達方式，因此 WannaCry 就是 want to cry，也就是遭勒索後會「想哭」的意思。

② swept 是動詞 sweep 的過去式，原是「打掃」之意，如「掃地板」為 sweep the floor。在此處 sweep 引申為「快速蔓延」或譯為「橫掃」，sweep the globe 也可說 sweep the world，而「快速蔓延全國」可說 sweep the country。

③ case of infection 是「感染的病例」，在此文境是指「電腦中毒事件」。infection 的動詞 infect 也常用於電腦中毒的情境，如 A computer can get infected with a virus.（電腦可能會中毒。）而「中毒的電腦」可稱為 infected computer。

④ CPC 是 Chinese Petroleum Corporation 的頭字詞，也就是「中國石油公司」，CPC 後面再加 Corporation，等於重複兩次 Corporation。

搭配詞練習

⚙ 請從方格中挑選正確的搭配詞來完成以下的句子。

release	run	developed	antivirus	update

1. Most of the tablets on the market _____ either Apple's operating system **software** or Google's Android **software**.
市面上大部分的平板電腦若不是**執行蘋果的作業系統軟體**，就是 Google 的 Android **軟體**。

2. We found a few bugs that are affecting battery life and will _____ a **software** _____ to address those in a few weeks.
我們發現幾個會影響電池壽命的程式錯誤，將在幾週內**發布軟體更新**來解決這些問題。

3. Microsoft has _____ the **software** for the PC's operating system.
微軟為個人電腦的作業系統**開發軟體**。

4. Windows PC users need a strong _____ **software** to ward off malware attacks.
Windows 個人電腦使用者需要有效的**防毒軟體**來阻擋惡意程式的攻擊。

解答：1. run　2. release, update　3. developed　4. antivirus

暖身練習解答：②

information

(n.) 資訊，資料

暖身練習

⚙ 請就以下中英譯文選出適當的搭配詞。　　　　▶ 答案請見 p. 243

Patients are dying because of a lack of **information** ① **exchange**
② **communication**.

因為缺乏**資訊交流**，病人都快死了。

　　information 可當「資訊」、「資料」、「消息」等解釋，也可簡寫成
info，是不可數名詞，因此沒有複數形。要形容「大量資訊」只能在前面
加上 a lot of, a great amount of, much 等，或使用量詞，如 three pieces
of information 為「三項資訊」。有時在口說或寫電郵時會使用 FYI 一詞，
這是 for your information 的頭字詞，也就是「提供資訊給對方參考」的
意思。

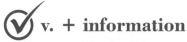 **v. + information**

v.	information	中譯
collect/gather		收集資訊
cover up		掩蓋資訊
disclose/reveal	information	揭露資訊
disseminate		散播資訊
download		下載資訊

exchange		交換資訊
extract/retrieve		擷取資訊
fabricate		捏造資訊
process	information	處理資訊
release		發布資訊
retain/withhold		保留資訊
verify		驗證資訊

搭配詞例句

- Washington will reveal the information at the appropriate time and place.
  美國政府將於適當的時間和地點揭露這項資訊。

- Some organizations such as the Queensland Police Service are using twitter to disseminate important information.
  某些組織如昆士蘭警方就使用推特來散播重要的資訊。

- Amnesty International has released similar information and is calling for an independent investigation into the incident.
  國際特赦組織已發布類似的訊息，並呼籲就此事件展開獨立調查。

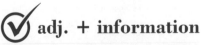 **adj. + information**

adj.	information	中譯
additional/further/more	information	進一步資訊
classified/confidential		機密資料

conflicting		矛盾的資訊
latest/up-to-date		最新資訊
related/relevant	information	相關資訊
tampered		遭竄改的資料
timely		及時的資訊

搭配詞例句

- His office often holds large amounts of confidential information.
  他的辦公室裡常常存有大量的機密資料。

- Please check directly with your airline for the most up-to-date information.
  請直接與您的航空公司聯繫，以了解最新資訊。

 **information + n.**

information	n.	中譯
	dissemination	資訊散播
	highway	資訊高速公路
	management	資訊管理
	network	資訊網路
information	overload	資訊超載
	processing	資訊處理
	security	資訊安全
	technology	資訊科技
	warfare	資訊戰

搭配詞例句

● The network employs 230 miles of fiber-optic cable as its information highway.
此網路系統使用 230 英里長的光纖電纜為其資訊高速公路。

● Learning strategies are very important in forming an individual information processing model.
學習策略對於形成個人的資訊處理模式非常重要。

● Information warfare has changed the nature of the battlefield.
資訊戰已經改變了戰場的定義。

相關詞彙之搭配使用

片語

the creation of an information society	創造資訊社會
to facilitate effective dissemination of information	促進有效的資訊散播
to fix dozens of information security weaknesses	修補數十處資訊安全上的弱點
to leak politically sensitive information	洩露政治敏感資料
to restrict access to confidential information	限制存取機密資料的權限

句子

● Information processing and dissemination have played a critical role in this transformation process.
資訊處理與散播在此轉換過程中扮演重要的角色。

段落

... the Internet's personality has changed. Once it was a geek with lofty ideals about the free flow of information. Now the web is <u>a sociopath with Asperger's</u>[①]. If you need help improving your upload speeds it's eager to help with technical details, but if you tell it you're struggling with depression it will try to goad you into killing yourself. Psychologists call this the <u>online disinhibition effect</u>[②], in which factors like anonymity, invisibility, a lack of authority and not communicating in real time <u>strip away the mores</u>[③] society spent millennia building. And it's seeping from our smartphones into every aspect of our lives. (*Time*)

……網路的性格已經改變。它曾是懷有崇高理想的奇才，致力實現資訊的自由流通，但如今卻像一個患有亞斯伯格症的社會病態者。如果你想要改善上傳速度，網路會很樂意提供詳細技術；但如果你說你正為憂鬱症所苦，它也會唆使你去自殺。心理學家把這種現象稱為線上去抑效應，各種因素如匿名性、隱身性、缺乏權威和無法即時溝通，去除了人類社會數千年來所建立的傳統，而且正從我們的智慧型手機逐漸滲透到生活中每一個層面。(《時代雜誌》)

說明

① sociopath 是「反社會人格者」，屬於「社會病態」，與「心理病態」的 psychopath（精神病患者）不同。我們可以從 socio-（社會）與 psycho-（心理）加上 path（pathology「病理學」的縮寫）來辨識學習。另外，Asperger's 就是 Asperger syndrome（亞斯伯格症候群），是依據研究此病症的奧地利小兒科醫師漢思‧亞斯伯格 (Hans Asperger) 的姓氏命名的。

② inhibition 是「抑制」，前面加上表示「相反」、「離去」的字首 dis-，disinhibition 就轉變成「去抑」，後面搭配 effect（效應）就譯成「去抑效應」。網路正好是讓人去除壓抑、無視規範而解放言行的世界，甚至造成 cyber bullying / cyberbullying（網路霸凌）現象。

③ strip 本義為「脫衣」，如「脫光」為 strip naked，「脫衣舞孃」為
stripper。但臺灣同學有時會將此字與 stripe（條紋）搞混。此處 strip
away 為固定搭配，指「去除」，後面接一個正式用字 mores（傳統），
換個例子如「消除壓力」就可說是 strip away stress。

搭配詞練習

⚙ 請從方格中挑選正確的搭配詞來完成以下的句子。

technology	user	confidential	information

1. **Information** _____ can be used as a tool to undermine national peace and security.
   資訊科技可用以損害國家和平與安全。

2. It is difficult to recover _____ **information** once it is made public.
   機密資料一旦公開就難以恢復原狀。

3. Google's search engine was created when most of the **Web's**
   _____ was open and available to anyone willing to capture it.
   當初創立 Google 搜尋引擎時，**網路資訊**大多是公開的，任由需要者取得。

4. Google has been compelled to hand over _____ **information** to the U.S. government.
   Google 被迫將**使用者資料**交給美國政府。

V. 環境災害類

pollution

(n.) 汙染

暖身練習 ⚙ 請就以下中英譯文選出適當的搭配詞。 ▶ 答案請見 p. 251

Nearly 40% of Americans live in areas with unhealthy levels of
① **smoke** ② **smog** pollution.
將近 40% 的美國人居住在**霧霾汙染**達有害健康水準的地區。

　　名詞 pollution 是「汙染」的意思，動詞是 pollute，如「汙染環境」爲 to pollute the environment。而形容詞「被汙染的」是 polluted，名詞「汙染物」則是 pollutant。人類不斷利用科技征服自然，結果產生 rubbish（垃圾）、exhaust fumes（廢氣）、noise（噪音）、toxic air（有毒氣體）、smog（霧霾，由 smoke 與 fog 組成）、hazardous waste（危險廢棄物）、nuclear/radioactive waste（核廢料），乃至於 carbon emission（碳排放）、radioactivity leakage（輻射外洩）、oil spillage（漏油）等不同型態的汙染和災害。

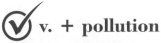 v. + pollution

v.	pollution	中譯
cause/create		引起汙染
combat/control/curb/fight/tackle	pollution	對抗 / 控制 / 治理汙染
cut/reduce		減少汙染

minimize		將汙染減到最低
monitor	pollution	監控汙染
prevent		防止汙染
suffer		受汙染之苦

搭配詞例句

- China's industries are reluctant to invest in new technology to combat pollution.
  中國的企業不願意投資新科技來對抗汙染。

- The EPA wanted power companies to minimize pollution from their coal-burning power plants.
  環保署要求電力公司將燃煤火力發電廠的汙染減到最低。

- Cities across the nation are developing programs to prevent the pollution of drinking water.
  全國各城市都在發展防止飲用水受到汙染的計畫。

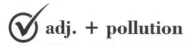 adj. + pollution

adj.	pollution	中譯
atmospheric		大氣汙染
chemical		化學汙染
environmental	pollution	環境汙染
industrial		工業汙染
local		區域汙染

	pollution	核汙染
nuclear		
widespread		大範圍的汙染

- Experts say nuclear pollution is an environmental problem that can last a long time because of the nature of radiation.
  專家表示核汙染因為輻射能的特質，會導致長期的環境問題。

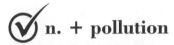 **n. + pollution**

n.	pollution	中譯
air		空氣汙染
heavy-metal		重金屬汙染
marine/ocean		海洋汙染
noise	pollution	噪音汙染
oil		石油汙染
smog		霧霾汙染
soil		土壤汙染

搭配詞例句

- Environmental problems like heavy-metal pollution have increased birth defects.
  如重金屬汙染這樣的環境問題，會增加嬰兒出生的先天缺陷。

• Noise pollution from sources like industrial work or outdoor transport is a proven source of stress.

來自工廠作業或戶外交通的噪音汙染已證明是壓力的來源。

相關詞彙之搭配使用

片語

a radiation leak at a crippled nuclear plant	受創核電廠的輻射外洩
damage to the environment	破壞環境
eco-friendly product	環保產品，對環境友善的產品
environmental impact assessment	環境影響評估
Environmental Protection Administration/ Agency (EPA)	環保署（臺灣）/ 環保局（美國）
measures to control industrial pollution	控制工業汙染的措施
nuclear waste storage facilities	貯存核廢料的設施
source of pollution	汙染源
sustainable environment	永續環境
to control greenhouse-gas emissions from airplanes	控制飛機所排放的溫室氣體
to enforce environmental protection laws	執行環保法規
to reduce diesel soot and nitrogen oxide emissions	減少柴油煙灰和一氧化氮的排放
to tackle carbon emissions from air travel	處理搭機旅行所造成的碳排放

句子

- EU has pledged to <u>reduce carbon emissions</u> to 20% below 1990 levels by 2020.

  歐盟承諾在 2020 年之前，<u>將碳排放量削減</u>至比 1990 年基準還低 20%。

段落

Air quality in southern Taiwan <u>reached hazardous levels</u>①, with the key indicator of fine particulate matter smaller than 2.5 micrometers (PM2.5) <u>hitting the highest level of 10</u>② in Kaohsiung, Pingtung and Tainan, the Environmental Protection Administration (EPA) said. The poor air quality was caused by <u>a lack of</u>③ wind to disperse atmospheric pollutants, the EPA said, urging residents in southern Taiwan who are sensitive to bad air to avoid outdoor activities. According to the EPA, level-10 PM2.5 <u>concentrations exceed</u>④ 71 micrograms per cubic meter and are considered extremely high, but measurements above level 7 are deemed severe enough to cause tangible discomfort and health problems. (*CNA*)

環保署表示，臺灣南部的空氣品質<u>已達危險等級</u>，高雄、屏東和臺南的空氣品質指標中，粒徑小於 2.5 微米的細懸浮微粒 (PM2.5) <u>濃度達最高的第 10 級</u>。環保署指出，<u>因沒有風吹散</u>空氣中的汙染物，導致空氣品質低劣，呼籲南臺灣對不良空氣品質敏感的民眾避免外出活動。根據環保署的標準，第 10 級細懸浮微粒 (PM2.5) 的<u>濃度為每立方公尺超過</u>71 微克，這是極為嚴重的程度，一般認為只要第 7 級以上即可引發身體不適和健康問題。(《中央社》)

> **說明**
>
> ① reach 當及物動詞用，後面搭配名詞 level。另外，在氣溫方面也可說 reach 36 degrees Celsius（達攝氏 36 度）。

② hit 與上述的 reach 一樣，可搭配 level 來表達「達到某水準」。

③ lack 表示「缺乏」，當名詞用時搭配介系詞 of，例如 His lack of self-discipline is evident.（他明顯缺乏自律。）但 lack 當動詞時是及物動詞，後面直接接名詞，例如 He lacks self-discipline.（他缺乏自律。）

④ 名詞 concentration 本來是「專心」的意思，但在此當「濃度」、「含量」解釋，後面可搭配動詞 exceed（超過）。

搭配詞練習

⚙ **請從方格中挑選正確的搭配詞來完成以下的句子。**

air	reducing	soil
local	nuclear	smog

1. Other urgent environmental problems to be solved, for example,
   _____ **pollution** by pesticides and _____ **pollution** by
   hydrocarbon use, were also considered important.
   其他亟待解決的環境問題，例如殺蟲劑造成的**土壤汙染**和碳氫化合物造成的**空氣汙染**，也都很重要。

2. The Obama administration's record in _____ _____ **pollution**
   is strong.
   歐巴馬政府在**減少霧霾汙染**方面的紀錄非常良好。

3. At least eleven-thousand Americans may have died of cancer as a result
   of _____ **pollution**.
   至少有 1 萬 1 千個美國人可能是因**核汙染**所導致的癌症而死亡。

4. Besides cooking the climate, aviation also **causes** _____ **pollution**.
   航空業除了造成全球氣候暖化，也會**引起區域汙染**。

解答：1. soil, air 2. reducing, smog 3. nuclear 4. local
暖身練習解答：②

typhoon

(n.) 颱風

暖身練習

⚙ 請就以下中英譯文選出適當的搭配詞。　　　　　▶ 答案請見 p. 257

We were supposedly in the middle of a ① **great** ② **heavy typhoon**,
and yet the waves were strangely hushed.
我們應該是處在**強烈颱風**之中，但海浪卻是出奇平靜。

　　大自然常見的風災有 typhoon（颱風）、storm（暴風）、hurricane（颶風）、tornado/twister（龍捲風）、cyclone（氣旋）等，因形成風災的地理位置和氣候條件不同而有各種名稱，但詞彙搭配的用法差不多。比較特別的是 storm 還可當動詞用，表示「猛攻」、「襲擊」，例如以下例句：

- Police stormed the building and arrested the criminals.
  警方猛攻這棟樓並逮捕罪犯。

　　以下以臺灣夏秋兩季常見的 typhoon 為例，介紹其搭配形式。

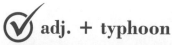 **adj. + typhoon**

adj.	typhoon	中譯
deadly		致命颱風
great/huge/powerful/raging/violent	typhoon	強烈颱風
monstrous		巨型颱風
super		超級颱風

搭配詞例句

- A huge typhoon downed trees and flooded streets in Manila, bringing traffic and commerce to a halt.

  強颱在馬尼拉吹倒樹木、淹沒街道，使交通和商業活動爲之停擺。

- Muifa was expected to be one of the most powerful typhoons to hit China in recent years.

  梅花預期是近年來侵襲中國最強烈的颱風之一。

- Now imagine a super typhoon lashing across this tiny island driven by winds exceeding 200 miles per hour.

  現在想像一個風速超過每小時 200 英里的超級颱風肆虐這座小島。

 **typhoon + v.**

typhoon	v.	中譯
typhoon	approach	颱風逼近
	batter/hit/lash/pound/rage/slam/strike	颱風侵襲
	destroy	颱風摧毀
	die down	颱風平息
	land	颱風登陸
	move	颱風移動
	reach	颱風抵達

搭配詞例句

- Typhoon Muifa lashed the Japanese island of Okinawa Friday with heavy rains and high winds.
  梅花颱風週五以強風豪雨侵襲日本的沖繩島。

- This year's drill was postponed because of Typhoon Fanapi, which landed on Taiwan on Sept. 19.
  凡那比颱風於 9 月 19 日登陸臺灣，今年的演習因而延期。

相關詞彙之搭配使用

片語

Central Weather Bureau (CWB)	中央氣象局
deadly winds of up to 130 miles per hour	時速高達 130 英里的致命強風
in the eye of the typhoon	在颱風眼之中
to issue a sea warning for typhoon	發布海上颱風警報
to lift a land warning for typhoon	解除陸上颱風警報
to raise money for victims of August's deadly typhoon in Taiwan	為臺灣八月發生的致命颱風的受害者募款
to rip roofs off hundreds of homes	掀掉了數百間房屋的屋頂
to wash away railway lines and bridges, knock out power and trigger landslide	沖走鐵路與橋梁，致使電力中斷並引發山崩
with peak winds of 90 miles an hour	最大陣風達時速 90 英里

句子

- The city asked the military to assist in <u>evacuating residents from low ground</u>.
  市政府請求軍方協助疏散居住在低窪地區的民眾。

- <u>The toll of dead and missing from the typhoon</u> reached at least one hundred.
  因颱風而死亡和失蹤的人數至少已達百人。

- Typhoon Muifa <u>continues heading north and is gathering strength</u>.
  梅花颱風持續朝北方行進並增強。

段落

At least six people are dead and 18 others missing after Typhoon Nock-Ten lashed the Philippines over the Christmas holidays. The unusually late storm first hit the eastern provinces on Christmas Day, flooding roads and farms, destroying homes and damaging ships as it crossed <u>the archipelago</u>[①], though the highly-populated Philippine capital was spared. Nock-Ten <u>took out power</u>[②] in many eastern provinces, with energy officials unsure when electrical services would be restored. More than 429,000 people <u>were preemptively evacuated from</u>[③] their homes in vulnerable areas and over 330 flights were cancelled. (AFP)

納坦颱風在耶誕假期期間襲擊菲律賓，造成至少六人喪生，18 人失蹤。這個遲至年底才形成的少見颱風橫掃菲律賓群島時，先是於耶誕節當日侵襲東部省份，洪水淹沒道路和農田，摧毀房屋和船舶，幸好人口眾多的首都馬尼拉逃過一劫。納坦颱風<u>導致</u>東部許多省份<u>停電</u>，能源官員也無法確定何時才能恢復供

電。在某些高風險地區有42萬9千多人預先撤離家園，還有超過330架次班機被迫取消。(《法新社》)

說明

① the archipelago（群島）指的就是前句的 the Philippines（菲律賓群島），英文新聞不喜重複相同用字，第二次提到 the Philippines 時就換用 the archipelago 來表示，讀起來才有變化。要注意 Philippines 的字尾有 s。

② took out power 的 power 是指「電力」。颱風一來容易造成「停電」，「停電」可用 power outage/failure, blackout 等方式表達。其他與 power 相關的搭配詞還有 power shortage（電力短缺）、power supply（電力供應）、power plant/station（發電廠）等。

③ 只要出現「從…撤離疏散民眾」的敘述，常用 be evacuated from... 這個被動語態的搭配。此處於 evacuated 前再插入副詞 preemptively（預先地），表示是颱風來襲前「預先撤離」。

搭配詞練習

⚙ 請從方格中挑選正確的搭配詞來完成以下的句子。

raged	hit	moving	great	approached

1. It was impossible to imagine that a _____ **typhoon** had once _____ here.

   無法想像這裡曾有**強烈颱風肆虐**過。

2. The **typhoon** was _____ northeast off Japan's Pacific coast, on course to _____ the capital region this weekend.

   颱風沿著日本太平洋海岸往東北方**移動**，按其行進路線預計本週末將**侵襲**首都地區。

3. Authorities in Nagoya advised more than one million people to leave as a powerful **typhoon** _____ the densely populated region of central Japan.

   因強烈**颱風逼近**人口密集的日本中部地區，名古屋當局勸告逾百萬市民趕緊撤離。

解答：1. great, raged　2. moving, hit　3. approached

暖身練習解答：①

earthquake

(n.) 地震

▶ 答案請見 p. 263

⚙ 請就以下中英譯文選出適當的搭配詞。

That **earthquake** ① **set off** ② **set up** a tsunami that killed more than 200,000 people around the Indian Ocean.
那場**地震引發**海嘯，造成印度洋沿岸超過 20 萬人喪生。

earthquake 也常用 quake 取代，而表示地震規模的單位是 Richter magnitude scale（芮氏地震規模），簡稱 Richter scale 或 magnitude，搭配的動詞為 measure（測量），例如以下例句：

- The earthquake was measured at a magnitude of 8.2 on the Richter scale.
  這場地震達芮氏地震規模 8.2。

- The city was badly shaken by a 7.6-magnitude quake that killed at least 700 people.
  這個城市遭規模 7.6 的地震重擊，造成至少 700 人喪生。

地震有個形容詞 seismic（地震的），因此「地震活動」也可稱為 seismic activity，而「地震學」為 seismology。其他與地震相關的字彙還有 epicenter（震央）、hypocenter（震源）、fault（斷層），而 aftershock 就是（餘震），例如以下例句：

- The two latest aftershocks shook New Zealand's city of Christchurch.
  兩起最新的餘震震動了紐西蘭的基督城。

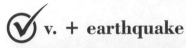 **v. + earthquake**

v.	earthquake	中譯
cause/generate / set off		引發地震
predict	earthquake	預測地震
survive		從地震中存活
withstand		抵擋地震

搭配詞例句

- The earthquake in California last week came without warning and highlighted the need for a reliable method of predicting earthquakes.
  上週加州無預警發生地震，凸顯出有效預測地震方法的重要。

⋯⋯⋯⋯⋯⋯⋯⋯⋯⋯⋯⋯⋯⋯⋯⋯⋯⋯⋯⋯⋯⋯⋯⋯⋯⋯⋯⋯⋯⋯⋯

- The building had survived the earthquake.
  這棟建築物曾歷經地震而屹立不搖。

⋯⋯⋯⋯⋯⋯⋯⋯⋯⋯⋯⋯⋯⋯⋯⋯⋯⋯⋯⋯⋯⋯⋯⋯⋯⋯⋯⋯⋯⋯⋯

adj. + earthquake

adj.	earthquake	中譯
devastating		毀滅性地震
great/huge/major/massive/powerful/severe	earthquake	強烈地震
mild/minor/moderate/small		輕微地震

- The Ministry of the Interior staged a drill to simulate a massive earthquake hitting the Hsinchu Science Park.
  內政部舉辦了模擬強烈地震襲擊新竹科學園區的演習。

- Aftershocks continue to rattle northwestern China, following a powerful earthquake.
  中國西北部遭強烈地震襲擊後,又持續發生餘震。

 **earthquake + v.**

earthquake	v.	中譯
earthquake	destroy/devastate/ravage	地震摧毀
	hit/strike	地震襲擊
	jolt/rattle/rock/shake	地震搖動
	occur	地震發生
	set/touch off	地震引發

- A powerful earthquake ravaged the northeastern district of Japan's Honshu Island.
  一場強烈地震摧毀了日本本州的東北地方。

- Although 70-80 percent of earthquakes hit eastern Taiwan, the heaviest casualties often occur in western Taiwan.
  雖然 70% 至 80% 的地震襲擊東臺灣,但最慘重的傷亡通常發生在西臺灣。

- A magnitude 6.4 earthquake followed by a series of strong aftershocks struck in a remote area of Alaska's Aleutian Islands.
  規模 6.4 的地震以及其後一連串強烈餘震，襲擊阿拉斯加阿留申群島的偏遠地區。

- A magnitude 4 earthquake jolted eastern Taiwan's Taitung County yesterday.
  昨日一場規模 4 的地震搖動了臺灣東部的臺東縣。

- A strong aftershock rattled the walls.
  強烈餘震撼動牆壁。

相關詞彙之搭配使用

片語

generating an earthquake around magnitude 7.5, perhaps up to magnitude 8.0	引發規模約 7.5 至 8 的地震
impending seismic disaster	逼近的地震災害
to trigger devastating landslides, tearing down homes and destroying roads vital to relief efforts	引發毀滅性山崩、房屋倒塌、救援道路中斷

句子

- Rescuers dug through rubble with their bare hands in a frantic search for survivors.
  搜救人員徒手挖掘瓦礫堆，拚命尋找生還者。

- Rescue workers are racing to save residents trapped in collapsed buildings.
  搜救人員急忙救援受困於倒塌大樓中的居民。

段落

At least 45,000 people <u>have been displaced by the powerful earthquake</u>[①] that hit Indonesia's Aceh province. The estimate of the number of homeless people continues to grow while <u>relief efforts</u>[②] fan out across the three districts near the epicenter of Wednesday's magnitude 6.5 quake. At least 100 people were killed and hundreds injured in the quake, which also destroyed or damaged more than 11,000 buildings, mostly homes but also several hundred mosques and schools. On Saturday, <u>sniffer dogs</u>[③] were again used in the search for bodies and possible survivors in the devastated town of Meureudu, where a market filled with shop houses was largely flattened. (*AP*)

強烈地震襲擊印尼的亞齊省，<u>造成至少4萬5千人流離失所</u>。無家可歸的預估人數持續增加，同時<u>救援行動</u>在週三發生規模6.5地震震央附近的三個地區展開。此次地震中至少已有一百人罹難，數百人受傷，並有超過1萬1千棟建物倒塌毀壞，其中大多數是房屋，但也有數以百計的清眞寺和學校。週六<u>搜救犬</u>再度出動，在受創嚴重的梅魯度鎮搜尋罹難者遺體和可能的生還者，當地商家林立的市場大部分都遭地震夷爲平地。(《美聯社》)

說明

① 動詞 displace 是「強迫離開」，如 displaced person 可指「流落異鄉的人」。此處使用被動語態 have been displaced 再接 by，後面接 the powerful earthquake（強烈地震），可知是因強烈地震而被迫離開家園。

② relief efforts（救援行動）是救難新聞中常見的搭配詞語，其他搭配還有 relief supplies/materials（救援物資）、relief measures（救援措施）、relief agency/organization（救援機構）或 emergency relief（緊急救援）、humanitarian relief（人道救援）等。

③ 動詞 sniff 是「嗅聞」的意思，此處 sniffer dog（搜救犬）就是以嗅覺敏銳的狗來尋找災區的罹難者和生還者，這些狗也可用於緝毒或偵查炸彈，是一種 detection dog（偵查犬）。

搭配詞練習

⚙ 請從方格中挑選正確的搭配詞來完成以下的句子。

quake	hit	jolted	powerful

1. A _____ **earthquake** struck the waters off western Indonesia, leaving at least one person dead.

   強烈**地震**襲擊印尼西部海域，造成至少一人死亡。

2. The 7.7-magnitude _____ **struck** 13 miles beneath the ocean floor.

   海床以下 13 英里處**爆發**了規模 7.7 的**地震**。

3. The magnitude 6.7 **quake** _____ a strait between the heavily populated islands of Negros and Cebu.

   規模 6.7 的**地震襲擊**人口密集的內格羅斯島和宿霧島之間的海峽。

4. A string of four **earthquakes** _____ Taiwan's northeastern Yilan area yesterday morning.

   昨日清晨連續四個**地震搖動**了臺灣東北部的宜蘭地區。

landslide/mudslide

(n.) 山崩 / 土石流

暖身練習

⚙ 請就以下中英譯文選出適當的搭配詞。　　　　▶ 答案請見 p. 268

Residents said there had been other ① **fatal** ② **dead mudslides** in
the last week.
居民表示，上週還曾發生過其他**致命的土石流**。

　　「山崩」的英文 landslide 由 land（土地）和 slide（滑動）組成，「小規模山崩」則稱爲 landslip。「土石流」mudslide 則是由 mud（泥）和 slide 組成。landslide 和 mudslide 的用法差不多，但 mudslide 還可分拆成名詞 mud 和動詞 slide into（滑入）的搭配來使用，例如以下例句：

- Two people were killed when mud slid into a quake-refugee camp.
  土石流入侵震災區的難民營，造成兩人喪生。

　　另外，landslide 還可以引申出「壓倒性」的涵意，例如「在選舉中獲得壓倒性勝利」就可說 to win a landslide victory in the election 或 to win a landslide vote。

v. + landslide/mudslide

v.	landslide/mudslide	中譯
cause / set off / trigger	landslide/mudslide	引發山崩 / 土石流
prevent		防止山崩 / 土石流

搭配詞例句

- Underground nuclear tests not only cause displacement in the earth, they also cause landslides, earthquakes, floods, typhoons and tidal waves.
  地下核武試爆不僅會引起土地位移，也會引發山崩、地震、洪水、颱風和海嘯。

- Heavy rains set off landslides and forced schools to be closed.
  大雨引發山崩，迫使學校關閉。

adj. + landslide/mudslide

adj.	landslide/mudslide	中譯
deadly/fatal		致命的山崩／土石流
devastating	landslide/mudslide	毀滅性的山崩／土石流
great/huge/major/massive/severe		大規模的山崩／土石流

搭配詞例句

- The search for six people still missing after a deadly landslide in Indonesia has been called off, bringing the presumed death toll to 18.
  印尼爆發致命的山崩後尚有六人失蹤，搜尋行動已宣告結束，推測死亡人數達 18 人。

- 1,500 people were killed in one devastating mudslide.
  1,500 人死於一場毀滅性的土石流中。

- Nine people were killed yesterday by a massive landslide.
  昨天的大規模山崩造成九人喪生。

....

 **landslide/mudslide ＋ v.**

landslide/mudslide	v.	中譯
landslide/mudslide	block/trap	山崩／土石流困住
	happen/occur	發生山崩／土石流

搭配詞例句

- The mudslides had trapped about 30 vans, buses and private cars.
  土石流困住約 30 輛小貨車、巴士和私人轎車。
  　說明　本句是以名詞 mudslide 搭配動詞 trap，為主動語態。描寫被土石流困
  住也可以用被動語態，例如 A few hundred tourists were trapped on the Suao-
  Hualien freeway because of the mudslide.（土石流導致數百名旅客被困在蘇花
  公路上。）

相關詞彙之搭配使用

片語

raising the risk of a landslide	提高山崩的風險
reduce the risk of landslides	降低山崩的風險
victims caught in a landslide	因山崩受困的受害者

句子

- Many of the homes were destroyed in the mudslide.
  許多房屋在土石流中被摧毀。

....

● He had <u>won by a landslide</u> in the Electoral College.
他在選舉人團中<u>贏得壓倒性勝利</u>。

段落

At least 141 people are missing after heavy rain <u>triggered a landslide</u>^① in south-western China. <u>A rescue mission was underway</u>^② after <u>approximately 40 homes were buried</u>^③ in Maoxian county in Sichuan province, the Xinhua news agency reported. The landslide hit the village of Xinmo at around 6 am and blocked a 2-kilometer section of a river, according to Xinhua. China has been experiencing weeks of heavy summer rains that have caused extensive flooding and triggered landslides. (*dpa*)

中國西南部的大雨<u>引發山崩</u>，造成至少 141 人失蹤。新華社報導，四川省茂縣有<u>近 40 戶民宅遭土石掩埋</u>，<u>搜救行動正如火如荼展開</u>。新華社表示，山崩約於清晨 6 點襲擊新磨村，並堵塞兩公里的河道。中國近幾週來的夏季豪雨已引發大量洪水和山崩。(《德新社》)

說明

① landslide 前面搭配的動詞為 trigger（引發），而「引起激烈反應」可以說 trigger a fierce response。另外，trigger 當名詞時意思是「扳機」，如「扣下扳機」就是 pull the trigger。

② a rescue mission 可代換成 rescue efforts，其後常接 be 動詞，再搭配形容詞 underway（進行中的），不過形容詞 underway 不可接在名詞前面。

③ 此處 ... were buried 是被動語態，也可用主動語態來形容土石掩埋情況，如 A massive landslide buried a mountain village.（大規模山崩掩埋了某個山村。）

搭配詞練習

⚙ 請從方格中挑選正確的搭配詞來完成以下的句子。

occur	set	massive	caused

1. Torrential rains _____ **landslides** and interrupted railway traffic.
   大豪雨**引發山崩**並中斷鐵路交通。

2. **Mudslides** and **landslides** _____ all over the world, and often happen in areas with plenty of vegetation.
   世界各地都會**發生土石流**和**山崩**，而且通常發生在植被茂盛的區域。

3. At least 540 **landslides** _____ **off** by rain were reported in published accounts around the world.
   世界各地的文獻記載，至少發生了 540 起由降雨所**引發**的**山崩**。

4. California's iconic Highway 1 near Big Sur has reopened 14 months after it was blocked by a _____ **landslide**.
   加州代表性的一號公路靠近大蘇爾路段因**大規模山崩**而封閉 14 個月之後，終於重新開放。

解答：1. caused 2. occur 3. set 4. massive
暖身練習解答：①

rain

(n.) 雨

▶ 答案請見 p. 274

暖身練習

⚙ 請就以下中英譯文選出適當的搭配詞。

① **Sour** ② **Acid rain** plagued the northeastern United States for years, harming trees and fish.
酸雨多年來危害美國東北部,樹林和魚類都受災。

rain 當動詞用指「下雨」,例如以下英文成語:

● It never rains but it pours. / When it rains, it pours.
禍不單行(指平日不下雨,但若一下雨則是傾盆大雨)。

而 rain 當名詞時意思是「雨」,臺灣同學在形容雨勢很大時,常會誤寫成 big rain 或 strong rain,這是受中文「大雨」和「強雨」干擾而寫出的中式英文,要盡量避免。常用寫法應為 heavy/pouring rain 或 downpour, downfall 等。相反地,「小雨」或「毛毛雨」可用 drizzle 或 drizzling rain 來表示。而「陣雨」為 shower,如 thundershower 為「雷陣雨」,sporadic/scattered/occasional showers 為「零星陣雨」。另外,「降雨量」可用 rainfall 或 precipitation 表示,例如以下例句:

● These windward mountain slopes receive abundant rainfall throughout the year.
這些迎風坡終年接受豐沛的雨量。

　　至於口語中經常使用的 May I take a rain check on that?（那件事我可以改天再做嗎？）一句的 rain check 與下雨無關，而是指「延期」或「改天再做」。

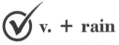 **v. + rain**

v.	rain	中譯
bring		帶來降雨
dump / pour with	rain	降下大雨
get caught in		被雨困住

> 搭配詞例句

- The storm has dumped a record 42 inches of rain in northeastern Taiwan.
  暴風雨在臺灣東北部降下破紀錄的 42 英寸（約 1,067 毫米）雨量。

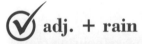 **adj. + rain**

adj.	rain	中譯
cascading/drenching/heavy/hurling/pouring/torrential		大雨 / 豪雨 / 傾盆大雨
drizzling/light/slight	rain	毛毛雨，小雨
falling		下雨
intermittent		間歇性的雨，陣雨

- The typhoon continues posing a severe threat with heavy rain.
  颱風帶來的大雨持續造成嚴重威脅。

- Torrential rains brought by Typhoon Megi have seriously affected Yilan.
  梅姬颱風所帶來的大豪雨重創宜蘭。

 **rain + v.**

rain	v.	中譯
rain	beat against	雨水敲打
	dribble/drip/trickle down	雨水流淌
	fall / pour down	雨水降下
	let up / stop	雨停
	pound	大雨重創
	topple	因大雨而倒塌

- Rain dribbles down his neck and soaks into his T-shirt.
  雨水沿著他的脖子流下，濕透了他的 T 恤。

- Up to 20 inches of rain has pounded the region over the past three days, forcing the evacuation of more than 10,000 people.
  過去三天高達 20 英寸（508 毫米）的大雨重創該地區，迫使一萬多人必須撤離。

- Steady rains toppled hillsides and turned streets into rivers over the weekend, leaving at least 12 people dead and three missing.
  週末期間持續的降雨造成山坡崩塌，街道也變成河流，造成至少 12 人死亡，三人失蹤。

相關詞彙之搭配使用

片語

annual spring plum rains	每年春天的梅雨
clothes sodden with rain / rain-sodden clothes	被雨水濕透的衣服
occasional showers	零星陣雨
partly cloudy with a chance of showers	局部多雲，有陣雨的可能
plum rain season	梅雨季

句子

- It is raining cats and dogs.
  傾盆大雨。

- Heavy rains and flash flooding have been reported in mountainous areas.
  山區已傳出大雨與暴洪的災情。

段落

Northern Taiwan was hit by[①] torrential rain, turning Keelung and the north coast into disaster areas. According to an initial report issued by the Central Emergency Operation Center, one person died, two went missing and five were injured, while 3,800 people had to be evacuated. Power and water supplies to about 15,000 households were disrupted and 970 sites were flooded. The <u>weather front moved</u>^② south, and central and southern Taiwan were also hit. (*Taipei Times*)

臺灣北部<u>遭到</u>大豪雨襲擊，使得基隆和北海岸都變成災區。中央災害應變中心的初步報告指出，目前有一人死亡，兩人失蹤，五人受傷，同時有 3,800 位民眾被迫撤離。另有約 1 萬 5 千戶家庭停水斷電，970 處地方淹水。<u>氣象鋒面</u>已經<u>南移</u>，臺灣中部和南部也受到重創。(《臺北時報》)

說明

① 陳述災難來襲的句型常用被動語態，如此處的 was hit 以及後面的 were disrupted, were flooded 等。

② front 是氣象術語，譯為「鋒面」，後面可搭配動詞 move（移動）。相關搭配還有 cold front（冷鋒）、warm front（暖鋒）。

搭配詞練習

⚙ 請從方格中挑選正確的搭配詞來完成以下的句子。

dumped	heavy	bring	plum	rainfall

1. Typhoon Megi _____ **heavy rains** throughout Taiwan.
   梅姬颱風在全臺各地**降下傾盆大雨**。

2. Taiwanese rescuers discovered a body after _____ **rains** brought by Typhoon Megi.
   在梅姬颱風帶來的**大雨**後，臺灣的搜救隊發現了一具屍體。

3. Temperatures are expected to cool down nationwide today with the arrival of the first _____ **rains** of the year.
   今年首波**梅雨**報到，全國今日氣溫預期將會下降。

4. The weather front is likely to _____ **heavy** _____ for the rest of the week in most regions, with temperatures ranging between 23°C and 29°C nationwide.
   氣象鋒面可能在本週為大部分地區**帶來大雨**，全國氣溫則介於攝氏 23 度到 29 度之間。

解答：1. dumped   2. heavy   3. plum   4. bring, rainfall

暖身練習解答：②

flood

(n.) 洪水

▶ 答案請見 p. 280

暖身練習

⚙ 請就以下中英譯文選出適當的搭配詞。

The **flood** ① **drowned** ② **swamped** homes and businesses, shut down roads, and led to sewage spills.

洪水淹沒房屋和商店，封閉道路，並使下水道汙水外溢。

flood 除了當名詞表示「洪水」之外，還可以當動詞用，意思是「淹水」，而且多用被動語態，例如以下例句：

- Several public buildings including a hospital were flooded.
  包括一棟醫院在內，好幾棟公共建築物都淹水了。

當動詞用的 flood 還可引申為「充斥」、「淹沒」，例如以下例句：

- China's exports of textiles and apparel have flooded the world market.
  中國出口的紡織品和服裝已充斥全球市場。

- In this complex society, we are flooded with information.
  在這個複雜的社會裡，我們常被資訊淹沒。

不過多數情況下 flood 還是當名詞使用，而且常用複數形 floods，或可用 floodwaters 取代。另外名詞 flooding 則強調洪水的狀況，也可譯為「洪災」。相關的搭配詞彙如下。

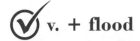 v. + flood

v.	flood	中譯
cause/trigger	flood	引發洪災
tame		治理洪水

搭配詞例句

- More rain is in the forecast for the region, but it is not expected to cause major floods.
  預報指出該地區還會持續降雨，但預期不至於引發洪災。

...

- Days of torrential rain triggered flash floods and landslides that have buried scores of victims.
  連續幾天的大豪雨引發暴洪和山崩，許多人慘遭活埋。

...

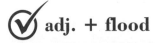 adj. + flood

adj.	flood	中譯
catastrophic/deadly/ destructive/devastating	flood	毀滅性的洪水
flash		突如其來的洪水，暴洪
great/severe		大洪水／嚴重的洪水

搭配詞例句

- The country began recovering from devastating floods.
  該國開始從毀滅性的洪災中復甦。

...

- Central Vietnam has recently been hit by two rounds of severe flooding, which killed 141 people.
越南中部最近遭受兩回嚴重洪水侵襲，造成 141 人死亡。

 **flood + v.**

flood	v.	中譯
flood	cause	洪水造成
	claim	洪水奪走（生命）
	hit	洪水襲擊
	ravage	洪水毀壞 / 肆虐
	reach	洪水抵達
	recede	洪水消退
	rise/surge	洪水上漲
	spread	洪水蔓延
	submerge/swamp	洪水淹沒
	threaten	洪水威脅

搭配詞例句

- The flood caused more than $10 billion worth in damage.
洪水造成逾 100 億美元的損害。

- The floods have claimed 26 lives.
洪水奪走了 26 條人命。

- Floods have reached the building at around one meter high.
  洪水已經淹到房子約一公尺高之處。

- Floodwaters have largely receded.
  洪水大多已消退。

- Malaysian authorities have shut down schools and evacuated more than 12,000 people as floodwaters rise in two northern states.
  因北部兩州的洪水高漲，馬來西亞當局已關閉學校並撤離 1 萬 2 千多人。

- Flash floods submerged more than a dozen vehicles.
  暴洪將十幾輛汽車淹沒在水中。

相關詞彙之搭配使用

片語

crossing on waist deep floodwaters	橫渡深及腰部的洪水
severe flood damage	嚴重的洪災損害
the country's worst floods in more than half a century	該國超過半世紀以來最嚴重的洪災
to rehabilitate the flood-devastated area	重建被洪水摧毀的區域

句子

- A total of 101 people have died or gone missing <u>due to flooding caused by heavy rains</u>.
  大雨所造成的洪災已導致共 101 人死亡或失蹤。

- <u>The flooding covered a swath</u> about two miles wide.
  洪災區域約兩英里寬。

- The flooding left a great deal of damage in Sichuan.
  洪水重創四川省。

段落

After a much-criticized delay[①], President Barack Obama visited flood-stricken Louisiana[②] Tuesday, defending his administration's response and urging citizens to pitch in[③] and help ravaged communities. At least 13 people have died and more than 100,000 people have registered for U.S. government emergency assistance as a result of the flooding. The National Guard has been deployed and the federal government has approved more than US$120 million in assistance for temporary rent, home repairs and flood insurance payments. (*AFP*)

飽受輿論批評救援行動遲緩後，歐巴馬總統週二視察遭洪水肆虐的路易斯安那州，為當局的救援反應辯護，並呼籲民眾同心協力來幫助受創嚴重的社區。此次洪災至少已造成 13 人死亡，超過 10 萬人申請美國政府的緊急救助。美國已部署國民兵部隊，聯邦政府也核准超過 1 億 2 千萬美元的援助經費，協助支應短期房租、房屋修繕和洪災保險等費用。(《法新社》)

說明

① much- 後面接形容詞可強化其形容的程度，常見字彙有 much-needed（亟需的）、much-anticipated（備受期待的）、much-loved（備受喜愛的），後面再接名詞。

② -stricken 前面接名詞，通常表示「受…打擊的」，如 quake-stricken（受地震打擊的）、drought-stricken（受旱災打擊的）、disaster-stricken（受災難打擊的）、poverty-stricken（受貧窮打擊的）等，其後再接名詞。

③ 動詞 pitch 本身有許多不同含意，例如「為…定音高」、「投擲」、「推銷」等，但此處 pitch 搭配介系詞 in，意思是「共同參與」。

搭配詞練習

⚙ 請從方格中挑選正確的搭配詞來完成以下的句子。

spread	ravaged	receded	swamped	flash

1. The **floods** have _____ to 38 of Thailand's 76 provinces although the **waters** have _____ in 11 of those.
   洪水已蔓延至泰國 76 省中 38 個省份，不過其中 11 省的水已消退。

2. **Floods** _____ Australia's northeast and _____ a major city.
   澳洲東北部洪水肆虐，一個主要城市慘遭淹沒。

3. The area was hit by early morning _____ **floods**.
   這個區域在清晨遭到突如其來的洪水襲擊。

解答：1. spread, receded　2. ravaged, swamped　3. flash

暖身練習解答：②

tsunami

(n.) 海嘯

▶ 答案請見 p. 286

暖身練習

請就以下中英譯文選出適當的搭配詞。

Navy ships packed with medicine and food headed to remote Indonesian islands that were pounded by a ① **10-foot** ② **10-feet** **tsunami**.

印尼偏遠島嶼遭 10 **英尺高海嘯**重擊，載滿醫療用品和食物的海軍艦艇前往救援。

　　tsunami 一字不論就發音或拼寫來看都不像英文，事實上這個字是從日文借用而來的。「海嘯」的日文漢字寫法是「津波」，意指「港口的波浪」。其實英文也有類似表達方式如 tidal wave（浪潮），不過其規模與「海嘯」無法相提並論；「海嘯」在英文中還有另一個說法為 seismic sea waves，指「地震引起的海浪」。不過因為日本是全世界發生海嘯頻率最高的國家，深具代表性，因此媒體在報導這類災難時還是常用 tsunami。

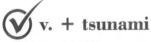 **v. + tsunami**

v.	tsunami	中譯
cause/produce / set off	tsunami	引發海嘯
prepare for / prevent		為海嘯的到來做好準備

搭配詞例句

● Each seismic shock produced a tsunami.
　每次地震都會引發海嘯。

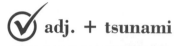 **adj. + tsunami**

adj.	tsunami	中譯
crushing/damaging/destructive/ devastating	tsunami	毀滅性的海嘯
ferocious/great/towering		強勁的海嘯

搭配詞例句

● International search and rescue teams rushed to Japan in the wake of a massive magnitude earthquake and crushing tsunami.
　發生大規模地震和毀滅性的海嘯後，國際搜救隊趕赴日本救災。

● Toyota has seemed to find its footing after the devastating tsunami in Japan.
　豐田汽車公司似乎已從日本毀滅性海嘯的打擊中重新站穩腳步。

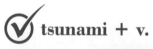 **tsunami + v.**

tsunami	v.	中譯
tsunami	assault/attack/pound/pummel/ravage/ slam/strike	海嘯襲擊 / 重擊
	engulf/swallow/ swallow up / swamp	海嘯吞沒
	sweep/wash away	海嘯沖走

搭配詞例句

- The tsunami assaulted Hawaii with seven-foot waves, although it caused little damage.
  海嘯以七英尺高的大浪襲擊夏威夷，不過並未造成嚴重損害。

- The death toll from a tsunami that pummeled remote Indonesian islands is expected to pass 500.
  海嘯重擊印尼偏遠島嶼，死亡人數預估超過 500 人。

- Residents have been ordered to high ground and stay away from the coast as tsunamis can strike in several waves.
  因海嘯可能多次來襲，居民已被下令撤離至高地，並遠離海岸。

- A tsunami in the Hawaiian Islands in 1869 washed away an entire town.
  1869 年發生在夏威夷群島的海嘯沖走了整個小鎮。

相關詞彙之搭配使用

片語

the most damaging tsunami on record	有史以來災情最慘重的海嘯
tsunami-warning system	海嘯預警系統
warnings of a tsunami of between six and 10 meters	警告將有 6 至 10 公尺高的海嘯來襲

句子

- A four-meter wave swamped parts of Kamaishi on the Pacific coast.
  四公尺高的海浪淹沒了太平洋岸釜石市的部分地區。

- The area was only accessible by motorcycle, foot or helicopter, and local police had few resources to search for survivors.
  災區只能靠機車、徒步或直昇機抵達，當地警方僅有少數資源搜尋生還者。

段落

Aid workers struggled to reach remote, tsunami-ravaged villages[①] in the Solomon Islands on Thursday, as the death toll rose[②] with more bodies found in wrecked homes and debris in the South Pacific island chain. At least nine people, including a child, were killed when a powerful earthquake set off a small tsunami that sent 1.5-meter waves roaring inland[③] on Santa Cruz Island, in the eastern Solomons, on Wednesday. Around 100 homes across five villages were damaged or destroyed. (AP)

搜救人員於週四奮力抵達所羅門群島中遭海嘯侵襲的偏遠村落，而隨著搜救人員在這個南太平洋群島的破瓦殘礫中找到更多屍體，死亡人數也不斷攀升。週三的強烈地震引發小規模海嘯，1.5 公尺高的海浪猛烈衝擊東所羅門的聖塔克魯茲島內陸，造成至少九人喪生，包括一名孩童。遍及五個村落約百餘間房屋受損或毀壞。（《美聯社》）

說明

① 名詞 tsunami 和動詞 ravage 是常見搭配，但在此處 ravage 加 -d 變成形容詞，而且兩個字用連字號組成 tsunami-ravaged（遭海嘯侵襲的）一字，修飾後面的名詞 villages（村落）。類似的詞彙還有 war-ravaged（受戰爭摧殘的）、earthquake-ravaged（遭地震侵襲的）等。

② 災難新聞中常會提到「死亡人數」，英文為 death toll，其後可搭配動詞 rise 來表示「增加」，例如 The death toll has risen to 100.（死亡人數已增加到 100 人。）

③ 1.5-meter 也是用連字號結合兩個字當形容詞用，因此 meter 要用單數，後面搭配的名詞 waves 才能用複數。另外，描述 waves 的動詞是 roar，意思是「咆哮」、「發出轟鳴聲」，在此搭配副詞 inland（往內陸）。

搭配詞練習

⚙ 請從方格中挑選正確的搭配詞來完成以下的句子。

slammed	devastating	ferocious
engulfed	caused	

1. The 8.9-magnitude earthquake **set off** a _____ **tsunami** that sent walls of water washing over coastal cities in the north.
   此規模 8.9 的地震**引發**毀滅性海嘯，滾滾海水衝擊北部沿海城市。

2. A _____ **tsunami** _____ Japan's eastern coast.
   強勁海嘯襲擊日本東部的海岸。

3. Towns and farms around Sendai city in northern Japan have been _____ by a seven-meter **tsunami**.
   日本北部仙台市附近的城鎮和農田都被七公尺高的**海嘯吞沒**。

4. **Tsunamis** are most often _____ by undersea earthquakes.
   海嘯大多是由海底地震所**引發**。

解答：1. devastating　2. ferocious, slammed　3. engulfed　4. caused

暖身練習解答：①

fire

(n.) 火災

▶ 答案請見 p. 294

暖身練習

⚙ 請就以下中英譯文選出適當的搭配詞。

Be sure you know how to operate your fire extinguisher and the right way to ① **fight** ② **destroy** a **fire**.
要確認你知道如何操作滅火器以及正確的**滅火**方式。

火災除了用 fire 表示之外，還可依火勢大小用 blaze/flame/flare（火焰）、wildfire（野火）、bushfire（叢林大火）、conflagration（大火）來表示，搭配方式也相當類似，例如以下例句：

- Gusty winds pushed flames 15 feet in the air.
  強風助長火勢，烈焰高達 15 英尺。

- The blaze is near an area where a wildfire burned almost 10 square miles last month.
  這場火災的地點靠近上個月燒遍近 10 平方英里的野火發生地點。

而以 fire 組成的字相當多，例如 firecracker（鞭炮）、firework（煙火）、firebug/firefly（螢火蟲）、fireplace（壁爐）、firearms（槍械）、firepower（火力）、fireproof（防火的）、fireman/firefighter / fire fighter（消防隊員）、firewall（防火牆）等。另外，fire 也常用在軍事或武裝活動上，如 fire 當動詞時有「發射槍砲」或「開火」的意思，例如以下例句：

- Toronto police said multiple shots were fired but no injuries have been reported.
多倫多警方表示，有多次槍擊發生，但未發現任何傷亡。

　　火災是常見的自然和人為災害，常造成重大損失，因此有關救火和防火的詞彙也相對較多。請見以下 fire 的搭配形式。

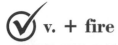 **v. + fire**

v.	fire	中譯
battle/extinguish/fight / put out		滅火
catch		著火
cease		停火
hold		暫停開火
make/spark/start	fire	點火
open		開火
return		回擊
set		縱火

搭配詞例句

- Firefighters took more than eight hours to extinguish a fire at a century-old mill.
消防隊員花了超過八小時才撲滅一座百年磨坊的大火。

....

- In Northern California today, hundreds of firefighters fought a wildfire in the Lake Tahoe resort area.
今日北加州有數百名消防隊員在太浩湖休閒度假區撲滅野火。

....

- Policemen armed with military equipment even opened fire to suppress the rioting.
武裝警察甚至開火鎮壓暴動的群眾。

- They set fire to the church to denounce Obama's election.
他們在教堂縱火以表達對歐巴馬當選的不滿。

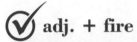 **adj. + fire**

adj.	fire	中譯
deadly/fatal		致命的火災
disastrous/serious		嚴重的火災
life-threatening	fire	威脅生命的火災
outdoor		戶外火災
residential		住宅火災

搭配詞例句

- Homeowners should take any steps they could to guard against life-threatening fires.
屋主應盡其所能防範會威脅生命的火災。

 **fire + v.**

fire	v.	中譯
fire	blaze/burn	火燒
	break out	火災發生

fire	claim	火災奪走（生命）
	damage/destroy	火災毀損
	engulf	大火吞噬
	erupt	爆發火勢
	go out	火熄滅
	rage	大火肆虐
	spread/sweep across spread/sweep through	火災擴散／橫掃
	start	起火

搭配詞例句

- It turns out that the fire burned for three hours.
  結果那場火燒了三小時。

- Australia's bushfires of 2009 claimed more than 170 lives.
  2009 年澳洲的叢林大火奪走超過 170 條人命。

- The fire erupted during a rock concert attended by as many as 4,000 people.
  多達四千人參加的搖滾演唱會上突然爆發火勢。

- Early this morning, a fire swept through a nursing home. Nine people were killed.
  今晨一所安養院慘遭祝融肆虐，造成九人死亡。

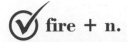 **fire + n.**

fire	n.	中譯
fire	alarm	火災警報器
	brigade/department/station	消防隊
	door	防火安全門
	drill/practice	消防演習
	engine/truck	消防車
	escape	逃生梯
	extinguisher	滅火器
	fatality	火災死亡人數
	hydrant	消防栓
	lane	防火巷

搭配詞例句

- They couldn't get on the phone with the fire department, because the lines were congested.
  由於電話線路壅塞，他們無法與消防隊聯繫。

- He goes back to his room, grabs his money, and escapes down the fire escape.
  他回房間抓了一把錢，就從逃生梯逃跑了。

- Is there a fire extinguisher in your home? And do you know how to use it?
  你家有滅火器嗎？你知道如何使用嗎？

● In the last 15 years, we cut our fire fatalities in half.
過去 15 年來，我們將火災死亡人數降低了一半。

相關詞彙之搭配使用

片語

a tongue of fire	火舌
be engulfed in flame and smoke	被火焰和濃煙吞噬
death from a fire	因火災喪生
to add fuel to the fire	火上加油
to enhance in-house firefighting systems	加強室內消防系統
to fight fire with fire	以其人之道還治其人之身
to set oneself on fire in protest at...	自焚抗議…

句子

● The blaze was sparked by an electrical fault.
這場火災是電線走火所引發。

● A natural gas leak can lead to fires and even explosions.
天然氣漏氣會導致火災，甚至引起爆炸。

● A little spark can cause a conflagration.
星火可以燎原。

● Arson is the single largest cause of fire in England and Wales.
縱火是英格蘭和威爾斯發生火災的最主要原因。

段落

The number of people missing and presumed dead[①] after this week's deadly London high-rise blaze now stands at 58. The number of confirmed deaths[②] previously stood at 30, but police had warned that the number may rise. Flames rapidly engulfed[③] the 24-storey[④] Grenfell Tower in the early hours of Wednesday. New cladding on the building has since been named as a potential factor in the spread of the fire. (*dpa*)

本週倫敦高樓致命大火的失蹤和推定死亡人數現為 58 人。之前宣布的確定死亡人數為 30 人，但警方警告人數可能會增加。週三凌晨大火快速吞噬這棟 24 層樓高的格倫菲爾塔。包覆大樓的新設層板被點名為此次火災蔓延的可能因素。（《德新社》）

說明

① 動詞 presume 是「假設」、「設想」的意思，字尾加 -d 成為形容詞 presumed，搭配名詞 dead，可譯為「推定死亡」。

② 動詞 confirm 是「證實」，字尾加 -ed 成為形容詞 confirmed，搭配名詞 death 或 dead，可譯為「確定死亡」。

③ 動詞 engulf 是「吞沒」，此處是主動語態用法，但也常用被動語態 be engulfed in...（被⋯吞沒），如 The building was engulfed in flames.（建築被大火吞噬。）

④ storey（樓層）是英式英文的拼法，美式英文的拼法為 story。此處 24-storey 因有連字號將兩字組成一字，當形容詞用，不能因為有 24 層樓而把 storey 寫成複數形 storeys。如「一幢三層樓的房子」應譯為 a three-storey house，如果 storey 單獨使用就可以寫成複數形，如 a house with three storeys。

搭配詞練習

⚙ **請從方格中挑選正確的搭配詞來完成以下的句子。**

drill	deadly	residential	alarm

1. Smoking caused 28 percent of all fatal _____ **fires**.
   致命性**住宅火災**有 28% 是吸菸引起。

2. Your family needs to hold a **fire** _____ at home to make sure everyone knows how to escape.
   你和家人在家必須做**消防演習**，確保每一個人都知道該如何逃生。

3. A student, who was smoking in a stairwell, started a small fire with his cigarette. It set off the **fire** _____.
   有個學生在樓梯間抽菸引起一場小火災，觸動了**火災警報器**。

4. A _____ **fire** swept through a prison in the town of Comayagua.
   致命烈火橫掃科馬雅瓜市的一座監獄。

volcano/volcanic

(n.) 火山 / (adj.) 火山的

▶ 答案請見 p. 300

暖身練習

⚙ 請就以下中英譯文選出適當的搭配詞。

Mount Fuji in Japan is actually an ① **alive** ② **active volcano**.
日本的富士山實際上是座**活火山**。

    volcano 是名詞，形容詞是 volcanic（火山的），很多與火山有關的詞彙可用 volcanic 來組成，例如「火山」也可稱為 volcanic mountain，「火山爆發」為 volcanic eruption。與火山相關的字詞有 lava（熔岩）、magma（岩漿）、crater（火山口）等。其他 volcano 和 volcanic 的搭配如下。

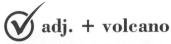 adj. + volcano

adj.	volcano	中譯
active		活火山
dormant		休火山
erupting		爆發的火山
extinct	volcano	死火山
powerful		威力強大的火山
sleeping		睡火山
volatile		反覆無常的火山

搭配詞例句

- In the U.S., there are 169 active volcanoes or volcanoes that are capable of reawakening
  美國有 169 座活火山或可能轉趨活躍的火山。

....

- The dormant volcano dominates the landscape.
  這座休火山是全幅景色的焦點。

....

 volcano ＋ v.

volcano	v.	中譯
volcano	erupt/explode/unleash	火山爆發
	force	火山迫使
	groan/rumble	火山隆隆作響
	push/spew	火山噴出
	reactivate	火山再次活動

搭配詞例句

- When volcanoes erupt, the lava releases some gases, including carbon dioxide and hydrogen.
  火山爆發時，熔岩會釋出一些包括二氧化碳和氫在內的氣體。

....

- Indonesia's most dangerous volcano forced international airlines to cancel flights to nearby airports.
  印尼最危險的火山迫使國際航空公司取消飛往附近機場的班機。

....

- Indonesia's most volatile volcano groaned and rumbled Tuesday.
  印尼最反覆無常的火山週二開始隆隆作響。

....

- The volcano spewed steam, other gas and rock debris across the landscape.
  火山噴出蒸氣、其他氣體和散落在地表的碎石。

- The volcano could reactivate at any moment.
  這座火山隨時可能會再次活動。

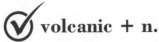 **volcanic + n.**

volcanic	n.	中譯
	ash	火山灰
	cone	火山錐
	eruption	火山爆發
volcanic	island	火山島
	lava	火山熔岩
	mountain	火山
	peak	火山峰

搭配詞例句

- The plume of volcanic ash over Europe this spring canceled more than one hundred thousand flights.
  今春歐洲上空團團的火山灰使得超過十萬架次的航班被迫取消。

- We can see volcanic lava that formed these large pillow-shaped pieces of rock.
  我們可看到形成這些大塊枕狀岩石的火山熔岩。

相關詞彙之搭配使用

片語

spewing hot gases and ash 12 miles into the sky	噴發出熱氣和火山灰，直上 12 英里高空
threats posed by hundreds of active volcanoes in the country	該國境內數百座活火山所帶來的威脅

句子

- Scientists warned that <u>the volcano could be heading toward an eruption</u>.
  科學家警告，<u>該火山可能即將爆發</u>。

- <u>Seafloor volcanoes do erupt violently</u>, but in relatively shallow water.
  <u>海底火山爆發確實很猛烈</u>，不過都是在相對較淺的海裡。

- The volcano <u>continues to threaten to coat this town with volcanic ash</u>.
  這座火山的<u>火山灰仍可能覆蓋這整個城鎮</u>。

- The volcano has been <u>in a constant state of eruption</u> since in 1995.
  這座火山自從 1995 年以來就<u>時常爆發</u>。

- The volcano is <u>showing a lot of signs of unrest</u> that probably presage an eruption.
  這座火山出現許多<u>蠢蠢欲動的跡象</u>，可能是爆發的前兆。

- After <u>three devastating months of volcanic activity</u>, the <u>lava flow</u> on Hawaii's Big Island has come to a near halt.
  經過<u>三個月毀滅性的火山活動</u>，夏威夷大島上的<u>熔岩</u>已幾近停止<u>流動</u>。

段落

The Alaska Volcano Observatory <u>issued its highest alert level</u>[1] Tuesday after a volcano erupted in the Aleutian Islands that reportedly sent ash thousands of feet into the air. The alert was downgraded hours later. Pilots told the observatory that a volcanic ash cloud rose to 34,000 feet. Three hours after that, the observatory said that <u>the alert level had been downgraded a notch</u>[2] because activity had apparently subsided. *(AP)*

阿留申群島一座火山爆發，火山灰據報噴飛上天達數千英尺高，阿拉斯加火山觀測所隨即於週二<u>發布最高層級警示</u>，而在數小時後又降低警示層級。有飛行員通知觀測所，一朵火山灰雲升高至 3 萬 4 千英尺的高空。三小時後，觀測所表示由於火山活動已明顯趨緩，<u>警示層級隨之降低一級</u>。（《美聯社》）

說明

① 「發布警示」的動詞可用 issue，而此處「最高層級的警示」即 highest alert level，其中 alert 當名詞用，意為「警報」，如 flood alert 為「洪水警報」、red alert 為「緊急警報」等。

② 「警示層級下降」的動詞可用 downgrade，而「降低一級」的「級」則可用 notch 或 level。

搭配詞練習

⚙ 請從方格中挑選正確的搭配詞來完成以下的句子。

exploded	pushing	eruption	ash

1. This **volcano's** _____ will likely be small.
   這座火山的爆發規模可能較小。

2. In 1883 a massive **volcano** _____ on the Indonesian island of Krakatau. More than 36,000 people were killed when the eruption generated giant, 120-foot waves.
   1883 年印尼喀拉喀托島上一座巨大**火山爆發**，引發高達 120 英尺的巨大海嘯，造成超過 3 萬 6 千人喪生。

3. **Volcanic** _____ has been disrupting air travel since mid-April.
   自四月中旬起**火山灰**就一直阻礙空中航行。

4. The **volcano** was _____ ash and smoke about two miles up into the sky.
   這座**火山噴出**約兩英里高的火山灰和煙塵，直上高空。

解答：1. eruption 2. exploded 3. ash 4. pushing
暖身練習解答：②

VI. 大衆傳播類

news

(n.) 新聞；消息

▶ 答案請見 p. 308

暖身練習

⚙ 請就以下中英譯文選出適當的搭配詞。

Upon hearing the news, U.S. Secretary of State Mike Pompeo expressed sorrow at a **news** ① **meeting** ② **conference**.
一聽到這個消息，美國國務卿蓬佩奧隨即在**記者會**上表達哀痛之意。

news 是不可數名詞，可以用 items/pieces of 等來形容數則新聞報導或消息，例如「兩則新聞」可說 two pieces of news。news 還可與許多字合成，例如 newspaper（報紙）、newscast（新聞廣播）、newsflash（新聞快訊）、newsman（新聞記者）、newsletter（通訊）、newsstand（報攤）等。與新聞相關的詞彙還有 press（新聞界），例如 press freedom 是「新聞自由」，press conference 是「記者會」。

在世界各地採訪新聞、拍攝照片並發布給各國媒體，供應各種新聞的機構就稱為「新聞通訊社」(news agency)。幾家知名的國際新聞通訊社的中英文名稱如下：

- The Associated Press (AP)：美聯社（美國）
- United Press International (UPI)：合眾國際社（美國）
- Reuters：路透社（英國）
- Agence France-Presse (AFP)：法新社（法國）
- Deutsche Presse-Agentur (dpa)：德新社（德國）

- Kyodo News：共同社（日本）
- ITAR-Tass：塔斯社（俄國）
- Xinhua：新華社（中國）
- Central News Agency (CNA)：中央通訊社（臺灣）

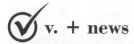 **v. + news**

v.	news	中譯
broadcast		播放新聞
censor		審查新聞
cover		採訪新聞
dominate	news	占據新聞重要版面
gather		收集新聞
make		登上新聞版面
spread		散播新聞

搭配詞例句

- Only national television stations controlled by the military were broadcasting news.
  只有軍方控制的國家電視台在播放新聞。

....

- The authoritarian governments of China, Cuba and Burma have been selectively censoring the news.
  專制政權的中國、古巴和緬甸一直選擇性地審查新聞。

....

- The upheaval in Egypt continues to dominate the news.
  埃及的動亂持續占據新聞重要版面。

....

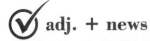 adj. + news

adj.	news	中譯
better-than-expected		比預期好的消息
breaking		突發新聞，最新消息
censored		受到審查的新聞
digital		數位新聞
domestic		國內新聞
fake/false/pseudo	news	假新聞，業配新聞
front-page		頭版新聞
global/international		國際新聞
headline		頭條新聞
online		線上新聞
running		持續報導的新聞

搭配詞例句

- Yahoo is teaming up with ABC News in a bid to create a digital news powerhouse.
  Yahoo 正在與美國廣播公司合作，致力打造一個數位新聞王國。

- In domestic news, the number one news story last year was the so-called plasticizer crisis.
  在國內新聞方面，去年最受矚目的新聞是所謂的塑化劑危機。

- Fake news is being spread through social media as part of an information war.
  假新聞在社交媒體上散播，是資訊戰爭的一環。

- Yahoo and ABC News said their "strategic online news alliance" will reach more than 100 million U.S. users each month.
  Yahoo 與美國廣播公司表示，他們的「策略性線上新聞結盟」，每個月將有超過一億個美國人收看。

 **news + n.**

news	n.	中譯
news	agency	新聞通訊社
	anchor	新聞主播
	archive	新聞資料庫
	article/coverage/report/story	新聞報導
	bureau	新聞社
	censorship	新聞審查
	correspondent	新聞特派員
	desk	新聞編輯部
	industry	新聞產業
	media	新聞媒體
	network	新聞聯播網
	release	新聞稿
	source	新聞來源
	station	新聞台

搭配詞例句

- Xinhua, China's state news agency, is considered a propaganda tool by press freedom organizations.

  中國的國家新聞通訊社新華社，被新聞自由組織視為宣傳工具。

相關詞彙之搭配使用

片語

foreign correspondent	國外新聞特派員
live broadcast	現場轉播
reporters' complaints of censorship	記者對審查制度的不滿
to gag/muzzle the press	箝制新聞自由
to hold a joint press conference	舉行聯合記者會

句子

- Scholars cite the incidence as further evidence towards <u>the plummeting of Taiwan news media into the realm of entertainment</u>.

  學者引用這個事件，作為<u>臺灣新聞媒體墮落至娛樂節目</u>的進一步證據。

- Taipei has been <u>picked by the Fox News website as</u> one of the top 10 budget travel destinations for 2012.

  臺北<u>被福斯新聞網選為</u>「2012 年 10 大地美價廉的旅遊勝地」之一。

- Google announced it would do more to <u>prevent fake news sites from making money through advertising</u>.

  Google 宣布將更加致力於<u>防制散播假新聞的網站從廣告中獲利</u>。

According to the British newspaper *the Guardian*, Google's Digital News Initiative (DNI) will provide a grant of US$805,000 to help Press Association develop an AI system that can automatically produce news stories by compiling information <u>issued to</u>[①] the public by parliament, law enforcement agencies and other government bodies. The project, which is to be carried out next year, will cover a wide range of topics, including crimes, health and employment. <u>In addition to writing the news</u>[②], the AI system will also select photos for the story. (*CNA*)

英國《衛報》報導，Google 的「數位新聞行動」(DNI) 基金會將提供 80 萬 5 千美元補助金，協助新聞協會開發人工智慧系統，該系統可收集編排國會、執法單位和政府機構公布給大眾的資料，並自動產出新聞報導。這項計畫預計於明年展開，將報導廣泛題材，包括犯罪、健康和就業等。除了撰寫新聞之外，此人工智慧系統還會為報導選取照片。(《中央社》)

說明

① issued（公布）前面省略了 which is，後面搭配介系詞 to 是指「公布給誰」，搭配介系詞 by 則是指「由什麼單位公布」。

② in addition to...（除…之外）是固定搭配，to 是介系詞，後面若接動詞要改成動名詞，如此處的 In addition to writing the news。in addition 則是另一種搭配，表示「此外」，等同於副詞 additionally，例如 The survey found that 51.8 percent of office workers regret making the choice that they did. In addition, 59.7 percent of office workers said that if they could go back, they would pick a different major.（調查發現，51.8% 的上班族後悔他們所做的決定。此外，59.7% 的上班族表示，如果能重來，他們會選擇不同的主修。）

搭配詞練習

⚙ 請從方格中挑選正確的搭配詞來完成以下的句子。

bureau	media	story	cover	coverage

1. The Associated Press opened its **news** _____ in Pyongyang, becoming the first international news organization with a full-time presence to _____ **news** from North Korea.
《美聯社》在平壤設立**新聞社**，成為第一個在北韓全天候**採訪新聞**的國際新聞組織。

2. It would be a great pity if the **news** _____ fail to follow moral rules in handling **news** _____.
如果**新聞媒體**在處理**新聞報導**時無法遵循道德規範，會是很遺憾的事。

3. Chinese netizens have turned to blockchain to share a **censored news** _____ about faulty vaccines given to small babies.
中國網民轉而透過區塊鏈，分享**受到審查**、關於嬰兒接種假疫苗**的新聞報導**。

解答：1. bureau, cover　2. media, coverage　3. story
暖身練習解答：②

media

(n.) 媒體

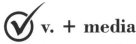
請就以下中英譯文選出適當的搭配詞。　　　　　　　▶答案請見 p. 315

China's ① **state** ② **country media** complained that farm subsidies in the United States and other Western countries distort international trade.

中國的**國家媒體**發出不滿，表示美國和其他西方國家的農業補貼政策扭曲了國際貿易。

　　media 是複數名詞，單數為 medium，不過一般來說 media 可以單複數通用。像這種單數字尾為 -um、複數字尾為 -a 的單字，還有「細菌」的單數 bacterium、複數 bacteria；「課程」的單數 curriculum、複數 curricula；「資料」的單數 datum、複數 data（data 也是單複數通用）。但 media 還是比較常當複數用，例如 multimedia（多媒體）、mass media（大眾媒體）等都必須用複數。在重視 media freedom（媒體自由）的美國，甚至把媒體稱為 the Fourth Estate，即「第四權」或「第四階級」，可見其重要性。以下為 media 的搭配詞彙。

✓ v. + media

v.	media	中譯
blame	media	譴責媒體
control		控制媒體

dominate	media	占據媒體重要版面
manipulate		操控媒體

搭配詞例句

- When a high school student in Hualien committed suicide recently, his parents blamed the media for having reported in detail on various methods of suicide.
  近來花蓮有一名高中生自殺，他的父母譴責媒體過度報導各種自殺的方式。

....

- In North Korea, the media is tightly controlled and used by Pyongyang to express official views.
  北韓嚴格控制媒體，利用媒體為平壤政府表達官方觀點。
  說明 此句為被動語態，動詞 controlled 位於主詞 media 後面。

....

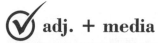 adj. + media

adj.	media	中譯
alternative		另類媒體
electronic		電子媒體
independent		獨立媒體
interactive	media	互動媒體
mainstream		主流媒體
official		官方媒體
social / social-networking		社交媒體
state / state-run		國營媒體

	media	
state-controlled		國家控管的媒體
visual		視覺媒體

搭配詞例句

- Nowadays, American children are heavily exposed to electronic media.
  今日美國的兒童大量接觸電子媒體。

....

- North Korea's official media condemned the U.S. deployment as a prelude to an attack on the North.
  北韓的官方媒體譴責美國的軍事部署，視之為攻擊北韓的序幕。

....

- China started a sweeping crackdown of its vibrant social-networking media over the weekend.
  中國在週末開始大規模掃蕩境內蓬勃發展的社交媒體。

....

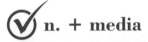 **n. + media**

n.	media	中譯
film		電影媒體
government		政府媒體
mass	media	大眾媒體
print		印刷 / 平面媒體

搭配詞例句

- The print media include newspaper, magazines and books.
  平面媒體包括報紙、雜誌和書籍。

....

 media + n.

media	n.	中譯
media	attention	媒體關注
	bias	媒體偏見
	censorship	媒體審查
	circus/frenzy/hype	媒體瘋狂報導 / 炒作
	coverage/report	媒體報導
	crackdown	打壓媒體
	empire	媒體帝國
	exposure	媒體曝光
	image	媒體形象
	mogul/tycoon	媒體大亨
	outlet	媒體管道
	reach	媒體影響力
	statement	媒體聲明

搭配詞例句

- One of the purposes of the media hype was actually to deliberately confuse people.
  這種媒體炒作的目的之一其實是故意要讓民眾搞不清楚。

......

- Popular podcasts can be a great media exposure tool for your business.
  受歡迎的播客可以是你公司一個很棒的媒體曝光工具。

......

- Media tycoon Rupert Murdoch refused a summons by Britain's parliament to answer questions over alleged crimes at one of his newspapers, leaving a senior executive from his media empire to face lawmakers.

  媒體大亨梅鐸拒絕英國國會傳喚，不去回答他旗下某報社被指控犯罪的問題，只留下他媒體帝國中一位高階主管獨自面對國會議員。

- Traditional media outlets such as television, radio, and the daily newspaper have long influenced what information reaches the public and how that information is packaged.

  電視、收音機和日報等傳統媒體管道，長期以來對於大眾所接收的資訊以及該資訊的包裝方式產生影響。

相關詞彙之搭配使用

片語

a medium of advertising	一種廣告媒介
to accuse the media of bias	指控媒體不公
to deny media reports	否認媒體報導
wide media coverage	媒體廣泛報導

句子

- The influx of media is exposing islanders to new ideas.

  媒體大量湧入讓島民接觸到新的觀念。

- China's official news media is often inaccurate and presents only the government's position.

  中國官方新聞媒體的訊息通常都不正確，而且只呈現政府的立場。

段落

Pressure on Turkey's media is nothing new. Ranked 155th out of 180 countries in the 2017 World Press Freedom Index, Turkey fared only marginally worse than it had the previous year, when it was ranked at 151. Some journalists in prison today have been there for years. Turkey has decimated the independent print media and <u>cracked down heavily on</u>[1] news websites and social media. Most of the journalists now imprisoned have not yet been convicted of any crime but <u>face trumped-up terrorism charges</u>[2]. Rights groups have criticized Turkey for decades for imprisoning journalists. (*AP*)

土耳其的媒體遭受打壓早已不是新聞。在 2017 年全球新聞自由指數報告的 180 個國家中，土耳其排名第 155 名，比去年的第 151 名還略遜一籌。有些現在被監禁的新聞記者已在監獄關了好幾年。土耳其大力剷除獨立平面媒體，並嚴格取締新聞網站和社交媒體。目前多數被監禁的新聞記者都尚未判決有罪，反被誣陷指控從事恐怖行動。人權團體幾十年來一直批評土耳其當局關押新聞記者的行徑。（《美聯社》）

說明

① crack down on... 是固定搭配，指「取締…，制裁…」，此處 crack down 和 on 之間加上副詞 heavily，強化其程度。而 crack down on 除了用來形容打壓媒體之外，英文新聞中也常用來描述「打擊犯罪」，如 to crack down on crimes。另外，動詞片語 crack down 也可組合成一字，成為名詞 crackdown，如 a new crackdown on crimes 為「新一波打擊犯罪」。

② 形容詞 trumped-up 是「虛構的」，後面搭配名詞 charges 就成為「虛構的罪名」，例如 He was arrested on trumped-up charges.（他被羅織罪狀而遭逮捕。）而 trumped-up evidence 就是「捏造的證據」。

搭配詞練習

⚙ **請從方格中挑選正確的搭配詞來完成以下的句子。**

medium	reach	electronic	mass	mainstream

1. Within the field of _____ **media**, the **film** _____ has the most universal appeal and impact.
   在**電子媒體**領域裡，**電影媒體**具有最普遍的吸引力和影響力。

2. The effects of television and other forms of _____ **media** are erasing regional dialects and localisms.
   電視和其他**大眾媒體**的影響力正在抹除地區方言和當地特色。

3. The Chinese government worries its story isn't being told fairly by the Western press, leaving it at a serious disadvantage in the realm of soft power. So it's spending billions to expand China's **media** _____.
   中國政府擔心西方媒體的偏頗報導將使其軟實力處於劣勢，因此投下數十億經費來擴大中國**媒體的影響力**。

4. Unlike the _____ **media**, citizen journalists are rooted in the local, and can dig up topics that the traditional media are unable to attend to.
   與**主流媒體**不同，公民記者紮根於地方，可以挖掘出傳統媒體無法關注的議題。

解答：1. electronic, medium　2. mass　3. reach　4. mainstream

暖身練習解答：①

newspaper

(n.) 報紙

暖身練習

⚙ 請就以下中英譯文選出適當的搭配詞。　　　　　▶ 答案請見 p. 322

Most people do not ① **watch** ② **read newspapers** anymore.
大多數人都不再**看報紙**了。

報紙內容通常可分為 straight news（直述性新聞）、feature（特寫）、editorial（社論）和 column（專欄）。另外，報紙新聞的結構通常又可分為 headline（標題）、lead（導言）和 body（本文）等。就報紙的尺寸而言，「一般報紙」稱為 broadsheet，內容強調重大公共議題；而尺寸較小的「小報」稱為 tabloid，就傾向腥羶聳動的八卦扒糞新聞。

在 print media（平面媒體）方面，傳播新聞的主要管道為報紙和雜誌。以下介紹幾家國際知名報紙和新聞雜誌的中英文名稱：

1. 報紙 (newspaper)：
   * The New York Times (NYT)：紐約時報（美國）
   * The Wall Street Journal (WSJ)：華爾街日報（美國）
   * The Washington Post：華盛頓郵報（美國）
   * The International Herald Tribune (IHT)：國際前鋒論壇報（美國）
   * The Times：泰晤士報（英國）
   * Financial Times (FT)：金融時報（英國）
   * The Guardian：衛報（英國）

- USA Today：今日美國報（美國）
- Yomiuri Shimbun：讀賣新聞（日本）
- Asahi Shimbun：朝日新聞（日本）
- The People's Daily：人民日報（中國）
- The China Post：英文中國郵報（臺灣）
- Taipei Times：臺北時報（臺灣）

2. 新聞雜誌 (news magazine)：

- Time：時代（美國）
- Newsweek：新聞週刊（美國）
- Businessweek：商業週刊（美國）
- Fortune：財星（美國）
- Forbes：富比士（美國）
- The Economist：經濟學人（英國）
- Common Wealth Magazine：天下雜誌（臺灣）

newspaper 和 magazine 的搭配詞彙差不多，以下僅列出 newspaper 的搭配。

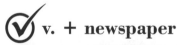 v. + newspaper

v.	newspaper	中譯
flick/flip/leaf/skim through		翻閱 / 瀏覽報紙
launch	newspaper	開辦報紙
publish		發行報紙
subscribe to		訂閱報紙

搭配詞例句

- He flicked through the newspaper as he didn't have time to read it properly.
  他沒時間好好看報紙，只能快速翻閱一下。

- In October 1986, three journalists launched a daily newspaper in Britain, *The Independent*.
  1986 年 10 月，三個新聞記者在英國開辦了一份日報，稱爲《獨立報》。

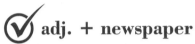 **adj. + newspaper**

adj.	newspaper	中譯
daily		日報
digital		數位報紙
independent		獨立報紙
influential		有影響力的報紙
largest-circulation		發行量最大的報紙
leading	newspaper	主要的報紙
muckraking		扒糞的報紙
national/nationwide		全國性報紙
state-run		國營報紙
weekly		週報

- A prominent daily newspaper in Japan says North Korea has agreed to five-party talks on its nuclear program.
  日本一家知名日報報導，北韓已經同意就其核子計畫進行五方會談。

- Senior government ministers have criticized one of the country's most influential newspapers.
  資深政府官員批評該國一家極具影響力的報紙。

 newspaper + n.

newspaper	n.	中譯
	article/report/story	報紙報導
	circulation	報紙發行量 / 銷售量
newspaper	columnist	報紙專欄作家
	headline	報紙標題
	publisher	報紙發行人

- Newspaper circulation has long been in decline.
  報紙銷售量長期持續下滑。

- War comes and goes through newspaper headlines, but it's a heavy constant in all military families' lives.
  戰事報導在報紙標題上來來去去，但在所有軍眷的生活中卻是揮之不去的陰影。

相關詞彙之搭配使用

片語

to generate ideas for follow-up stories	激發後續報導的想法
to reach a circulation of 8,000 copies	發行量達到 8,000 份
to spark ideas for new stories	激發新報導的想法

句子

- Good quotes can back up your lead and substantiate information in your story.
  好的引言可以支持報導中的導言，讓訊息有憑有據。

....

- Newspapers often seek local angles by writing how people in their areas are affected by the news.
  報紙通常會尋求在地觀點，寫出當地民眾如何受到該新聞的影響。

....

段落

The number of Americans reading print newspapers, magazines and books is in rapid decline①. Substantial percentages of the regular readers of leading newspapers now read them digitally②. Currently, 55 percent of regular *New York Times* readers say they read the paper mostly on a computer or mobile device, as do 48 percent of regular *USA Today* and 44 percent of *Wall Street Journal* readers. Many readers are now shifting to digital platforms to read the papers. (*CBS*)

美國閱讀紙本報紙、雜誌和書籍的人口正急速下降。幾份主要報紙的大量忠實讀者現在都改用數位閱讀。目前有 55%《紐約時報》的忠實讀者表示他們大部分都是在電腦或行動裝置上讀報，48%《今日美國報》的忠實讀者、44%

《華爾街日報》的忠實讀者也都是如此。許多讀者現在都轉移到數位平台閱讀報紙。（《哥倫比亞廣播公司》）

> **說明**
>
> ① in decline（下降）是常用搭配，也可用 on the decline 來表示。此處 decline 前面搭配形容詞 rapid（迅速的），另可用 precipitous（猛衝的）、sharp（急劇的）、steep（陡直的）、dramatic（戲劇性的）、sudden（突然的）說明各種快速下降的程度。
>
> ② read them digitally（用數位閱讀）的 them 所指的是前面提到的 leading newspapers（主要報紙），而此段描述數位閱讀的搭配還有 read the paper mostly on a computer or mobile device 和 shifting to digital platforms to read the papers。另外，「數位報紙」為 digital newspaper。

搭配詞練習

⚙ 請從方格中挑選正確的搭配詞來完成以下的句子。

publishing	weekly	digital	independent

1. They discussed the feasibility of joining together in _____ a nationwide **newspaper**.

   他們討論合作**發行**一份全國性**報紙**的可行性。

2. After working on a couple of local papers for a number of years, Jason and a number of colleagues **launched** a _____ **newspaper**.

   傑森和幾個同事為幾份地方報紙工作數年後，**開辦**了一份**週報**。

3. A new _____ **newspaper** being established in central Queensland is set to shake up the region's print news industry.

   澳洲昆士蘭中部誕生了一份全新的**獨立報紙**，將撼動該地區平面新聞產業。

4. *The Daily*, a _____ **newspaper** created by Rupert Murdoch's News Corp., has been launched as an application for the iPhone. *The Daily*, as an independent news product, has a subscription price of US$1.99 per month for iPhone users.

   梅鐸的新聞集團創立的**電子報**《每日報》，已在 iPhone 上推出應用程式。《每日報》是獨立的新聞媒體，iPhone 使用者的訂閱費用為每月 1.99 美元。

解答：1. publishing　2. weekly　3. independent　4. digital

暖身練習解答：②

television

(n.) 電視

▶ 答案請見 p. 329

暖身練習

⚙ 請就以下中英譯文選出適當的搭配詞。

Ever since legalization of ① **wire** ② **cable television** in Taiwan, the demand for programming has increased dramatically.
自從臺灣的**有線電視**合法開放之後，節目製作的需求量就大增。

　　觀賞電視節目是一般人主要的休閒活動，美國的節目型態五花八門，除了 television news（電視新聞）之外，還有許多吸引觀眾的節目，例如 series（影集）、reality show（真人實境秀）、soap opera（肥皂劇）、situation comedy（情境喜劇，簡稱 sitcom）、quiz show（益智節目）、variety show（綜藝節目）、talk show（談話節目）、documentary（紀錄片）等，很多節目也會在臺灣播出，並深受觀眾喜愛。以下為幾個世界知名的電視頻道中英文名稱：

- Cable News Network (CNN)：有線電視新聞網（美國）
- American Broadcasting Company (ABC)：美國廣播公司
- National Broadcasting Company (NBC)：國家廣播公司（美國）
- Public Broadcasting Service (PBS)：公共廣播電視（美國）
- British Broadcasting Cooperation (BBC)：英國廣播公司
- Nippon Hoso Kyokai (NHK)：日本放送協會
- China Central Television (CCTV)：中國中央電視台
- Al Jazeera / Jazeera Satellite Channel (JSC)：卡達半島電視台

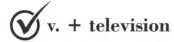
v. + television

v.	television	中譯
appear/go on make appearance on	television	出現在電視上，上電視
watch		看電視

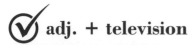
搭配詞例句

- The President went on national television to reply to accusations he had been involved in corrupt real estate deals.
  總統親上全國性的電視，回應他涉及不動產貪汙的指控。

....

- Gaddafi's death has made the headline news, as per usual when Gaddafi makes any appearance on TV.
  格達費死亡的消息登上頭條新聞，就像以往格達費出現在電視上一樣受人注目。

....

adj. + television

adj.	television	中譯
commercial		商業電視
high-definition		高畫質電視
live		現場電視直播
national	television	全國電視
portable		手提電視
public		公共電視
smart		智慧型電視
state-run		國營電視

- The image carried on live television around the world was the tearing down of a tall statue of Saddam Hussein in Baghdad.
  巴格達一座巨大海珊銅像被拆毀的影像，透過現場電視直播傳送至全世界。

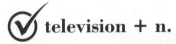 **television + n.**

television	n.	中譯
television	ad/advertisement/commercial	電視廣告
	channel	電視頻道
	network	電視聯播網
	ratings	電視收視率，電視分級制
	series	電視影集
	transmission	電視播送

- A television ad about the U.S. national debt has been deemed too controversial by major networks.
  幾家大型電視聯播網認為一支關於美國國債的電視廣告爭議性太大。

- Ambrose's book "Band of Brothers" was turned into a television series for HBO.
  安柏思的書《諾曼第大空降》被拍攝成 HBO 的電視影集。

相關詞彙之搭配使用

片語

a veteran news anchor/anchorman/ anchorwoman/ announcer	一位資深新聞主播 / 播報員
Academy Awards / The Oscars	奧斯卡金像獎（美國表彰電影的獎項）
closed-circuit television (CCTV)	閉路電視
commercial break	電視廣告時間
Emmy Awards	艾美獎（美國表彰電視節目的獎項）
Grammy Awards	葛萊美獎（美國表彰音樂的獎項）
Liquid Crystal Display (LCD) TV	液晶電視
Plasma Display Panel (PDP) TV	電漿電視
rating battle/war	收視率大戰
remote control devices	遙控器
set-top box	機上盒
to center on the development of HDTV and flat-display screen technology	專注開發高畫質電視和平面顯示器技術
to make channels available to subscribers on all screens at all times	使頻道的訂戶隨時隨地都能收看電視
Tony Awards	東尼獎（美國表彰劇場表演的獎項）
TV distributors and channel owners	電視經銷商與頻道業者

句子

- Since it <u>first aired</u> in 1989, *The Simpsons* has never been afraid to <u>touch on the key issues of the day</u>.

《辛普森家庭》自 1989 年<u>開播</u>以來，從不畏懼<u>觸及時代的重要議題</u>。

> **說明** 此句中的 air 與「空中」無關，而是動詞「廣播」、「播送」之意。

- <u>Cable TV and satellite TV</u> are the most practical and widely-used options available for people who want to <u>watch their favorite shows</u>.

<u>有線電視和衛星電視</u>是人們想要<u>觀賞喜愛的節目時</u>最實用、也是最常採用的選擇。

- The television industry designed <u>a TV ratings system</u> to give parents more information about <u>the content and age-appropriateness of TV programs</u>.

電視產業設計了<u>一套電視分級系統</u>，讓家長更加了解<u>電視節目的內容和適合觀看的年齡</u>。

段落

News organization Reuters is stepping into the <u>modern streaming age</u>[①] with a new mobile TV news service, aptly called Reuters TV. Available for the iPhone, the new app lets users view curated, personalized news coverage from anywhere, on demand. No more sports news for those who <u>couldn't care less</u>[②], or political reports for folks who like to <u>keep out of</u>[③] the D.C. drama[④]. (*Digital Trends*)

新聞通訊機構路透社邁入串流新時代，推出新型行動電視新聞服務，就稱為路透社電視。這個新的應用程式可在 iPhone 上使用，供使用者隨時隨地依個人喜好收看整理過的新聞報導。對運動毫無興趣或是對政壇戲碼敬謝不敏的人，再也不會收到這些新聞。(《數位趨勢》)

說明

① stream 原是名詞，指「河流」，當動詞用時意思是「流動」，而此處 streaming 則是電腦術語「串流」，指一種透過網路傳輸影音媒體的技術，讓觀眾可即時觀賞影像。另如 live video streaming 為「直播影音串流」、stream media 為「串流媒體」。

② couldn't care less 按照字面意思是「無法在乎得更少」，容易使人誤解，既然「無法在乎得更少」，意思就是「完全不在乎」，在此譯為「毫無興趣」。另一個類似用法為 couldn't agree more，是指「完全同意」，例如 I couldn't agree with you more.（我完全同意你的意見。）

③ keep out of... 是「避開…」，如 keep out of the sun 是「避免陽光照射」；公共告示牌上寫著 keep out，就有「禁止入內」之意。

④ D.C. 是指美國首都 Washington, D.C.，其中 D.C. 是 District of Columbia 的頭字詞，中文譯為「華盛頓哥倫比亞特區」，在此引申為美國的政壇。

搭配詞練習

⚙ 請從方格中挑選正確的搭配詞來完成以下的句子。

national	networks	appeared	channel	broadcasts

1. Iraqi President Saddam Hussein _____ **on** _____ **television**, predicting a victory over U.S.-led forces.
伊拉克總統海珊**出現在全國電視上**，預言將大勝美國領導的盟軍。

2. Video footage broadcast on global **television** _____ showed Gaddafi's bloodied corpse lying on the ground.
格達費血跡斑斑的屍體橫陳在地上的錄影畫面，在全球的**電視聯播網**播出。

3. The official China Central **Television** _____ in English, French, Russian and Arabic in addition to Chinese.
官方的中國中央**電視台**除了中文之外，也以英語、法語、俄語和阿拉伯語**播出**。

4. The state-run Xinhua news service has launched an English-language international **television** _____, CNC World.
國營的新華社開辦了一個以英語播送的國際**電視頻道**：中國電視網。

解答：1. appeared, national 2. networks 3. broadcasts 4. channel

暖身練習解答：②

book

(n.) 書籍

暖身練習

⚙ 請就以下中英譯文選出適當的搭配詞。　　　　▶ 答案請見 p. 338

If you are self-publishing your book, the decision of the **book**
① **name** ② **title** is purely up to you.
如果你是自行出版，就由你自己全權決定**書名**。

　　book 大多當名詞用，意思是「書籍」、「簿冊」。以「書籍」來分類，大致上可分為 fiction（虛構）和 non-fiction（非虛構）兩大類，而 fiction 中最常見的是 novel（長篇小說），以字數還可細分為 novella（中篇小說）和 short story（短篇小說）；以內容區分則可分為 literary fiction（文學小說）、historical fiction（歷史小說）、science fiction（科幻小說，簡稱 sci-fi）等。至於 non-fiction 的種類繁多，包括 reference book（參考書）、encyclopedia（百科全書）、almanac（年鑑）、biography（傳記）、popular science（科普）、textbook（教科書）等。除了紙本書之外，現在也有愈來愈多的 audiobook（有聲書）和 electronic book / E-book 或 digital book（電子書）可供選擇。而 book lover（愛書人）或 bookworm（書呆子）一定擁有 bookcase（書櫥）和 a pair of bookends（書擋，書立）。

　　book 也可以當動詞用，意思是「預訂」，如 be fully booked 就是「預訂已滿」；而「預訂」的名詞則為 booking，如 advance/early booking 為「提早預訂」。另外，動詞 book 後面可搭配名詞如 flight（班機）、hotel

（飯店）、accommodation（住宿）、room（房間）、seat（席位）、table（桌位）等，例如以下例句：

- We booked our own flights and hotels; we didn't use a travel agency.
  我們自行預訂班機和飯店，沒有找旅行社幫忙。

另外，多數英語學習者都知道名詞 book 前面常搭配動詞 read（閱讀），但其實 read 當名詞時也有「讀物」的意思，例如：

- A good read is something you have to finish once you've started.
  一本好書，就是你一旦開卷就非讀完不可的書。

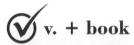 **v. + book**

v.	book	中譯
author/write		撰寫書籍
compile		編纂書籍
dedicate		把書獻給
edit	book	編輯書籍
flick/flip/leaf/skim through		翻閱 / 瀏覽書籍
launch		發表新書
plagiarize		抄襲書籍
proofread		校對書籍

搭配詞例句

- I would like to dedicate this book to my wife Liwen, who provides me with constant support and encouragement in my work.
  我要將這本書獻給妻子麗雯，感謝她對我工作的不斷支持和鼓勵。

- Some people may skim through books they find boring.
  有些人對沒興趣的書可能只會瀏覽翻閱而已。

- A dispirited student decides to plagiarize an obscure scholar's book for his doctoral dissertation.
  沮喪的學生決定要抄襲一位名不見經傳學者的書，作為他的博士論文。
  說明 「博士論文」的英文為 dissertation，「碩士論文」則常用 thesis。

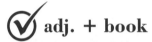 adj. + book

adj.	book	中譯
award-winning		獲獎書籍
best-selling		暢銷書
children's		童書
classic		經典書
comic		漫畫書
electronic	book	電子書
hardback/hardcover		精裝書
illustrated		繪本
out-of-print		絕版書
paperback		平裝書
second-hand / used		二手書

self-help	book	自助 / 勵志書

搭配詞例句

- *The Bible* is the best-selling book of all time with over 5 billion copies sold and distributed.

《聖經》是有史以來最暢銷的書籍，銷售和流通超過 50 億本。

說明「暢銷書」也可用 best seller 或 bestseller 表示，如美國最具代表性的「紐約時報暢銷書排行榜」就是 The New York Times Best Seller List，而「紐約時報暢銷書作者」可稱為 The New York Times best-selling author。

- Comic books are full of superheroes and a dazzling variety of characters, but in the early days of the industry one thing was conspicuously rare: black characters.

漫畫書中充滿超級英雄和各式眩目耀眼的角色，但在漫畫產業發展初期，黑人的角色卻出奇地少。

 **book + n.**

book	n.	中譯
book	critic/reviewer	書評家
	exhibition/fair	書展
	launch	發表新書會
	review	書評
	royalty	版稅
	signing	簽書會
	title	書名

搭配詞例句

- A woman described as the most influential book critic in the English-speaking world, is stepping down because she wants to instead write about politics and culture under the administration of Donald Trump.
  一位被稱為英語世界中最有影響力的書評家不寫書評了，因為她要轉換跑道，撰寫川普政權下的政治和文化現象。

- The Frankfurt Book Fair is the world's largest event of the publishing industry.
  法蘭克福書展是全球出版產業最盛大的活動。

相關詞彙之搭配使用

片語

award-winning author/writer	得獎作者 / 作家
copy editing	審稿
copy editor	核稿編輯
copy writer	文案撰稿人
digital printing	數位印刷
leaf through the pile of children's books	翻閱成堆的童書
list price of a book	書的訂價
literary agent	作家經紀人
pocket reference book	口袋參考書
print on demand (POD)	隨需列印（有需求時才將書籍列印出來）
publishing house/company / publisher	出版社

the Booker Prize the Man Booker Prize for Fiction	英國曼布克文學獎（布克獎）
the Nobel Prize in Literature	諾貝爾文學獎
the Pulitzer Prize	美國普立茲獎
to co-author a book with a bestselling author	與暢銷書作者合著出書
to do something by the book / to go by the book	照章行事

句子

● Don't judge a book by its cover.
不要以貌取人。

● A majority of new authors are usually offered a low advance and low royalty percentage.
大部分新進作家通常只會拿到很低的預付款和版稅率。

● Famous Taiwanese writer Wu Ming-Yi, whose book "The Stolen Bicycle" has been nominated for an international literary award, said that he objected to being listed as a national of "Taiwan, China" on the Man Booker Prize website.
以《單車失竊記》一書入圍國際文學獎的知名臺灣作家吳明益表示，他反對曼布克獎的網頁將其國籍列為「中國‧臺灣」。

● Books can be revised and republished: each revision is considered a new edition of the same book.
書籍可修訂和重新出版，每次的修訂可視為同一本書的新版。
說明 書籍每次再版就是一個 edition，如「第二版」為 the second edition；但若是就原書重印，內容並未修訂，那就是再刷，如「第三刷」為 the third printing。另外也有將厚重原文加以精簡的「刪節版」，稱為 abridged edition。

• The art of <u>cosplay</u> was on vivid display at LA <u>Comic Con</u>.

<u>角色扮演</u>的藝術在洛杉磯<u>動漫展</u>上鮮活展現。

　說明 此句中的 cosplay 是日式英文，從 costume play 兩字合併簡化而成，現已成為英文的一部分，中文常譯為「角色扮演」，而「角色扮演者」則稱為 cosplayer。Comic Con 是美國 comic book convention 的簡稱，不過參展作品已不限於漫畫，近年更加入 manga（日本漫畫）、animation（動畫）、anime（日本動畫）、video games（電玩）、science fiction films（科幻電影）和角色扮演等流行文化元素，中文稱之為「動漫展」。

段落

SUNBURN, by Laura Lippman. (Morrow, $26.99.) This <u>thriller</u>[1] may be set in a small town in Delaware in the mid-1990s, but it <u>draws its inspiration from the noir romances</u>[2] of the 1940s: Two strangers with secrets meet in a town where nobody goes. Our <u>reviewer</u>[3], Harriet Lane, writes that the novel, "though cool and twisty, has more heart than expected. It's generous in other ways, too. <u>The particular atmosphere</u> of unlovely Belleville <u>is deftly conveyed</u>[4] ... yet there is beauty here too. You see the huge red sun sinking into the cornfields; you feel the dew underfoot." (*The New York Times Book Review*)

《SUNBURN》，蘿拉‧李普曼著（Morrow 出版，美金 26.99 元）。這部<u>驚悚小說</u>的背景雖然設定在 1990 年代中德拉瓦州的小鎮，但其<u>靈感源自於</u> 1940 年代的<u>黑色羅曼史</u>：兩個身懷祕密的陌生人在一個人跡罕至的小鎮相遇。本報<u>書評家</u>哈莉特‧連恩如此評論這本小說：「儘管情節冷酷曲折，但比預期來得感人，在其他方面也展現溫度，<u>生動傳達出</u>貝爾維爾這個小鎮惹人嫌的<u>特殊氛圍</u>……但也有可愛之處。你可看到巨輪的夕陽沉落在玉米田中，也可感受到腳下的露珠。」（《紐約時報書評》）

說明

① thriller 為「驚悚小說」或「驚悚電影」，其他相近的小說類型有 mystery（偵探／推理小說）、crime（犯罪小說）、horror（恐怖小說）、fantasy（奇幻小說）。

② 此處又出現另一種小說類型 romance（愛情小說，羅曼史），而 noir 是法文「黑色」之意。此外，「從…擷取靈感」可用 draw inspiration from... 來表示。

③ 此處 reviewer 是指 book reviewer（書評家），而比較正式嚴謹的書評家可稱為 book critic 或 literary critic。另外，「電影評論家」則為 film/movie critic。

④ The particular atmosphere of ... is deftly conveyed 是指「把…的特定氛圍熟練地表現出來」，其中 deftly 是副詞，意為「熟練地」。

搭配詞練習

⚙ 請從方格中挑選正確的搭配詞來完成以下的句子。

Exhibition	self-help	fairs	launch	Used

1. President Tsai Ing-wen opened the 2018 Taipei International **Book**
_____ by lauding Taiwan's diversity and freedom, saying those are
elements that gave birth to one of the most important **book** _____
in Asia.
蔡英文總統在 2018 年臺北國際**書展**開幕儀式上，讚揚臺灣的多元和自由，表示這是使臺北書展成為亞洲重要**書展**的因素。

2. The most admired thinkers—Plato, Aristotle, Cicero, and Seneca—all
wrote _____ **books**, whose aim was to teach us to live well.
最受景仰的思想家如柏拉圖、亞里斯多德、西賽羅和塞內卡都曾寫過**勵志書**，教導我們如何活得有意義。

3. _____ **textbooks** can save you hundreds of dollars a year over
the list price.
二手教科書比起原訂售價，每年可為你省下好幾百美元。

4. A virtual **book** _____ is really no different than a regular book
launch, except that it is limited to activities done online such as social
media, blogging, email marketing, etc.
虛擬的**新書發表會**其實與一般的新書發表會沒有什麼不同，除了虛擬新書發表會的活動僅限於線上舉辦，例如透過社交媒體、部落格或電子郵件行銷等。

解答：1. Exhibition, fairs　2. self-help　3. Used　4. launch
暖身練習解答：②

journal

(n.) 日報；期刊

▶ 答案請見 p. 344

請就以下中英譯文選出適當的搭配詞。

Publishing **journal** ① **theses** ② **articles** by faculty members is a necessary requirement for advancements in a position.
發表**期刊論文**是教師升等的必備要求。

　　journal 的意義很多元，可指每日發行的「報紙」，如財經權威《華爾街日報》，英文名稱為 The Wall Street Journal；journal 也可以指定期出刊的「雜誌」，包括學術「期刊」，如英國的《文化研究期刊》為 Journal for Cultural Research；journal 還可以指私人撰寫的「日誌」，意思近似 diary，而且 journal 也可當動詞用，意思是「寫日誌」，例如以下例句：

- Research shows that people who journal their intake of food ate less and made healthier choices.
  研究顯示，會寫日誌記錄食物攝取的人吃得較少，並作出較健康的選擇。

　　journal 也與新聞有關，例如「新聞學」是 journalism，「新聞記者」是 journalist，「新聞文體」是 journalese 等。近年來因數位科技和網路平台興起，一般民眾也能自主從事社會觀察的採訪、評論和報導。有別於主流傳統媒體的新聞發布，這種業餘的新聞工作者稱為「公民記者」，即 citizen journalist 或 citizen reporter。

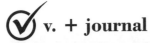 **v. + journal**

v.	journal	中譯
keep		寫日誌
publish	journal	出版期刊
subscribe to		訂閱期刊
write for		為期刊撰寫文章

搭配詞例句

- You can keep a journal in a notebook, in computer files, or in letter form.
  你的日誌可以寫在筆記本上、記在電腦檔案中或寫在信紙上。

- He has written an article on how to write for psychological journals.
  他曾寫過一篇文章，闡述如何為心理學期刊撰寫文章。

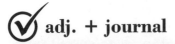 **adj. + journal**

adj.	journal	中譯
academic/scholarly		學術期刊
cited		被引用的期刊
distinguished/highly-ranked/ prestigious/reputable	journal	聲望卓著的期刊
leading/major		主要期刊
peer-reviewed		同儕審查的期刊
professional/specialized		專業期刊

搭配詞例句

- The writing quality is especially important when you are seeking to be published in an academic journal.

  若你想在學術期刊上發表文章，就要特別注意寫作品質。

- In accounting, the most frequently cited journal is *The Accounting Review.*

  會計學裡最常被引用的期刊是《會計學評論》。

- A major criterion for evaluating teachers for promotion purposes required that faculty members publish a certain number of articles in reputable journals.

  評鑑教師升等的主要標準，是教師在聲望卓著的期刊上發表一定數量的文章。

 **journal + n.**

journal	n.	中譯
journal	archives	期刊資料庫
	article/paper/publication	期刊文章 / 論文
	reporter	新聞記者
	reviewer	期刊論文審查者

搭配詞例句

- The professors often ask us to make critical comments on journal articles.

  教授經常要求我們對期刊文章提出批判性意見。

- He has authored or co-authored about 30 journal publications.
  他已撰寫或與人合寫了約 30 篇期刊論文。

相關詞彙之搭配使用

片語

news journal with in-depth and updated local news	深入且即時的地方新聞報紙
to develop a journal-keeping habit	培養寫日誌的習慣

句子

- Effective academic journal writing should always be supported by citations and references.
  有效的學術期刊寫作應該有引用和參考文獻的支持。

- The journal is available on the Internet as well as in print.
  這本期刊有線上版和印刷版。

段落

Exasperated by rising subscription costs charged by academic publishers[1], Harvard University has encouraged its faculty members[2] to make their research freely available through open access journals[3] and to resign from publications that keep articles behind paywalls. A memo from Harvard Library to the university's 2,100 teaching and research staff called for action after warning it could no longer afford the price hikes imposed by many large journal publishers[4], which bill the library around $3.5m a year. (*The Guardian*)

學術期刊出版社高漲的訂閱費用惹惱了哈佛大學，該校鼓勵教員透過對外開放的期刊免費提供研究成果，並請辭收費期刊的編務工作。哈佛大學圖書館發送給全校 2,100 位教員和研究員的備忘錄中呼籲大家採取反制行動，並警告說圖書館已無力支付許多大型期刊出版社不斷調漲的費用，每年高達約 350 萬美元。（《衛報》）

說明

① academic publisher（學術期刊出版社）專門出版 academic journal 或 scholarly journal（學術期刊）。而 rising subscription costs 中的 rising 是形容詞，也可用 soaring（高漲的）來搭配名詞 costs（費用）。

② faculty members（教員）通常是指大學的各級教師，包括 full professor（正教授）、associate professor（副教授）、assistant professor（助理教授）、lecturer（講師）等。

③ open access journals 是指開放給大眾取用的免費學術期刊，又稱為 open access publishing（公開取用出版），通常是線上期刊。

④ 英文新聞傾向以不同字詞來表達相同概念，此處 price hikes 與第一句的 rising costs 同義，指「高漲的費用」；journal publishers 也與前面的 academic publishers 同義，都是指「學術期刊出版社」。

搭配詞練習

⚙ 請從方格中挑選正確的搭配詞來完成以下的句子。

wrote	kept	peer	articles	reviewed

1. She _____ **journal** _____ on vocal technique and vocal interpretation.

   她**撰寫**過發聲技巧和發聲詮釋的**期刊論文**。

2. However, a wide range of health policy researchers and _____-_____ **journal articles** disagree with these conclusions.

   但是許多衛生政策研究者和**同儕審查的期刊論文**並不同意這些結論。

3. Many influential leaders have _____ **journals**, meticulously maintaining a detailed account of their day-to-day lives, thoughts and feelings.

   許多有影響力的領袖都有**寫日誌**的習慣,詳細記錄他們日常的生活、想法和感受。

解答:1. wrote, articles   2. peer, reviewed   3. kept

暖身練習解答:②

advertisement
(n.) 廣告

▶ 答案請見 p. 350

暖身練習

⚙ 請就以下中英譯文選出適當的搭配詞。

Sara has become a ① **living** ② **walking advertisement** for her hair stylist.
莎拉已成為她髮型設計師的**活廣告**。

advertisement 常簡寫為 ad，是指在各種大眾媒體如報紙、雜誌、電視、收音機上刊登播送的「廣告」。但若指「電視或廣播電台的廣告」，也常用 commercial 一字，例如以下例句：

- Super Bowl commercials have become a cultural phenomenon.
  美式足球超級盃的電視廣告已成為一種文化現象。

另外，在街上發送或塞到信箱的「廣告傳單」稱為 flyer，貼在牆上的「廣告海報」稱為 poster，至於大型的戶外「廣告看板」則為 billboard。

 v. + advertisement

v.	advertisement	中譯
carry/issue/place/publish/put/run		刊登廣告
make	advertisement	製作廣告
regulate		規範廣告
take out		移除廣告

搭配詞例句

- American Tobacco Company ran a full-page advertisement on the back cover of every issue of the publication.
  美國菸草公司在這份刊物每一期的封底都刊登全版廣告。

- Many nations currently regulate advertisement to children, and in some cases, advertisement to children has been banned or severely limited.
  許多國家目前都有規範針對兒童的廣告，在某些情況下，針對兒童的廣告是被禁止或有嚴格限制的。

 adj. + advertisement

adj.	advertisement	中譯
anti-drug		反毒品的廣告
classified		分類廣告
controversial		有爭議的廣告
full-page	advertisement	全版廣告
online		線上廣告
paid		付費廣告
walking		活廣告

搭配詞例句

- A full-page advertisement appealing for support for the multi-seat single vote model was put in two Chinese newspapers.
  兩份中國報紙上刊登了全版廣告，呼籲支持多議席單選票制。

- Online advertisements are becoming more personalized based on your online behavior.
  線上廣告是基於你的網路行為來運作，變得愈來愈個人化。

....

- The church might consider placing paid advertisements, highlighting forthcoming events which could be made especially attractive to the outsider.
  該教堂可能考慮刊登付費廣告，主打即將舉行特別用以吸引教外人士的活動。

....

 n. + advertisement

n.	advertisement	中譯
campaign		競選廣告
print	advertisement	平面廣告
recruitment		招募廣告

搭配詞例句

- A recruitment advertisement may describe an ideal job candidate as possessing excellent communication skills.
  招募廣告中可能會提到，理想的工作人選需要具備優異的溝通技巧。

....

相關詞彙之搭配使用

片語

airing a commercial during the Super Bowl	在轉播超級盃期間播出電視廣告
influence of advertisements on child health	廣告對兒童健康的影響

句子

- The success of a <u>television advertisement</u> depends to a large extent on <u>how well its script has been written</u>.
  電視廣告成功與否，有很大程度取決於<u>腳本寫得好不好</u>。

- <u>Advertising of tobacco</u> on television or at sporting events <u>is banned</u>.
  電視上或運動比賽時<u>禁止廣告香菸</u>。

- Place your <u>print and online ads</u> through one of our websites.
  透過我們的網站來刊登您的<u>平面和線上廣告</u>。

段落

Vietnam on Thursday called on all companies doing business in the country to <u>stop advertising on</u>[①] YouTube, Facebook and other social media until they find a way to halt the publication of "toxic" anti-government information. The communist country is <u>putting increasing pressure on advertisers to</u>[②] try to get YouTube owner Google and other companies to remove content from foreign-based <u>dissidents</u>[③]. (*Reuters*)

越南於週四要求境內所有企業<u>停止在</u> YouTube、Facebook 和其他社交媒體上<u>刊登廣告</u>，直到政府找到防堵「有毒的」反政府資訊流通的方式為止。這個共產國家<u>正向廣告商大力施壓</u>，要他們向 YouTube 背後的老闆 Google 以及其他公司要求移除國外<u>異議人士</u>提供的內容。(《路透社》)

說明

① advertise 是動詞「刊登廣告」，字尾加 -ing 的 advertising 即名詞「廣告業」。不過這裡的 advertising 來自動詞 advertise，因為前面有動詞 stop，advertise 必須改為動名詞 advertising，後面搭配介系詞 on 再接媒介，表示「在…上刊登廣告」。

② put pressure on ... to... 是「對…（人）施壓，使其做…（事）」，而
advertise 字尾加 -r 變成 advertiser，即「廣告商」。

③ dissident 當名詞時表示「意見不同者，異議人士」，如 political dissident
是「持不同政見者」。dissident 也可當形容詞用，意思是「意見不同
的」，如 dissident view 是「不同的意見」。

搭配詞練習

⚙ 請從方格中挑選正確的搭配詞來完成以下的句子。

controversial	online	carry	campaign	classified

1. The magazine is criticized by the authority for ignoring a warning not to
_____ the _____ **advertisement**.
這本雜誌無視警告刊載那則有爭議的廣告，飽受當局批評。

2. You need to learn how to find properties on the popular _____
_____ **advertisement** website.
你要學著在大家常用的線上分類廣告網站上搜尋房地產的訊息。

3. There's an element to American political campaigns that everyone hates
and almost everyone loves to denounce: the negative _____
advertisement.
在美國的政治選舉活動中，眾人痛恨且樂於譴責的就是負面的競選廣告。

解答：1. carry, controversial　2. online, classified　3. campaign

暖身練習解答：②

附 錄

新聞英文
搭配詞
學習資源

線上中英對照新聞

　　免費線上英文新聞常以豐富多彩的圖文報導最新脈動，而且議題包羅萬象，不論政治、經濟、文化、科技、環境、運動或影劇等領域，只要讀者有興趣，都可以搜尋到相關文章。如果閱讀全英文新聞覺得辛苦，不妨從中英對照的文章開始讀起。以下列出幾個國內外提供中英版本的知名新聞媒體連結：

- 台灣光華雜誌：
  https://www.taiwan-panorama.com/

- 自由時報中英對照讀新聞：
  http://iservice.ltn.com.tw/Service/english/

- 讀紐時學英文：
  http://paper.udn.com/papers.php?pname=POH0067

- 紐約時報中文網：
  https://cn.nytimes.com/

- 英國廣播公司 BBC 英倫網：
  http://www.bbc.com/ukchina/simp

- 金融時報 FT 中文網雙語閱讀：
  http://big5.ftchinese.com/channel/ce.html

線上語料庫和詞典

　　除了紙本的詞典和專書之外，讀者也可使用以下線上語料庫和詞典來檢索英語搭配詞語。這些線上資源都是免費的，而且可快速找到英語的各種搭配形式，使用方式相當簡單，大部分只需鍵入想要查詢的中英字彙，就可得到各種搭配結果和例句，而且這些語料庫的網站上也會提供使用說明，讀者可自行參考學習。

1. 中英雙語：

- TANGO（搭配詞檢索）：

  http://candle.cs.nthu.edu.tw/collocation/webform2.aspx?funcID=9

- English-Chinese Parallel Concordancer（英中平行關鍵詞檢索）：

  http://ec-concord.ied.edu.hk/paraconc/index.htm

- Linguee（英中詞典及譯文例句搜索）：

  https://cn.linguee.com/?chooseDomain=1

- iCIBA（詞霸）：

  http://www.iciba.com/

- Dict.cn（海詞）：

  http://dict.cn/

- Jukuu（句酷）：

  http://www.jukuu.com/

- Youdao（有道）：

  https://dict.youdao.com/

- 國家教育研究院雙語詞彙、學術名詞暨辭書資訊網：
  http://terms.naer.edu.tw/

- 國教院華英雙語索引典系統：
  http://coct.naer.edu.tw/bc/

- 香港中文大學傳譯資源網：
  http://www.interpreting.hku.hk/glossary/

2. 英文：

- Linggle（線上搭配詞檢索）：
  http://www.linggle.com/

- Online Collocation Dictionary（線上搭配詞典）：
  http://www.freecollocation.com/

- Just the word（線上搭配詞檢索）：
  http://www.just-the-word.com/

- FRAZE.IT（線上搭配詞檢索）：
  https://fraze.it/

- Ludwig（線上搭配詞典）：
  https://ludwig.guru/

- Netspeak（線上搭配詞檢索）：
  http://www.netspeak.org/

- Corpus of Contemporary American English（美國現代英文語料庫）：
  http://corpus.byu.edu/coca/

- Corpus Concordance English（英語語料庫檢索）：

  http://lextutor.ca/conc/eng/

- WordNet Search（字網搜尋）：

  http://wordnetweb.princeton.edu/perl/webwn

- ozdic.com（OZ 字典）

  http://www.ozdic.com/

- StringNet（字串網）

  http://nav4.stringnet.org/

參考書目

　　新聞英文的搭配詞語眾多，形式豐富，並不是本書篇幅能夠含括。讀者如有進一步寫作或學習需求，也可查閱以下書目。

1. 新聞英文：

《焦點新聞英文》，(2018)，臺北：敦煌。

《柯林氏新聞英語》，(2003)，臺北：書林。

《新聞英文閱讀與翻譯技巧》（增訂版），(2014)，臺北：眾文。

2. 中英雙語搭配詞典和專書：

《牛津英語搭配詞典》（第二版），(2015)，北京：外語教學與研究出版社。

《英文研究論文寫作：搭配詞指引》，(2008)，臺北：眾文。

《麥克米倫高級英漢雙解詞典》，(2008)，臺北：書林。

《英語搭配大辭典》，(2006)，北京：外語教學與研究出版社。

《實用英語詞語搭配辭典》，(1995)，香港：朗文。

3. 英文搭配詞典和專書：

Academic Vocabulary in Use. (2008). Cambridge: Cambridge University
　　　Press.

*English Collocations in Use: how words work together for fluent and
　　　natural English*. (2005). Cambridge: Cambridge University Press.

Key Words for Fluency: Intermediate Collocation Practice. (2005).
　　　London: Thomson.

Key Words for Fluency: Upper-Intermediate Collocation Practice. (2004).
　　　London: Thomson.

LTP Dictionary of Selected Collocations. (2005). Hove, UK: Language
Teaching Publications.

Macmillan Collocations Dictionary. (2010). Taipei: Bookman Books.

Oxford Collocations Dictionary for Students of English. (2nd ed.) (2009).
Oxford: Oxford University Press.

The BBI Combinatory Dictionary of English. (3rd ed.) (2010). Taipei:
Bookman Books.

MEMO

MEMO

MEMO

MEMO

MEMO

MEMO

國家圖書館出版品預行編目 (CIP) 資料

新聞英文搭配詞：學會 collocation, 擺脫中式英文 / 廖柏森作 .
-- 初版 . -- 臺北市：眾文圖書，2018.09　面；公分
ISBN 978-957-532-516-9（平裝）　1. 新聞英文 2. 詞彙 3. 句法
805.12　　　　　　　　　　　　　　　　　　　　　　107014647

SE076

新聞英文搭配詞：學會 collocation，擺脫中式英文

定價 450 元

2018 年 9 月　初版 1 刷

作者	廖柏森
責任編輯	蔡易伶

總編輯	陳瑠琍
主編	黃炯睿
資深編輯	顏秀竹・蔡易伶
編輯	何秉修・黃婉瑩
美術設計	嚴國綸
行銷企劃	李皖萍・王盈智
發行人	黃建和
發行所	眾文圖書股份有限公司
	台北市 10088 羅斯福路三段 100 號
	12 樓之 2
網路書店	www.jwbooks.com.tw
電話	02-2311-8168
傳真	02-2311-9683
郵政劃撥	01048805

ISBN 978-957-532-516-9

Printed in Taiwan